Know You
by Heart

by

Laurie Winter

Warriors of the Heart, Book 5

Know You by Heart

Cover Art by *Tina Lynn Stout*

The Wild Rose Press, Inc.
PO Box 708
Adams Basin, NY 14410-0708
Visit us at www.thewildrosepress.com

Publishing History
First Sweetheart Rose Edition, 2019
Print ISBN 978-1-5092-2832-4
Digital ISBN 978-1-5092-2833-1

Warriors of the Heart, Book 5
Published in the United States of America

"Who was that?"

"A friend who's still in the service. She called from a base overseas to tell me one of our CST sisters was KIA yesterday. Gail was on a mission, and the team came under fire. She took five bullets." A sob escaped her mouth.

"I'm so sorry." Meaningless words were not enough, but he had no idea what else to say. Her pain ripped through him. After a minute of crying, Alice pulled back her emotions.

"Her body will be flown back to the States for burial." She leaned forward and cupped her head in her hands. "I'll need time off to go to the funeral."

"Take all the time you need." He had no problem with her leaving but didn't want her going alone. "I'll come with you."

Straightening, she shook her head. "You don't have to do that. Gail's won't be my first military funeral."

He firmly held her hand, which felt like ice. "You've done so much for me. Let me do something for you."

"You don't have to…"

"I want to."

She lifted her gaze, and a single tear fell, landing on his hand covering hers. Micah used his thumb to wipe off the dampness from her cheek. Seeing her hurting gave rise to a fierce protectiveness—a feeling stronger than anything he'd ever felt. Unfortunately, his physical strength couldn't fight off her grief. He'd need to dig deeper. "I know you're capable of taking on the world, but what I'm saying is, from now on, you don't have to do it alone."

Praise for Laurie Winter

Dedication

To the courageous women
of the Cultural Support Team,
to author Gayle Tzemach Lemmon,
and in memory of 1st LT Ashley White.
A huge thank you to Sergeant Janiece Marquez,
whose interview was instrumental
in bringing Alice to life.

Chapter One

When Alice Liddell chose her legal name at the age of eighteen, she meant it as a symbol of her new life. Like Alice in Wonderland, she'd visited strange lands, met distrustful people, and barely survived a brush with death. She'd been afforded more than one second chance, something she was grateful for every day.

Now, she straightened her spine and stepped through the walkway, toward a 747 bound for Texas and the next part of her journey. Where life would take her next, she didn't know. Hopefully, her destination, a veterans' retreat, would help guide her in the right direction.

The attendant escorted her to a large, leather seat at the front of the plane.

Her first-class accommodations were definitely an upgrade from the military cargo planes and assault helicopters she'd grown accustomed to traveling in. Physically spent after the long walk through the airport, Alice breathed a sigh of relief. For the next several hours, she could sit and relax.

As she limped over to her window seat, she winced at the sudden muscle cramp in her right leg. She eased herself down and used her strong fingers to knead out the ache, just as her physical therapist instructed. After a minute, the cramp subsided, and she sat upright, begging her body to cooperate for the remainder of the flight and resist any more bursts of pain.

People walked by and down the aisle, rolling small suitcases and carrying bags, travel pillows, and children. One woman wearing a purple pantsuit clutched a designer bag in her hands while whispering words of comfort to the small dog tucked inside. Outside the window, baggage carts hurried around the tarmac.

She hoped both her suitcases would arrive in Austin. Spending two weeks wearing the same outfit would stink, literally.

"Excuse me." A deep voice sounded from the aisle. "Would you mind if we switched seats? I prefer to sit on the inside, away from the aisle."

She turned her attention from the action outside to the man speaking, and her gaze moved up the length of his athletic body, finally settling on a striking pair of brown eyes. After several seconds of flipping through her recently unreliable memory bank, she placed a name with the face. He had the look of a young Keanu Reeves, circa *Point Break*. Despite the fact she recognized him, she wouldn't give Micah Palmer the satisfaction.

Why did he want the interior seat? Maybe to hide from obsessive sports fans, which she was, but neither of him nor his team. "Sure." *Why not?* As long as she remained in first-class, the location of her seat didn't matter. She stood and shuffled out into the aisle.

He was tall, beating her by a few inches, and his hands were large. She imagined he had no trouble keeping a tight grip on a football. Micah was the star quarterback of the Timber Lake Warriors, or more accurately, the former star. After last year, his standing with the team and its fans dropped.

"Thanks." He smiled and stepped back to make room. He moved his gaze from her face to her lower half. "Is your leg okay?"

Forcing her face to remain relaxed, she blocked out the pain radiating from the entire right side of her body. "I'm fine. It's just stiff."

Once Micah was in her old spot, Alice settled herself into the aisle seat and the ache in her leg subsided. At least in her new location, she could stretch her leg into the aisle every so often.

Curious, she subtly peeked at her new neighbor. He was more handsome close-up than on TV. Most people would be thrilled to sit beside a professional football star, but not her. Or, at least, not when the star was Micah Palmer. First, she was a huge fan of the Arizona Scorpions, the Warrior's biggest rival. Second, Micah Palmer missed most of last season due to a torn ACL. Third and most important, she'd read reports about his excessive partying and alleged drug use.

The flow of boarding passengers trickled to a final few people.

She reclined her head on the chair's soft headrest and closed her eyes, listening to the sounds of the attendant preparing for take-off mixed with passengers' chit chat. A phone chimed beside her, and she lifted her eyelids to peer over.

Micah cleared his throat. "Hey…I'm on the plane and need to shut off my phone. What do you need?" After a brief pause, he rubbed his face. "I told you I'll be out of reach for the next two weeks." Another pause. "No, I can't have any guests while I'm there…I got to go…bye."

His groan of obvious frustration made her smile. Alice heard enough through the phone's speaker to concur the caller had been a female admirer. *Poor guy.* All he wanted was two weeks of peace. His phone chimed again, and Alice almost rolled her eyes.

"Cassidy, I'm so glad you called. I wanted to let you know where I'm staying." He straightened in his chair. "Oh, okay." He paused. "That's fine. I should get off my phone anyway, so I'll talk to you soon. Maybe tonight after I get settled in." Micah picked at some lint on his khaki shorts. "Sure, I forgot you're leaving with Ray. Have a good trip…bye."

Another female caller, but she'd received the gold-star treatment. Alice turned her head to gaze upon the seemingly most popular man in the world.

He clicked off his phone. "Sorry about that." He grinned and shrugged. "You know how it is…people need to reach you every second of the day."

"No…I don't know how it is." She returned the smile then mentally slapped the grin off her face. Don't want him thinking she was another flirty, star-struck girl. From what she'd read in news reports, his ego didn't need any more stroking. "I'm lucky if I get a call once a month." Her circle of friends was small and tight. Most of her Army Cultural Support Team sisters were either deployed or busy with their civilian jobs. Her only family was her cousin—a newlywed. Kate had other things on her mind.

"Consider yourself lucky. I'm unplugging these next two weeks. Get off the grid so to speak." Micah slipped his phone into his carry-on bag then showed her his empty palms. "If you see me pull out my phone during the flight, feel free to slap me."

Alice laughed at the invitation. During previous football seasons, she would have loved to do just that. Especially during the game when Micah threw a touchdown pass with eight seconds left for the win, knocking her beloved Scorpions out of the playoffs. "You'll be safe with me. My fighting days are over."

The plane bumped with sudden movement, and then glided away from the gate.

Alice jolted with an increasing tempo in her pulse, either the result of the stress of flying or the nearness of Micah Palmer. So what if he was cute? Good looks weren't necessarily a reflection of a good soul.

She'd brought along a book about helping women in third-world countries become business owners. She opened it in an attempt to read through a couple chapters.

After about fifteen minutes, she gave up, unable to concentrate on the printed words on the page. She had a bad case of the jitters and couldn't calm her over-analytical mind. Flying normally didn't make her nervous. She'd jumped out of planes with nothing but a parachute strapped to her back. Maybe she'd feel better after a nap.

Alice closed her eyes and visualized what might await her when she got off the plane in Austin. She had no idea what to expect. Her friend, former Special Ops soldier Heath Carter, helped start the retreat, and she attended at his invitation. She'd gotten to know Heath when she'd served alongside him in Afghanistan. He was a good man and soldier—actually, the best.

She'd never made a secret of her injuries as a result of an IED and how she still suffered. Heath traveled to visit while she was at Walter Reed and witnessed firsthand the wounds marking her body. He hadn't needed a PhD to understand the damage done to her mind.

Two of her soldier brothers lost their lives to the same IED. Yet, she was still breathing, with a few scars to show as souvenirs. The majority of the fire in her soul had been extinguished, though she safeguarded the small spark that remained.

After two weeks at the retreat, she hoped to discover the answer to the question keeping her wide awake at night—why had she lived?

****

Micah reached across the form of the sleeping woman sitting beside him to accept the glass of ice water with lemon from the attendant. Not exactly what his body craved, but he'd come too far to start over again. Sixty-three days sober. Sixty-three days since he flushed the last of his pills down the toilet.

With this trip, he'd complete the final part of his recovery, like throwing the football into the end zone to win the game. Two more weeks until he'd start serious workouts. His knee injury had fully healed, but the media still questioned his professional abilities, along with his personal integrity. The football stadium was where he belonged. Micah would do anything necessary to earn his way back into its fold.

Working his way back to the top would be a struggle, and he wouldn't want success any other way. Challenges fanned the fire of his inner drive and forged him into a champion before. Why not again?

To focus his active mind on something other than worrying about football, he glanced at his seat partner. Should have asked her name before she fell asleep. He watched as her thick eyelashes fluttered over the dark, sunken skin under her eyes. If he had to guess, he'd say she was in her late twenties. Her delicate features and pretty face appeared as a facade, like a jewel-encrusted scabbard.

She hadn't recognized him, which normally would make him happy. But he was left strangely disappointed by her indifference. Maybe when she woke, he'd drop a few hints and let his celebrity crack the ice. Making small talk with a beautiful woman always helped pass the time.

Unfortunately, she stayed asleep until their plane began its descent into Austin, and then stirred.

The hum of the wheels being lowered filled the plane, and his ears began popping. Micah returned the sports magazine he'd been reading to his duffle-bag then adjusted his baseball cap. "I'm impressed you can sleep on an airplane." He glanced over with a grin. "I can never get comfortable enough."

She stretched her arms overhead and yawned. "I've slept in less comfortable places than a first-class airline seat. If I'm tired enough and have the opportunity, I can sleep anywhere."

"Since I can't snooze during flights, I study the people around me." He exhaled in relief at the bump of the plane touching down. "I use the exercise to clear my mind. I'll pick someone and guess their story."

"Okay…sounds interesting. What's your take on that guy?" She pointed toward the man sitting across the aisle.

Leaning in, he lowered his voice. "His hair is too dark for his age, which means he likely dyes it to cover the gray. The style of his jeans and shirt are too young.

He's also jittery. My bet is he's traveling to meet a younger girlfriend."

"I'd buy that." She nodded. "Do you think he's married?"

"No ring, but he could have removed it. I'll save some hope for humanity and say he's single and not traveling to Texas to cheat on his spouse."

She leaned her head a little closer. "Let's definitely go with single."

Micah's breath caught as her long, brunette ponytail brushed over the skin of his arm. "Now, the lady sitting next to him is on a business trip. She's spent the entire flight reviewing spreadsheets. My guess is she has a big presentation that will either make or break her career." He laughed at himself. Why was he admitting his weird mental game to a stranger? She probably thought he was a creep.

"What did you come up with about me?" She widened her eyes and arched her eyebrows.

"Well, let's see." Micah pretended like he hadn't been studying her while she slept. Again, he wanted to avoid coming off as super creepy, especially if at some point, she recognized him. "I don't see a ring, so I assume you're single. Since you slept through most of the flight, I guess you're sleep-deprived and have small kids."

She scrunched her brows.

But she hadn't interrupted to contradict him, so he continued. "You're traveling for a fitness event. You're tall and built like a volleyball player. You might be a coach."

"Very interesting analysis." She set a lime-colored bag on her lap.

Micah lifted his duffle from underneath the forward seat. The plane's door would open soon, and they'd disembark—each going in a different direction. "So, how did I do? I usually don't get a chance to ask."

She frowned. "Well, I'm not married, so you're right about that, but I don't have children. Earlier in my life, I was very physically active, but that's no longer the case."

"Your leg." Micah thought back to how she'd limped when exiting her seat to switch. "Sport's injury?" If so, he could relate.

The flight crew made the final announcement, and the plane door opened. Other passengers stepped into the aisle to remove their baggage from the overhead bin. After a minute, the line moved toward the front of the plane.

His seat partner stood. A pained grimace emerged on her face.

"When I was injured, the job I was engaged in wasn't a game. It was nice to meet you, Mr. Palmer. Good luck with next year's season."

Micah slumped back in his window seat, watching her turn to face the front of the plane. After a short delay, she moved away with the crowd of people exiting.

So, she had known who he was, but he hadn't gotten her name. Which was okay. He didn't have the time or energy to chase women, not if he wanted to regain his good reputation. And not if he strived to once again become the top quarterback in the National Football League.

Micah strode off the plane and toward the baggage claim. The cool air inside the airport made him shiver.

While he waited for his suitcases to appear, he glanced up at the guitar sculptures displayed above the conveyor belt, which made for an interesting distraction. Only a dozen people asked for an autograph, either on the plane or at the airport. Not like a few years ago, when he couldn't take more than four steps without being mobbed. Nowadays, the only way he made the news was for bad behavior off the field. Come July, the course of his career would change when he'd step onto the practice field for training camp, healthier than ever.

Once he retrieved his suitcase, he searched for the guy who'd drive him to the retreat where he'd volunteered to help. Micah scanned the crowd and noticed the dark-haired woman who'd sat beside him on the plane. She let out a whoop before hugging a lucky guy. Boyfriend maybe?

Wait—the man she embraced looked like the photograph of the guy from the veterans' retreat he was supposed to meet. Micah stepped closer to get a better look. If she knew the guy from the veterans' retreat, then…. The story he'd invented about her on the plane had been wrong. Yes, she was physically fit but not because she was an athlete. The woman with hazel eyes and a long brown ponytail was a soldier.

Chapter Two

"I'm so happy to see your scruffy face." Alice hugged Heath Carter one final time before grabbing the handle of her suitcase. Her tall, dark haired friend served as a real and solid reminder of her time with the Army CST had been real, not a contrived memory.

Heath took hold of the other suitcase. "Happy to see you, too, Lipstick."

His thick beard couldn't hide his amusement from using her old Army nickname.

"Let's not go there, Carter." She bumped him with her hip, causing a slight burn in her muscles. "At least not yet."

"Before we can take off, I need to find the volunteer I'm driving to the retreat. He should have come in on your flight." He glanced around the large space filled with fast-moving people.

"What does he look like?" Alice glanced toward the baggage claim and saw Micah Palmer heading in her direction. The rate of her heart increased. She couldn't shake the guy.

"That's him." Heath stepped toward Micah and held out a hand. "Hey, man, welcome to Texas."

The men shared a handshake—the polite method the male species used to size up one another. Glancing between the two muscular men, she could almost smell the testosterone. "You're volunteering at the Liberty

Veterans' Retreat?" Alice's eyebrows rose. Of all the sport celebrities who donated their time to charities, she'd bet money Micah Palmer was not at the top of the list.

"My teammate, Reagan Harrison, suggested I spend a few weeks volunteering before heading back to training for next season."

Micah flashed a smile as white and bright as a new pair of sneakers. She half-expected him to remove a halo out of his back pocket and set it over his head. In his world, filled with millionaire athletes, good works were done for show. Who had time to help others when he was busy negotiating his next contract?

"Good of you to come down and join us." Heath nodded and walked toward the sliding glass doors. "Our director, Dr. Thompson, has lots of work planned."

As they left the airport and entered the parking structure, Alice walked beside Heath, with Micah trailing behind. She'd decided to ignore him, not wanting to hint at her small excitement from being in the presence of a famous athlete. When they arrived at Heath's SUV, she handed him her suitcase then pulled herself up without much grace into the front seat. During the hour ride to Liberty Ridge, she and Heath reminisced about old times.

Eight years ago, she'd been a member of the first class of female soldiers attached to a Special Operations team. When she'd arrived at their firebase in Afghanistan, Heath and his Special Forces team had not rolled out the welcome mat. For months, she worked hard, earning their respect and a true place on their team. "How's your son doing?" She was delighted to find him happily married and a father after pushing through a battle with PTSD.

"John's growing like a weed." He shook his head and scratched at his beard. "He'll turn two next month. Before I know it, he'll be asking for the key to my Harley."

Chuckling, Alice patted his shoulder. The recent absence of comfortable camaraderie made her appreciate her time spent with Heath. "Seems like just yesterday we were kicking butt out in the Afghan desert. Now look at us…I'm hobbling around, and you've been totally domesticated."

"Not totally. I still have my bike." Heath steered the vehicle onto a gravel drive. Up ahead a wooden sign read, *Welcome to the Liberty Veterans' Retreat.*

Micah stirred in the backseat.

Her and Heath's conversation must have bored him to sleep. Oh, well.

Once parked in front of a huge house, Alice stepped out into the fresh, country air. The pain in her leg returned with a vengeance, radiating down from her hip. After the long car ride, she held onto the SUV for support. Wincing, she rode the wave of throbbing cramps rolling along the right side of her body, while Micah and Heath got the luggage out of the vehicle.

Instead of cursing, she reminded herself she was lucky to still have her right leg. With her leg mangled by shrapnel, the medics worked hard to save it. The price tag was a little pain likely for the rest of her life. She could handle pain. The memory of the source still brought her to her knees. She counted deep breaths until the agony faded. The tinkling vibrato of a glass wind chime filled the air, calming her soul.

The front door opened, and a woman stepped

outside. "Welcome, Alice. I'm Colleen Thompson. So thrilled you're here." Wearing a large smile, she hopped down the porch steps. She was petite, with short blonde hair, and dressed in jeans and a purple plaid shirt.

Alice, standing with the straight posture the Army successfully drilled into her, towered over the shorter woman. By the age of fourteen, Alice had grown to her full height of six feet. If sports had been available where she'd lived, she would have excelled. Instead, her family had cast her as a freak. Too bad their disdain for her height hadn't stopped her parents from arranging a marriage to a man three times her age on her fifteenth birthday. Her stomach churned at the memory.

"Thank you for inviting me, Dr. Thompson." Alice shook the doctor's hand. "Your retreat is beautiful and so peaceful."

"Please call me Colleen. Heath will show you to your cabin, and you can get settled. Take some time, and then when you're ready, come find me in the main house, and we can go over the services available."

Colleen gazed at the man standing to her left. "Welcome to you, as well, Mr. Palmer. I'm delighted you're here to help. Don't worry. I don't plan on working you too hard. We need you in top shape for next season."

Alice glanced over at Micah, who stood with less-than-perfect posture and rocked back on his heels. He appeared unsure, which surprised her. The Micah Palmer she watched on TV and read about in the news burst with over-confidence. Maybe away from the football world, he was just like everyone else.

He stepped forward and flashed a million-watt

smile at Dr. Thompson. Then, he turned that smile on Alice.

Her knees trembled, and her heart knocked in her chest.

Just like the rest of them? Okay…maybe not.

****

Since joining the NFL, Micah had grown to expect to be the center of attention wherever he went. But with these people, he'd been relegated to an afterthought. During the car ride, Heath and Alice had chatted while completely ignoring him. Then, when the retreat's small-in-stature director greeted them, she'd welcomed Alice first. In his youth, he'd been taught a lady should always go first. With that lesson still residing in his brain, he swallowed his ego-filled pride.

"Let me show you to your room, Micah." Dr. Thompson led him in the opposite direction of Alice and Heath. "I set aside a nice, out-of-the-way spot for you in the main building."

He entered through the wide main doors. Inside, he passed a reception desk and several offices, then he entered a tall-ceilinged great room. Dominating the space was a large stone fireplace, which was surrounded by several sofas and chairs.

"This area is the retreat's gathering space. It's a safe zone where the veterans can interact and unwind. We also hold group therapy here." Dr. Thompson pointed to a wide staircase placed at the side of the room. "Your room is upstairs."

He followed her, grumbling internally over being treated like an average volunteer. His presence would give the little retreat some good press. Maybe the director planned something special for later. He'd sign autographs and take pictures with the veterans. Then he'd send a few good pics to his agent.

The team doctors had lectured him that volunteering would be beneficial for his recovery. He couldn't slip back into popping painkillers like they were candy. Most importantly, though, he needed the public back on his side. A few good deeds done in the public eye would certainly help his cause. When he entered his room, he lurched to a halt. "You want me to stay in here?"

"Sure." She glanced at him and smiled. "Don't worry. You won't be in your room for anything other than sleeping. I plan on keeping you very busy." Stepping back through the doorway, she pointed to the left. "Bathroom is down the hall that way. Dinner is outside on the patio at six. Tonight, our cook is grilling steak. Don't be late."

She left him standing in a room the size of a storage closet. A standard twin bed hugged the wall. He imagined he'd sleep with his feet hanging over the end. The only other furniture was a chipped yellow dresser that had seen better days. Fighting a growing sense of indignity, Micah tossed his suitcase on the bed and strolled over to the window.

He shouldn't complain. His childhood bedroom had been smaller than this one, and nobody besides his grandma cared enough to give him space in their house or their heart.

At least the view was good—spectacular, actually. Behind the main building stood a row of ten cabins. Beyond lay acres of rolling, green farm fields. He fixed his focus on the beauty of the retreat, instead of the lackluster welcome and meager lodgings.

He scanned the landscape until his gaze rested on the statuesque woman standing on a cabin porch. Alice—now she was a tall glass of tequila and lime. And those long legs—they stretched to infinity.

She might no longer be in the Army, but her military bearing remained. Even with her limp, she walked with a long stride.

She sat on a rocking chair and took out a book. Then she opened it and began writing.

His first instinct was to go over and claim a seat on the rocker next to hers. Instead, he'd give her space. Later, he'd find an opportunity to get to know her better.

Lucky for him, he'd see a lot of her over the next few weeks, giving him plenty of time to uncover the true story of Alice.

****

It's too quiet here. Alice lay in bed, her eyes wide open, staring into the darkness. Resisting the urge to peek at the digital clock on the bedside table, she flopped over to face the other direction and punched her pillow. Why couldn't she fall asleep? Normally, she could fall asleep anywhere. Memories of her multiple deployments and what she witnessed held her hostage inside her own head—blood-soaked fatigues, hungry children, and buildings turned into rubble. The sounds of bomb blasts and rapid rifle fire rang in her ears. She had no escape and nowhere to run. Her past dogged her like a rabid animal.

While resting on her side, she struggled for breath, which grew heavy and strained. Accepting defeat, she crawled out of bed and slid on a pair of shorts and a sweatshirt. Outside, the air was still and held a touch of chill. She focused on breathing in and out. *Inhale…Exhale…Relax, you're safe.*

She contemplated her plans for the future—building a path to carry her through the rest of her life. But at thirty years old, she had no idea where to begin. She'd devoted eleven years to the United States Army. Now, she was physically injured and emotionally drained. Could she find a passion that her body would allow her to pursue? One thing she knew for sure, she wouldn't continue living in the pit of sinking sand she'd become trapped inside. Though fear kept her paralyzed. Would one wrong move cause her to sink farther?

What came next after the retreat? Back to her apartment in South Carolina? Then what? She came here to find direction. Only one certainty remained—wherever she decided to go next, she'd go alone.

The fresh, night air returned her sense of calm. She went inside and climbed back into bed, giving sleep another chance. The next morning, she walked to the main building for breakfast. As she approached the kitchen, the smell of bacon made her mouth water. At the voice inside her head reminding her of her vow to eat healthy, she gritted her teeth. Instead of the bacon and pancakes she wanted, she helped herself to a lightly buttered bagel and fresh fruit.

Several tables stood scattered on the floor—a slight improvement from an Army mess hall—with more outside on the patio. The temperature was still cool, but she preferred chilly weather to sitting at a table with other people. Those present might be fellow soldiers but to her, they were still strangers. Alice balanced her plate, fruit bowl, and mug in one hand and reached for the patio door handle.

"Let me get that." Micah appeared at her side.

"Thanks." She stepped aside to let him slide open the door.

He followed her. "Do you mind if I join you? It's getting crowded in there."

She should tell him no. She'd come outside to be alone. She was better off alone. Instead of telling him to get lost, she hauled out her dusty good manners. Alice shrugged and sat at an empty table. "I don't care."

"Let me grab some grub. I'll be right back." Micah hustled inside.

Gifting her with a nice view of his round, blue jean-covered backside. *Great.* Worse than eating at a table full of fellow veterans was sitting alone with one pesky football star. Shouldn't he prefer to stay with a group of guys who obviously thought he walked on water? Judging from the festive reaction he'd received last night at dinner, Micah Palmer could be nominated for sainthood.

Did anyone else care that last year he'd partied instead of concentrating on his recovery from the ACL tear? What about the rumors of drug addiction? Just because he could toss a ball farther than most people didn't get him off the hook for bad behavior.

Micah exited through the patio doors. "What's with the scowl?"

He set down a plate so full of food, the white china looked like it would snap in half.

Pulling out a chair, he placed himself directly across from her.

"I don't scowl. I have a resting grumpy face." She flicked a gaze over at the bagel in her hand, then took a bite.

"You don't fool me. I've seen your very pretty smile."

"Haven't had many reasons to smile lately." She lifted her fork and twirled it between her fingers, watching the flash of her reflection in the shiny metal. She had a sparkle in her eyes that hadn't been there earlier that morning. When was the last time she'd really laughed? She remembered the night before the raid that changed her life. She and a few fellow soldiers played poker outside in the hot, dusty space between two tents, set up on a rickety table, telling one crazy story after another until four in the morning. Twenty-four hours later, one of those storytellers was dead.

"And why is your smile hiding these days?" Micah gazed from across the table.

Her stomach tightened. "I'm staying at a veterans' retreat that specializes in helping soldiers with PTSD. You've seen me walk and appear to be a smart guy. I'm sure you can figure it out." She studied the bowl of fruit by her plate.

His smile faded. "I'm sorry if you think I'm prying. From now on, I'll stick to safe topics…like the weather, or how the NFL shouldn't allow female referees." Micah waved his fork in the air. "Like really, what do girls know about football?"

Alice choked on the coffee she'd begun swallowing. "You better not be serious." Micah's laughter was deep and rich.

"See, I knew you had a smile in there."

Her widening grin had a mind of its own. The man was incorrigible.

"Do you watch football?" Micah asked.

"In full disclosure, I'm a huge Arizona Scorpions

fan. The Warriors are enemy number one." She held up an index finger.

"Then I guess our conversation is over." He stood and took several steps toward the door. "My contract states I can't associate with Scorpion's fans."

Another smile pulled on her lips. "Please. If anything, I shouldn't be talking with *you*."

He walked backward and returned to his seat. "Why is that?"

Because she was just as messed up as him. "You're one of the best quarterbacks in the league. Maybe *the* best. Once you're back to full strength, the Warriors will be unstoppable." *And I'm seeing you as a human being, a nice guy, not just a celebrity ball player.*

"Those reasons sound like you should want to hang around me." He wiggled his dark eyebrows.

"Sure, if you weren't playing for the Scorpions' chief rival."

Nodding, he waggled a finger. "The Scorpions are a solid team, and their quarterback is a good guy. I enjoy playing against them. Good competition brings out the best in both teams."

"Do you miss playing?" Alice rested her arms on the table and leaned in.

Micah exhaled a long breath and brushed back his floppy bangs. "Football is my life. When my injury took away what I loved most, I didn't deal well."

Without the thrill of football, she figured he was left with a gaping hole, similar to when she'd been medically discharged from the Army. Only she hadn't turned to drugs or alcohol. Though she'd been blessed with privacy. Her coping mechanisms hadn't been made public, unlike Micah. "You're fully recovered now, right? Will you attend training camp in July?"

"I'll be there, ready to rock-n-roll." Micah balled up his napkin and rocketed it into the garbage can across the patio. The paper ball bounced off the rim and onto the ground. With a shrug, he walked over and deposited it inside. "Good thing I stayed with football, not basketball."

Alice finished her breakfast. She was ready to take her dishes inside then return to her cabin but felt awkward leaving him to sit alone. Since her therapy session didn't start for an hour, she saw no harm in hanging around a little longer. "So, why did you come here to volunteer? I'm sure you could find plenty of other places closer to home."

He took a bite of waffle, chewed, and then cleared his throat. "If you follow football, you'll have heard of Reagan Harrison. He's a teammate and has helped me through some rough times. Anyway, he's married to Julie, whose late husband was Heath Carter's friend, John Ellis." His smile faded. "You might have heard about the cover-up regarding his death?"

Hearing John's name filled her with sadness. Yes, she had. John Ellis had been killed in action before her time in the Cultural Support Team. Heath had talked about John and the guilt he carried over his best friend's death. "John Ellis is well known by those of us who served alongside Special Forces."

He slumped in his chair. "Reagan encouraged me to take some time before training camp to *yank my head out of my rear*...his words, not mine. Also, I remember him threatening to *fold me into a taco if I screw up*."

Alice chuckled at the image of the linebacker giving his all-star quarterback a bit of tough love. "So, you volunteering at the retreat is not just a PR stunt?"

"Honestly, I need some good PR. I've struggled during the off-season. Reagan views volunteering as a personal growth opportunity." He narrowed his eyes. "I'm focused on getting back onto the football field." Micah finished eating.

They stood in sync and cleared off their dishes.

Alice turned to face him and not for the first time felt the pull of attraction, which produced tiny flutters in her chest. She'd never fully trust her heart to any man. She loved the men she considered her military brothers, yes. Some of her best friends were men.

Micah seemed like a nice guy. He could grow to become another friend. A cute friend, but she had plenty of those already. No big deal. A handsome face and sexy smile didn't have the power to make her melt. Or set aside her conviction to live her life as a single woman. As long as she lived alone, she wouldn't be subject to someone else's demands.

She entered through the rear entrance of the main building and stopped inside the now-empty dining area, glancing at Micah. "I didn't leave the Army voluntarily. I had a career-ending injury and understand how you feel, craving something to the point where the infection eats away all your peace. You've been granted a two-week reprieve from the pressures of football. Take the break as a gift and turn your focus on helping others."

"The pressures of football never leave, not even here." Micah swirled a finger at their surroundings. "I'm sorry about what happened. I hope you find enjoyment here. But for me, the only way I'll get back my life is throwing touchdowns again."

He was lucky. Micah would recover what he'd lost.

Alice, on the other hand, had a body and mind too damaged to fulfill her dreams.

Chapter Three

"You want me to do what?" Micah stood beside a small, red barn, arms crossed over his chest. He'd known the retreat shared land with an organic farm. The expectation to provide manual labor for said farm was a surprise.

Storm Thompson clenched his jaw and held out a sheet of paper. "Here's the instructions. The lumber is over there. Chicken wire, staples and all the tools you'll need are in the barn. It's a small chicken coop. Should take you only a few hours, tops."

"I understand what you want me to do, but I don't understand why. Don't you have hired hands for this kind of stuff?" He stepped back. No way was he, a high-paid professional athlete, spending even an hour constructing a farm building.

Storm snatched the instructions out of Micah's hand. "Fine. You can't build a chicken coop. I'll get someone else."

Micah took back the plans with a huff. "I didn't say I couldn't."

The corner of Storm's mouth lifted in a smile. "Great. Have fun. Call if you need help."

He wouldn't need help. Of course, he could build a stupid chicken coop. How hard could it be? After reading over the directions twice, he conceded the task was harder than anticipated. But he'd never admit his uncertainty to Storm. He'd build the darn chicken coop if it took him all day.

Unfortunately, he worked on the project for most of the day, despite, or more likely, due to his bravado. The first boards he'd nailed together were crooked, which then made everything erected afterwards look like a drunk tried his hand at carpentry. He disassembled the entire thing and started over.

Now, the sound of the dinner bell echoed across the field. Stretching the chicken wire across the last side and stapling it into place was his final task. Dinner would wait. He wasn't leaving until his job was completed.

At seven o'clock, he finally entered the dining room—officially the last one through the line. Micah accepted a plate of cold ham, corn, and scalloped potatoes, and the cook gave him a sympathetic-looking nod. He sat alone and listened to the sounds of conversation and laughter drifting out of the great room.

Lifting the fork to his mouth, he groaned from the agony radiating from his right shoulder. How could he be sore from swinging a hammer? Micah rotated his shoulder a few times in an attempt to loosen the muscles, and the sharp pain made him whimper. Fortunately, no one around to witness his humiliation.

"Rough day?" Alice appeared through the kitchen door. "I can rub your shoulder muscles and see if I can work out the knots."

She looked tall and lean in tight jeans and a snug, long-sleeve shirt. "It's nothing." He scooped up a chunk of ham, pretending like the act of lifting a fork wasn't killing him.

She stood behind him.

The warmth of her body surrounded him. The heat of her hands set fire to his shoulder.

"I took physical therapy classes before changing my major, but I remember a few tricks." She pressed the palm of her hand into the upper trapezius on his left side.

"What was your rank in the Army?" He needed a distraction from the mixing sensations of pain and release coursing through his body. Letting his head drop, he braced his hands on the table and closed his eyes.

"First Sergeant, but started as an Intelligence Officer. I was deployed four times…once to Iraq, the final three to Afghanistan."

"Impressive. Did you see much action?" he asked before her finger pushed into a nerve. "*Ow*."

"Sorry. I'll be gentler."

The sound of her quiet laughter made him smile.

"My early days were spent mostly behind a desk. Toward the end of my career, I was attached to several Special Operations teams, which is how I met Heath. I accompanied the team on village stability operations and intelligence-gathering missions. My job entailed handling the women and children found at each location."

"Were you a commando?"

Her laughter filled the otherwise quiet room. "No, but close. The men on my team nicknamed me Lipstick, because I always wore makeup when we went on a mission. Their teasing was mostly in good fun. I had to identify myself quickly as a woman when dealing with the Afghan women. Wearing makeup and perfume was an easy way to communicate my femininity across language barriers."

Had she been injured on one of those missions? He reached up and covered her hand with his own. His temper burned at the thought of someone intentionally hurting her. "I can't imagine everything you must have experienced." How could he when he played football for a living?

"My job was rough but very rewarding. I had to keep up with the tough guys doing the door kicking. Serving with those men was the best time of my life."

He kept quiet, even though he craved to know everything about her. Too much information could be risky. Especially when his attraction came dangerously close to caring.

Alice lifted her hand off his shoulder. "There…feel better?"

After a few rotations, he felt the muscles loosen. Her painful kneading had worked. "Almost as good as new. Thanks."

"No problem. Well…see you later."

As he watched her long stride take her out of the room, he wondered what she hid under her tough exterior. On the surface, she seemed calm and totally put together. But then again, so did he. Every day, he balanced on the tightrope of returning to the comfort of pills and striving for greatness. He couldn't have both. He'd tried and failed. Shooting to his feet, he held his plate to return it to the kitchen. Could he stay clean and get back to the top? Or would his hunger for winning and fame leave him an empty shell of addiction and failure?

****

The next morning, Alice picked at the lint balls decorating her sweater and waited for her therapy session to begin. Today marked her second session with Dr. Thompson. She was scheduled to meet for individual counseling once a day but could request more, if she felt the need. Asking for more help was as likely as asking for an extra helping of cooked peas. Not pleasant but sometimes the healthiest option.

So far, once a day was more than enough. She was guarded with what she shared with anyone, even a psychiatrist. Alice refused to talk about her life before the Army. Her early years had no bearing on the person she was today.

"How do you find the facilities?" Dr. Thompson sat on the navy upholstered chair across from her.

Colleen, as she preferred to be called, was slim, with short blonde hair and bright blue eyes, which could be either soothing or piercing, depending on how cooperative Alice was. "Everything is very nice. I went for a walk yesterday and explored the property. You really have a lovely location." Easy enough question to answer.

"I'm glad you feel comfortable here. Have you taken the opportunity to meet the other veterans yet?"

Not really, and she had no desire of doing so. A few of the men were here with their spouses. She was the only female soldier at the retreat. Why would she engage with soldiers whom she hadn't served with and never would? Alice clenched her fists. "I'm here to find myself, not make new friends. I'm sure the guys are good men, but I can't be burdened with their problems, too."

"I understand." The corners of Colleen's mouth

lowered. "Sometimes, listening to another's struggles can help you."

A tickle built in her throat, and she coughed. Hadn't she said that exact thing to Micah yesterday? "Okay, I'll try."

"Don't put yourself in a situation where you feel uncomfortable, but don't close yourself off, either. I know you were very close to the other women in the Cultural Support Team and also the Special Ops soldiers you served alongside. Do you struggle from losing those connections?"

"I still keep in touch with some, but it's not the same. My discharge hit me like a death. The Army was my family, and now, I'm separated from the community." Nerves fluttered in her gut.

"What about your natural family? Mom, Dad, brothers or sisters? Are you close?" Colleen wrote on a notepad in the open folder on her lap.

A sickening tightness grew in Alice's gut. *They can't hurt you anymore. You're dead to them, just like they are to you.* "I don't talk about my biological family."

Colleen lifted her gaze and blinked. "Not even in a safe setting? What you say in here is confidential."

Pain stabbed her temples at the memories. She had no idea the horror Alice had lived with for sixteen years. How could she explain her history without burning with shame? No words would heal those scars. Alice's real name had been Esther Wolf. She was the tenth child of her creep of a father. Besides a few whippings, he hadn't physically harmed her. But she knew his heart was as black as the gun he kept under his bed. She'd witnessed the way he dominated his wives and children, hurling verbal abuse and threats.

Her dad had six wives and promised her to another polygamist when she reached the age of seventeen. The man who'd wanted her as his wife, Lyle Walters, was equally dark-hearted and cruel. If she hadn't run away, she would have become Lyle's fourth wife.

With the hindsight of an adult, she couldn't comprehend how grown men treated teenage girls and women like property and have not paid for their crimes. But their community lived in an isolated compound deep in rural Arizona. While living there, she hadn't once seen a member of law enforcement. The leader of their sect was the only law the group knew. After she ran away, she finally understood how royally messed up her upbringing had been. "I don't talk about anything in my life that happened before the age of eighteen," Alice said, firmer than was necessary. Her back stiffened.

"Let's drop the subject of your family…for now, and focus on your future. Where do you see yourself in five years, or even ten?" Colleen rested back in her chair.

Good question. And one Alice had no good answer for. She could easily take her military training and convert those skills into a well-paying civilian job. Although the thought of being chained to a desk for the rest of her working life lacked appeal.

Six months ago, a fellow CST veteran had offered her an assignment with her consulting company, training women for entrepreneurship in third-world countries. She'd been tempted but at the time, felt too weak to travel overseas. Even now, she didn't know if she had the stamina. "In five years, I'd like to do something that leaves me fulfilled…something that challenges me. What that is, I don't know. Ten years out is too far removed to even consider."

"And what makes you happy?" Colleen asked.

"Before, I was happiest when I exercised, keeping my body in top shape." She grimaced. "Now, I can't even walk without pain. The idea of being inside the gym again makes me anxious. When I was active duty and serving on the Cultural Support Team, my life had meaning. I was doing something groundbreaking. I enjoyed helping others and being part of a team." She swallowed hard. "Then my purpose was stripped away by the terrorist who planted that IED. Right now, I have no purpose and for me, that's scarier than facing another bomb."

"Coming to terms with a life-changing event is difficult." Colleen smiled. "The physical after-effects make moving on even harder. Here's my homework for you…journal experiences during the day that make you both happy and sad. Take time at the retreat to reassess your future. Next time we meet, we'll discuss what you've discovered."

The session ended, and Alice left the building, finding the breeze refreshing to her overwhelmed mind. Long-buried memories stirred. Thinking about her future was almost as unsettling.

She'd spent her entire adult life running from the demons of her childhood. Besides her cousin, Kate, no one in her family knew her new name or where she lived.

Panic rose from deep in her core into her chest. Her left hand tingled, then grew numb. She leaned against one of the porch beams for support. Black spots drifted across her vision.

"Are you all right?" a deep voice sounded from behind.

She blinked to clear her vision. "Yes…no. I need to sit down."

Micah stepped alongside her. He held her elbow and supported her as she lowered onto the porch step. "Can I get you something to drink?"

"No, thanks." She rested her forehead on her knees and took long, deep breaths. Micah's thigh brushed against hers. The reassurance of his presence helped ground her back to the here and now. A tingling sensation ran from her leg to the back of her neck, causing her to shiver. A reminder that her attraction to Micah meant she was still very much alive.

****

Micah sat helplessly beside Alice. The waves of her brown hair reflected the sunlight as it cascaded down around her like a protective curtain. A curtain he itched to peel back and discover what hid behind.

After a few minutes, she lifted her head and blew out a breath. "That freak out was embarrassing."

"Don't be embarrassed. My grandma suffers from anxiety attacks. What happens to your body during an attack is out of your control."

"I don't know what happened. One second I was fine, the next…my body shut down."

Micah patted her hand, which was cool to the touch. "Have you had panic attacks before?"

"I've had bouts of anxiety but nothing so sudden and intense. I'm feeling better." Breathing heavy, she stood on unsteady legs. "Thanks for your help."

Placing his hand under her elbow, he helped her

keep her balance. "Your body might need time to flush out the excess adrenaline. Take a break and relax. I'll walk you back to your cabin."

"I need to stay outdoors." She swept off strands of brunette hair stuck to her damp forehead. "Go back to whatever you were doing. I'm fine."

She didn't look fine, not with her hands shaking and skin as pale and gray as fog. "I was on my way to check in with Storm to find out what new form of torture he's come up with for today. Trust me, you'd do me a huge favor by letting me hang out with you."

She laughed.

He loved hearing the sound—light and easy—a contrast to the tough-as-nails woman.

"What did you think you'd do here as a volunteer, pose for pictures?" Alice met his gaze and grinned.

"Something like that." He hid the truth under the joking tone of his voice. When he'd agreed to volunteer, he had expected photo ops and maybe a few arts and crafts. "Pounding nails all day yesterday almost destroyed my shoulder."

"You're a professional quarterback. Aren't you supposed to be in shape or something?" She patted his bicep.

"I haven't played since last September." Micah fought against the memory of the game that changed everything and the stabbing pain after his injury when he lay crippled on the playing field.

Her gaze dropped to the long scar on the outside of his knee. "How about we take a walk? I found a nice trail that leads to a pond. We both can escape for a little while."

"Sounds good." He really liked Alice. Not in a I-have-the-hots-for-you way. She was easy to talk to and liked football, even if she did cheer for another team. Plus, too many questions about her remained unanswered.

They walked side by side toward the path, and Micah stole quick glances. She was very pretty—a tall brunette with wide hazel eyes that reminded him of a cat. "How often does your injured leg bother you?"

Crossing her arms over her body, she shrugged. "Some days are better than others. Most of the damage from the IED blast was done to my leg, but some shrapnel found its way into my side and arm. I make a pretty picture in a swimsuit." She grunted and shook her head.

Despite her blunt self-assessment, he pushed forward with the subject. He imagined the scars would only add to her appeal. "You survived, which is something to be proud of."

Dry grass crunched under their shoes in a catchy staccato. The twitters of barn swallows and the buzz of insects filled the air.

She remained silent for several minutes. "I was lucky. Another soldier pushed me out of the way when the IED went off. Two other soldiers never saw another sunrise. I feel guilty for being here right now, while their families are living without them. I have no children, no husband, and no parents who'd mourn me." She shook her head. "Why did I come home and they didn't?"

"You were handed a second chance. The real question is…what will you do with it?"

He should ask himself the same question. His knee had recovered. He'd kicked his painkiller addiction. He had a second chance to redeem himself—not only in the fans' eyes but his own. And then Cassidy—the one that got away. He'd lost her because of his bad behavior and refusal to seek help.

Cassidy moved on with one of Micah's friends, no less. If he could prove he was a reformed man, would he have a second chance with the love of his life?

Alice stopped and peered over with one eyebrow cocked. "Have you been talking to Dr. Thompson?"

"No." Micah shook his head. "Why?"

"She's after me to make decisions about my future. My plan had been to serve in the Army until I retired." Frowning, she grunted. "Now, I feel like a kid who's discovering what she wants to be when she grows up."

"Let me tell you a story." He began walking. "Growing up, I lived mostly with my Korean grandmother. She was never overly impressed with my athletic ability. She'd say 'Micah, just because you throw a ball far doesn't mean you are more special than anyone else.' "

Alice laughed. "She sounds like a very wise woman."

Yes, and Alice was wise not to get hung up on his talent for football, as well. "She is the smartest person I've ever met, but at the time, I thought she didn't understand how hard I worked at earning my spot on a professional football team. I hated taking college classes. All I wanted was to play football. Luckily, you aren't as thick-headed as me. You have options."

"You're part Korean?" she asked.

"Is my ethnicity all you took away from my heartfelt speech?" He placed a hand over his heart and tipped his head to the sky. "And I thought I channeled my inner Dr. Phil. Yes, I'm a quarter Korean, the rest is a mixture of Italian, Russian, and German." Micah patted his chest. "I'm a regular United Nations."

The narrow path opened into a wide field. Ahead, the sun glinted off the calm water of a pond. Tall grass and Texas Yellowstar flowers swayed with the breeze.

"What about you?" He stopped at the water's edge. Little sparrows darted through the blue sky. "What was your family like growing up?" Her face, which slowly regained its rosy color, drained pale.

"I don't talk about my family." She walked away, around to the other side of the pond.

Micah's own parents were losers—both in jail by the time he could walk. His paternal grandmother had taken him in and raised him, and the family living next door had unofficially adopted him. Their son, Jamal, had been Micah's best friend.

He understood Alice keeping private about her family but sensed something deeper. Not much he could do to help when he had issues of his own. Even on a beautiful day like today and walking with an attractive woman, he couldn't shake the darkness and fear inside. Who would he be without football? A regular guy living an average life. Who was he now? A man willing to risk everything for another shot at becoming the best.

He glanced down at the pond, saw his image in its smooth water, and wasn't sure he liked what reflected back.

Chapter Four

For Alice, sitting in group therapy was as unpleasant as a twenty-mile ruck hike. How many more sob stories would she listen to before the group was dismissed? She could sympathize with these men. Too well. But she simply hated reliving the worst parts of deployment over and over again.

Personally, she'd rather remember the good times—the forged bond of the CST sisterhood, her first mission with a Special Ops team, the rush of adrenaline when she served as the team's gunner while they rode across the bumpy streets of Kabul.

Her chest ached with yearning. How had she gone from desert soldier to sitting around talking about her feelings? From the fidgeting of the men around her, she guessed they shared similar thoughts.

Their therapist, Becky Moore, handed them each a piece of paper. When she sat again, she crossed her jean-clad legs and smiled. "Look to the person on your left and focus solely on the exterior. What is your initial impression? Write the reasons you think he or she is here."

Alice peered to her left. The man was young, maybe early twenties. He had burn scars on his left arm and across a portion of his face. His left leg was amputated below the knee.

What was her first impression? She glanced at both

of her feet, still attached to her body and encased in brown boots. Should she write her true feelings? He hadn't been as lucky as she had. Instead, she wrote that he looked too young to have to deal with the damaging effects of war.

The group of fifteen handed their papers to the therapist, who then read each statement aloud. She'd tasked the group to guess which one was being described.

Becky unfolded the next sheet. "She's probably a victim of sexual assault, since women don't have combat-related trauma."

Alice ground her teeth. *Typical*. She had seen combat many times during her service. If anyone had tried to rape her, he would have gone home minus a few parts.

Everyone's gaze rested on her.

"Alice, the comment was obviously meant for you," Becky said. "What do you have to say in reply?"

She stared at the man to her right—a middle-aged guy with buzzed blond hair—causing him to squirm in his chair. "What can I say? He's generalizing because of my gender."

"I didn't mean…" the man stammered.

"I know exactly what you meant." Alice waved a hand to cut him off. "Let's move on."

Fifteen minutes later, group therapy ended. She escaped the torture cell and immediately strode outside to inhale fresh country air. On her way back to her cabin, she saw Heath coming toward her.

"*Ciao, bella*." He jogged to meet her at the cabin stairs. "Just the person I want to see."

"You speak Italian now?" She snickered.

"I'm a man of many talents. How about you come over to the ranch for the afternoon? I'd love to introduce you to Grace and my little guy."

"You are my knight in shining armor." She sighed and pulled him into a hug. A break was exactly what she needed—time to clear her mind and refocus on her goal.

Heath lowered his eyebrows and gazed at her. "What's going on? You look upset."

"I'm fine. Let me grab my purse, and we can talk on the way." Alice darted to her cabin, picked up her hot pink leather bag from the bedside table, and ran outside to join Heath by his SUV. She climbed into the front seat.

Micah appeared from around the corner of the storage shed, pushing a wheelbarrow. He waved. "Hey! Where do you think you're going?"

"Day trip to Heath's ranch. Looks like you're having fun." She watched as Micah tripped over a board and barely recovered his balance.

The momentum forced the wheelbarrow to tip, waver, and fall to its side. Dirt and weeds spilled out over the grass.

"Please take me with you?" Micah kicked at the pile of dirt, sending up a shower of pebbles and dark soil. "I didn't volunteer for manual labor."

"You volunteered to help in whatever way the director deemed necessary," Heath interjected through the open car window of the driver's side. "Storm thought you'd be useful helping with the chores, and look, you're being useful…kind of."

"I don't like pushing around dirt." Micah set the wheelbarrow upright, only to have it fall over once

40

again. He slumped and hung his head.

Alice disregarded the urge to walk over, rub his back, and tell him everything would be okay. He looked so dejected. For all Micah's outward bravado, she'd noticed a vulnerable side. He was a man who not only craved attention, but also approval.

"We have to go." Heath put the vehicle in Drive. "Don't worry, I'll have Ms. Liddell back before sundown."

As Alice and Heath drove away, she glanced backwards at Micah.

He gave the tipsy wheelbarrow a kick before reaching down to scoop up spilled dirt.

Alice turned her attention to the road ahead and ignored the hitch in her heart. Maybe she should have invited him to come along. How had she gotten so attached to him in only a few days when she worked so hard to keep her distance from others? The charming Micah Palmer had totally blown past all her defenses.

****

Micah deposited the wheelbarrow from hell back in the shed. After slamming closed the door, he went inside the main building and hid in his room before Storm handed out more chores. He grabbed his phone and flopped onto his tiny bed. Two voicemails waited.

The first was from Carl, his agent, who'd approved of Micah volunteering at the retreat before the kick-off of the preseason. "It will be good for your image," he had said. "We need to win back both the fans and sponsors."

In the voicemail, Carl stated he'd scheduled a reporter for an on-site interview. He straightened his posture. Just what Micah had been waiting to hear.

He'd pose for good publicity shots with the veterans and speak about how he'd grown as a person since last season. He would convince the sports world he was totally committed to football.

The second came from Hailey, a woman he'd met during his drug-haze days. Since the moment he'd entered rehab, Micah cut contact with anyone who threatened his recovery. He deleted the message from Hailey, then tossed the phone facedown onto the bed. The only person he wanted a call from was Cassidy, who was in Rome, mixing work and a holiday with her new boyfriend.

After breaking up, she'd quickly moved on. If only she'd waited for him to clean-up his life. But she hadn't. She'd said loving an addict broke her heart, so she'd left him to hit bottom on his own.

Now, that dark part of life was behind him. He'd recovered and stayed clean for twelve weeks. Maybe someday, Cassidy would give him another chance to prove himself worthy. Six months from now, he could possibly have everything back he valued—his career and the love of his life.

A knock on the door jolted him from sleep.

"Micah, man…you in there?"

Couldn't a guy get a few minutes peace?

The knocking sounded again.

"Yeah." He scrubbed his hands down his face. "What do you need?"

"I could use your help," Storm yelled through the door. "Meet me by the sheep pen."

At the sound of Storm's boots retreating down the hall, Micah cursed. Just when he thought his day couldn't get any worse.

****

"It's been almost a year since I visited you at Walter Reed." Heath drove toward True Horizon Ranch, one hand on the wheel. "A couple days ago, when I saw you at the airport, I said to myself…there's the Alice I know and love. My warrior princess."

"I'm not a warrior princess." The bomb blast had knocked all the fight out of her. Sorrow built in her chest. She rested her elbow on the door panel and set her forearm against the cool glass of the window. Outside, acres of green farmland spread over the rise of low hills for as far as her eyes could see. "To be honest, Heath, I don't know who I am anymore."

"You are who you've always been…Alice Liddell." Heath tapped on the steering wheel. "Your heart hasn't changed."

She hadn't trusted anyone with the true story of her upbringing. No one but her cousin knew she legally changed her name at the age of eighteen. On that birthday, she was born again—a birth by fire. She was no longer Esther, a scared child on the run. "My identity was a soldier with the US Army. Now that's gone. In the past, I've always been confident in my plans and pursued them without doubt. Why does every path forward now feel uncertain?" Alice enlisted as soon as her name change became legal. Joining the military had been her goal since a few months after leaving the compound when she'd seen a picture of a female soldier in a magazine. The woman had appeared strong and tough, exactly what Alice wanted to become.

"You were always more than that," Heath said. "Remember the scones you used to bake on base? You had guys hanging around your place, begging for one because they were so good."

Funny how those little, mundane things in life became buried under more emotionally powerful events. She'd forgotten that when she was stressed, she'd spent hours baking in her kitchen. The smells coming out of her little apartment at Fort Bragg would draw in hungry soldiers like stray dogs to a meat shop. "You're right. My blueberry scones were to die for."

"You could open a little bakery." Heath turned onto a long driveway, then drove underneath the metal arch of True Horizon Ranch. The colorful tattoos covering his arms glowed under the sunlight beaming through the windshield. "Many parts of you have nothing to do with the Army. Your fitness obsession could easily translate into a job as a personal trainer."

"I haven't stepped into a gym since the explosion. I'm very out of shape." Under her clothes, she felt the lack of muscle. Her once-toned stomach was slightly rounded. After her injury, she'd steadily lost weight and muscle mass. She'd grown soft and avoided looking at her body in the mirror.

Heath parked beside a large, white farmhouse and turned. "I have an idea. Our friend Micah Palmer could use a bit of tough love and needs to get in top shape for training camp. Let him be your guinea pig. The retreat has a little gym, and I know you have a good imagination. Try out your trainer skills on him and maybe find a new career."

Heath jumped out of the SUV before she could form a reply. He waved for her to follow him to a huge barn.

Inside, brightly lit horse stalls stood in long rows on either side of the aisle. The smell of fresh hay tickled her nose, causing her to sneeze.

"Bless you," a voice called out. A woman exited one of the stalls, holding a dark-haired toddler. She held out her free hand. "I'm Grace Carter. It's nice to meet you, Alice."

A soothing comfort filled her at meeting the woman who'd saved Heath from self-destruction. Alice shook her hand. "It's a pleasure. I never imagined wild Heath as a rancher, but I have to admit…country life suits him."

"Yes, it does." She laughed, and the little boy in her arms reached over for Heath. "Except for his fear of horseback riding."

Now in Heath's arms, the little boy stopped squirming and rested his head on his dad's broad shoulder.

"I'm not afraid of riding horses." Heath stroked the dark hair on the back of baby John's head. "They just have it out for me."

Alice's heart swelled in pride for Heath and how far he'd come. He'd spent a long time grieving the loss of a good friend, fought guilt and anger, survived a death wish, and somehow found love and peace. Despite her own lack of faith in the institution, she thought marriage was good for Heath. How did anyone promise forever?

Love and marriage might be the answer for some people, but not for someone like her. Would her wounds ever heal enough to change her mind?

****

A Star Wars movie marathon was scheduled for that evening. The retreat staff would show the original three, projected on a big screen outside. Watching movies was an activity Micah's tired body could get behind. The earlier sheep incident almost sent him packing his bags to leave. What a shock to learn fuzzy sheep were really stubborn beasts. He'd almost lost a finger from his throwing hand due to their snappy temper.

He sat on a lawn chair toward the back of the open grassy area and watched others filter in, chatting in small groups before filling in the empty chairs. The night air was still warm, and the buzz of conversation relaxed him. A line of tall oak trees stood behind the big screen set up for the movie, and their branches swayed with the light breeze.

Across the dimly lit yard, Alice appeared and stood alone on the stone paver patio.

When he caught her attention, he waved her over. "I've saved you a seat." He patted the empty chair next to him. "But only if you can tell me what planet Princess Leia was from."

"Alderaan." She sat, then relaxed into the lawn chair. "Easy question. What substance was Hans Solo frozen in at the end of *The Empire Strikes Back*?"

He snorted. "You mock my intelligence. Solo was frozen in carbonite. Get this last one right, and I'll go get the popcorn."

"Bring it." Alice cocked an eyebrow.

"In which country were the Tatooine scenes filmed?"

She chewed the corner of her lip. "I know it's in Africa. Does that count?"

Did Alice have any idea how cute she looked? He enjoyed those moments when she let down her guard and he caught a glimpse of a fun-loving girl who lived life to the fullest. "Nope. I will need the name of the country for the win." He counted off the passing seconds with clicks of his tongue.

"Tunisia," she shouted out.

"I thought I had you." Micah stood and stretched his exhausted legs. "Do you take butter and salt?"

"Of course." She smiled. "Is there any other way?"

A few minutes later, he returned with one large bowl and set it down on Alice's lap. "Only one bowl left. Okay if we share?"

"Sure. Thanks." She dug a hand in to grab some popcorn. Within seconds, the opening lines of the movie rolled onto the screen. "Good to meet a fellow movie geek," she whispered.

When he reached across and grabbed another handful of popcorn, he accidentally brushed his fingers against Alice's hand. His heart skipped from the brief contact. A physical attraction to her did come as a surprise, but he felt a stirring of something more growing under the surface. He'd have to be careful not to allow a deeper connection to take root.

"What did you do this afternoon?" She glanced at him wearing a smirk. The light off the projector screen glowed on her skin.

"You mean what cruelty did Storm come up with? Shearing sheep."

"Really? That sounds like fun." Alice tossed another handful of popcorn into her mouth and munched.

He shook his head with strong conviction, not missing the glint of humor in her eyes. "Not fun. Sheep are evil."

"Sheep aren't evil. They're very sweet and gentle.

In Afghanistan, we dealt with sheep and goats. They never gave us much trouble." She passed him the popcorn bowl. "Except for the time a goat took a particular liking to one of the operators on our team. I offered to plan the wedding."

He snorted a laugh. "You've never met Storm's sheep. I think he paid them to act up. They tried to eat me."

In the background, the beeps of droids reminded him he was not paying attention to the movie. The woman sitting beside him was more interesting.

"I'm sorry you had a rough day." She patted his hand.

"I heard from my agent. He's sending a reporter down at the end of the week. If I get a nice story, I might leave early to go home and start training." And begin earning back the respect of his team and the fans.

Alice returned her gaze to the movie screen. "Sure. If good press is the only reason you're here."

How could he make her understand his sole motivation was his love of football? He leaned in, putting his head closer to hers, in order to keep his voice low. "Remember the movie *The Karate Kid*? That's me here. All I'm doing is waxing cars and painting fences."

"Wax on, wax off…I get it. But Mr. Miyagi had a reason for all that seemingly meaningless work." She didn't take her gaze off the movie screen.

"Storm's only motivation is to torture me." He recognized the whiney tone of his voice and shut his mouth. When had he turned into such a baby?

"If you only came here for good PR then you've missed the point of the retreat." She turned and narrowed her eyes. "A little humility would do you good."

Stunned by her candor, Micah stared back, slack-jawed. "You think I'm arrogant?"

"You're not arrogant. Well…not too much. You're just used to being treated like you're special." Alice tossed a puff of popcorn at his head. "I've spent a long time in an environment where I had to be blunt."

"But I *am* special." He cracked a smile. Acting a regular guy was fun, too. Especially with Alice as a companion. She had a way of keeping him grounded, and if his ego threatened to float too high, she'd yank him right down to earth. During rehab, he'd worked on maintaining a humble spirit. Tough when he'd lived so many years being treated like sports royalty. He'd also practiced taking responsibility for his actions, and not only the ones that won football games—a hard but necessary lesson important in his effort to stay clean.

"Sure, you're special all right." She threw more popcorn. "Now, be quiet so we don't get kicked out of here." Alice scooted her bottom forward so her head rested on the back of the chair.

That plastic bar digging into her head couldn't be comfortable. He left his seat and slipped into the kitchen in search of a clean towel. After returning outside, he stood behind Alice's chair and lifted her head then set the makeshift pillow in place. Pleased to see her more comfortable, he sat. In the past, he'd assumed grand gestures were needed to impress a woman. Maybe he'd been turned around. Were small, thoughtful gestures more meaningful, if done from the heart?

"Thanks." She reclined her head against the thick

49

towel draped over the back of the chair. "Your grandmother raised a gentleman."

If only he could win back Cassidy that easily. He doubted a little trick with a kitchen towel would erase all the damage he'd done to their relationship. If he ever got another chance with Cassidy, he'd prove his stay in rehab, as well as the retreat, helped mold him into a better, more caring man.

Chapter Five

Alice shivered in the morning air. Due to the movie marathon the night before, she hadn't seen her bed until two a.m. Despite her sleep-deprived state, she'd woken before dawn with the remnants of a nightmare drifting over her like strands of a spider web.

Now, she entered the main building and headed toward the kitchen, crossing her fingers the staff had started the coffee. Instead of the comforting scent of strong brew, she found Storm and Heath engaged in conversation.

"Morning, sunshine." Heath tipped his head toward the line of carafes on the counter. "No coffee yet, sorry."

"Bummer. What are you doing here so early?" Alice walked over to the guys standing at the other side of the room. She hadn't spent much time with Storm, but he seemed like a good guy. Heath liked him, and in her eyes, his approval was enough to earn her confidence.

"I'll head outside and make sure all the equipment is ready." Storm turned toward Alice and patted her on the shoulder. "Morning. You'll have fun. Promise." He exited the room.

Heath scratched at his brown beard. "We're doing a team-building challenge today. Storm and I wanted to finalize a plan before we gathered you all together."

Her panic spiked, quickening her pulse. She had no desire to play games with the other veterans here. Alice grabbed his arm. "I'm not doing team building. Everyone here sees me as a girl soldier who'd rather carry a purse than a gun. I don't have the time or the energy to prove them wrong."

"Don't make assumptions. And even if they're true, you should want to go out and prove them wrong." Heath patted her on the shoulder. "Educate them on your background and your contribution to the Special Ops community."

She straightened her spine to stand perfectly erect. "They think I'm here because I was raped." Just saying the word made her sick. Sexual assault was unfortunately a serious issue in the military. She held a strong disgust for any man who'd use his strength or authority to attack another.

Heath's eyebrows lowered, and he frowned. "Will you dismiss a group of good people because you won't let them get to know you?"

Alice huffed and jerked her chin. "I'm not doing team building. I'd rather shear sheep with Micah." For some reason, her comment made Heath smile.

"You really are the most obstinate woman I've ever met. And that includes my wife, who is as bullheaded as…well, a bull." He slapped his thigh.

"I'm sorry, Heath. I don't mean to be difficult." She sighed. Heath was right. Since day one, she'd put up her guard, which meant no one here had learned her story. Well, with the exception of Micah. "You know how hard I worked to break into your band of brothers in Afghanistan. In this situation, I have nothing to prove."

"No point in arguing with you, is there?" He picked at the dirt under his fingernails. "I'll talk to Colleen about finding you another activity."

"You're the best." She leaned over to plant a kiss on his scruffy cheek. As warmth filled her chest, she was reminded she hadn't totally closed herself off to human connection. Good, trustworthy people still existed in the world. "Thanks for inviting me. My experience so far has been positive."

"Does hanging out with a certain handsome quarterback qualify as positive?" He winked.

With speed, Alice looped her arm around his neck and placed him in a headlock. Showing just as much hustle, he slipped out of her reach.

"Whoa!" He laughed. "Glad to see you're still as feisty as I remember."

"And you're still a troublemaker." For a few minutes, she'd regained her free-spirited humor. At one time, she'd been the life of the party and excelled at cracking jokes with her dry humor. Was there hope she'd ever feel the same light happiness again?

A few veterans entered the room and glanced at Alice and Heath, then disappeared into the dining area.

"They don't know what to make of you, that's all." Heath squeezed her shoulder. "Remember, everyone here is struggling with their own demons."

"I know." Alice nodded. A good reminder. The other veterans' struggles and pain were as important as her own. "I need a swimming-pool-size cup of coffee, then I'll find someplace quiet to think in peace." She didn't mean to be ungrateful, but she had no desire to make short-term friends. Well, maybe with one exception. Micah had the sneaky ability to lower her defenses. Funny to think she was now friends with the Warrior's star quarterback, proving her life was a series of unpredictable twists and turns.

Once Heath left the kitchen, Alice hung around and chatted with the staff until the room filled with fresh-brewed goodness. With coffee in hand, she went outside to find a discreet spot to savor her warm drink. She'd taken a few sips when she spotted Heath and Storm walking toward her. Both men moved with quick-paced, long strides, like they were on a mission. *Now what?*

"Yo," Heath hollered. "We have a proposition."

She had plenty of experience with Heath and his propositions. About five years ago, when they were stationed in Afghanistan, he'd suggested to Alice and a few others in their unit that they capture the goat who'd recently wandered close to the base and sneak it into the detachment commander's room. She'd gone along with the prank, thinking it funny at the time. Once she learned the goat had eaten one of the commander's uniforms, she experienced an instant shot of regret. Then had another when she was caught and had to clean bathrooms for a month. "I have one for you, too—don't say another word until I've finished my coffee." She lifted a finger.

Storm cleared his throat. "Alice, listen to what we have to say and don't rush to judgment."

She calmly set down her coffee mug and stood. Now, she looked Storm straight in the eyes. "You've interrupted my coffee meditation. Your idea better be good."

****

"Tell me again why this fence needs to be

repainted?" Micah asked Storm, who'd quickly become his nemesis.

"Colleen doesn't like the shade of brown. She says it reminds her of cow poop." Storm set a gallon of paint on the grass. "A white fence is less offensive."

"Then *you* paint it white." Micah's mood nosedived from bad to worse. Ever since leaving rehab, he'd struggled to find fulfillment. Without football or pain pills, he'd fought against sliding into a depression. Right now, negative emotions swirled in his gut and voices sounded in his head, declaring him a failure. Even though he no longer physically craved the drugs, he longed for the easy high they provided.

Volunteering here was theoretically meant to kick him out of self-centered thinking. So, why couldn't he stop wallowing under the weight of his failures? Maybe he'd feel better if he actually worked with the veterans instead of performing farm chores. None of the other retreat volunteers were working on the farm. As far as he noticed, the others who stayed to help were actually helping the retreat. After each day spent in manual labor alone, he felt more useless.

Storm's little girl, Harper, ran toward them. A white dog followed at her heels. "Daddy, Kitty wants to eat."

Micah glanced from the girl to the dog. Who named their dog Kitty? A four-year-old girl, that's who.

"I'll help you in a minute." Storm kissed his daughter on top of her strawberry blonde head. "So, Micah…you good here?"

He hooked his thumbs into the front pockets of his shorts. "I hate sounding like a pampered brat, but I didn't come here to donate labor to your farm. I need the good PR from working with the veterans."

"Why doesn't your attitude surprise me?" Storm took off his baseball cap and whacked it on his jean-covered thigh, sending dust raining onto the ground. After a few more pats with his hand, he set the cap back on his head. "I've asked you to help with what we need. I apologize if physical labor doesn't fit into your public relation strategy."

Across the field, Micah noticed a group of veterans playing football. "I'd be more useful over there." He pointed to the action. Tossing around a ball was preferable to painting any day. "I'm better at football than I am at painting. Since you've seen my handiwork so far, you should realize that by now."

Storm crossed his arms. "Here's a deal for you. How about you use the time here to get a jump-start on your training for next session?"

Even the mere thought of training sent a shot of adrenaline through his veins. Beads of sweat formed on his brow, and his heart raced. Unfortunately, a retreat in central Texas was not the time or place. "I'd love to, but a reporter is coming to do a story on my volunteer work, and I wouldn't look good holed up in a gym."

"You'd work with a veteran." He pointed in the direction of the retreat, which was over the hill about a quarter of a mile away. "This person was once a gym rat but now struggles with her future. Let her train you. You'd motivate her as much as she would you."

Her? He didn't doubt Alice could run his sorry butt into the ground, but training a professional athlete took precision. He couldn't take the risk of becoming reinjured. "You want Alice to train me? I don't think so."

"Alice will work off a plan we've received from the Warrior's head trainer. You'll be in good hands." Storm slapped him on the back before grabbing hold of Harper's hand, stopping the little girl who'd been running circles around their legs. "Your choice is to paint the fence or train with Alice?"

He snorted. *I know when I'm being played.* "Where's Alice?" He gazed off into the distance, toward the retreat's buildings. Only a few of the cabins weren't hidden from the rolling landscape. Together, they'd come up with something else to do. Something more fun than painting or training. She was likely as reluctant as him.

"Waiting for you in the workout room." Storm smiled. "Good luck."

"Thanks." He had a feeling he'd need it. Although, what if Alice was the kick he needed to shake off his funk. During rehab, he'd learned the importance of a good support system. Spending time with her was like having his energy tank refilled. And physical exercise would give him an endorphin boost that might keep away thoughts of failure.

He walked across the field to the retreat area and entered the gym to find Alice leaning against the back wall. The space was a small building outfitted with a few weight machines, a treadmill, an exercise bike, and free weights.

"You sure about training me?" At the sight of her—looking tall, slim, and attractive—he lost most of his will to fight the arrangement. Working with her might not be so bad.

She grunted and pushed off the wall then strode toward him. "I'm just as much of a victim as you. I've been assigned the role of Mr. Miyagi. No more wax on, wax off. Today, your real training begins, Micah-son." Hands pressed together, Alice bowed.

He laughed. "They exploited my dislike of farm work, but you're a guest here. You can't be forced to be my trainer."

"Oh, they got me, too. Either I work with you or participate in team-building exercises and group therapy." She lifted a small hand-weight off the shelf and did a few arm curls.

"Why would those be so bad?" Alice circled him like a tiger would its prey. Her gaze roamed over his body, making him suddenly and unexpectedly very self-conscious.

"Take off your shirt," she instructed.

"What?" He wore an old T-shirt and athletic shorts. No way was he stripping down in front of her.

"I want to see what I'm working with." She rolled her hand in a waving motion. "Come on, don't be shy." Her eyebrows arched over wide, hazel eyes.

"This isn't the NFL combine, you know." Despite his protests, he lifted the hem of his shirt and removed it before tossing it on the floor. Micah now stood bare-chested in the middle of the gym. During the combine, he'd stood before NFL medical staff and coaches while they judged his worthiness to play professional football. He'd proven himself during each drill, earning the respect of staff and press alike. But now, while Alice studied him, he wondered if despite all his pride and bravado, she found him lacking. His body and face grew warmer by the second.

Alice stood before him.

Silent and serious as a painted saint. The intensity

of her gaze caused him to shiver.

When she met his gaze, she smiled.

Was it too late to change his mind and go back to painting?

****

Alice wasn't the type to swoon over a man's muscular physique. The men she'd served with had all been ripped and loved to show off. With them, she'd rolled her eyes and gone about her business. Micah, on the other hand, caused beads of sweat to roll down her back. As she looked him over, she sucked in a breath then released it slowly.

He was the perfect blend of strength and lean muscle. With wide shoulders and muscular biceps, he possessed the build of a man who worked with his body for a living. His broad chest narrowed down to a flat stomach and trim waist. And his legs weren't too shabby either.

The right side of his body was slightly more defined, highlighting the fact he was right-handed. Her gaze was a traitor as she roamed over Micah. When she finally got a hold of herself, she glanced at his face to meet his gaze. She recognized in his eyes a mixture of pride and insecurity. Was he concerned she'd find fault with him? With a body like a Greek god, he had nothing to worry about.

"Your turn," he said with a smirk.

She grabbed his shirt off the floor and tossed it to him. The man had a wicked sense of humor. Just the type of guy who could crack her defense. "Dream on. I needed to find out where you can use extra work."

"And what's your verdict?" He slipped on his shirt.

That he was perfection. Avoiding his gaze, she

walked to the bench where she'd set the packet of information from the Warrior's trainer. "We'll work on balancing the strength on both sides of your body. Also, your muscles seem tight. I'll share stretching techniques and yoga postures that will help."

"I'll agree to follow your instruction only if you sweat alongside of me." He strolled over to stand at her side. "No sitting around eating doughnuts while I do pushups."

The heat from his body danced across the bare skin of her arm. "I'm too out of shape." She glanced down and pretended to read over the notes the trainer sent her earlier. She'd completely embarrassed herself keeping pace with Micah.

"No excuses." He bumped her with his hip. "We're training together."

How could she explain that ever since the explosion, insecurity had melted away her former ice-cold self-confidence? Just agreeing to train Micah had been a struggle. "You don't understand."

"Yes, I do. Better than you know." He stepped back and looked her up and down. "Hurry and go change into shorts, and then we can get to work."

Alice groaned. She'd compromise to get started with training but only for today. "I'm fine in pants. Let's start warming up."

"Let me see your scars." His gaze lowered to her covered legs.

Once he saw the ugliness hidden under the leg of her pants, he'd either look at her with disgust or sympathy. Coming from a man as handsome as Micah would be mortifying. "No."

"Lift up your pants leg and show me." He pointed

to the lower portion of her right leg.

"No." Her stomach twisted with nerves. Shaking her head, she moved toward the door. The man should learn how to back down from a challenge.

"I'm not moving until you do." His smile faded into lips pressed firm, and he set his hands on his hips.

Of all the men in the whole wide world, why was she stuck with this headstrong one? "You really are a pain."

Micah's grin was wide, and creases formed at the corners of his eyes. "I know."

Fine, just for a second. She'd let him get a quick look to satisfy his curiosity, and then they could move on. Taking a deep breath, she raised her pants leg, stopping at her knee. The sight of the lightly colored bumps and scars roiled her gut. Dizziness blurred her vision, making the floor below spin. Suddenly, she felt the warmth of Micah's hands brush across the rough skin on the outside of her leg. The world stilled, and her breath caught in her throat.

"You standing here is a miracle." He rose to face her. "How close were you to losing your leg?"

Sorrow burned inside her chest. "Too close." The memory of pain, along with the touch of the man, caused her to shiver. "I had a team of very skilled surgeons. They not only saved my leg, but they saved my life."

"I understand why you might feel embarrassed, but I hope you don't with me." He slowly lowered her pants leg. "I think your scars are something you should take pride in."

Tears welled in her eyes. "I'll be right back." Alice turned to head to her cabin and change clothes, then she'd work him 'til he begged for mercy.

A half an hour later, she wished she'd never agreed to be Micah's trainer by proxy. The stitch in her side threatened to double her over, her legs quivered, and her feet ached. That Heath and his bright ideas. He must have known she'd be forced to exercise, too. The last time she'd visited a gym was a year ago, on a base in Afghanistan. Back then, she'd worked out every day. Now, she couldn't run one mile without stopping to catch her breath. Before the blast, she competed in half marathons, even coming in first in her age group at one race.

"Come on, drill sergeant." Micah jogged backward to meet her. "Running was your idea."

"My idea was for *you* to run," she huffed out in between breaths. "And I'd watch from a comfortable chair." Her lungs burned with the struggle to take in enough oxygen. Her right leg and hip had turned mutinous. With each step, she feared she'd never walk again.

After four more steps, she collapsed onto the grass next to a small animal enclosure. "Go on...leave me behind."

Micah, who was about twenty feet ahead, U-turned and jogged to where she lay. "Are you okay?"

As he towered above, he blocked out the sun. She groaned and punched the ground. *Ouch*...now her hand hurt, too. "No, I'm not okay. Didn't you hear me say I'm out of shape? Plus, I have a bum leg."

He knelt beside her. "I'm sorry. I thought we were going slow enough."

"Don't be sorry." The concern in his voice washed away her self-pitying mood. Despite being proud, which at times bordered on egoistical, Micah was a sweet guy. "I'll survive. But you on the other hand, need to finish your run."

The loud clucking of chickens sounded. A flock of hens bobbed around a fenced-in area.

She counted twenty with colors ranging from a deep red-orange to a snowy white. Her family had raised hens and roosters, and she used to love gathering the eggs—an effective excuse to spend time outside.

"I built this." Wearing a wide smile, Micah pointed toward the pen. "My first project."

"Impressive." She sat upright to get a better look. The wire was crooked, and the posts weren't straight in the ground. A strong wind could likely blow over the enclosure. In her opinion, the chickens didn't mind the shoddy workmanship, though. A long-necked rooster strutted toward her, squawking and flapping its wings. "Your skills are wasted on the football field. You should work as a carpenter."

Rising from off his knees, he laughed. "You're very funny. I'll go finish my run. How about I meet you at the main building in thirty minutes?"

Alice nodded, then admired the view until he ran out of sight. The more time she spent with Micah, the more unsure she grew of which was in greater danger of crashing and burning—her body or her heart.

****

As much as the admission pained him, Micah now understood the merit of Storm and Heath's plan. Training with Alice helped her own recovery.

After dinner, he escorted Alice to her cabin. They sat on the only two chairs on the porch and talked about sports, movies, and travel. Hills rolled over the landscape as far as he could see. A brisk breeze carried scents of the earth—clean and organic. The setting sun transferred a spectrum of periwinkle, flame orange, and pink onto the low clouds.

As he took the time to appreciate the beauty around him, he remembered youthful days spent playing outdoors until sunset. The same, light-hearted feeling filled him. In truth, no amount of money or fame gave him such a deep sense of satisfaction as his current perfectly tranquil mood. For the first time since the deepest pit of his addiction, he felt wholly connected to not only a place but a person. How could he bottle up these positive emotions to tap into once the pressure began building?

At the sight of Alice's yawn, he checked the time. Amazing how quickly three hours passed when spent with good company. After saying goodnight, he returned to his tiny bedroom, alone. He checked his phone and saw a text from Cassidy, lowering his spirits. Regret replaced his earlier contentment. Every day, he woke up to the memory he'd hurt her, and no quantity of apologies would atone.

An ache slashed at his heart. He pressed a hand on his chest, pushing down the pain. He longed to see her and share his experiences at the retreat. Because of the time difference in Rome, he couldn't call. Just as well. Instead, he powered up his laptop and opened a new email.

Cassidy,

How is your trip? I know you're making a great impression on the Italian fashion buyers. I'm at the veterans' retreat. After three days, I can honestly say I'm happy I agreed to come. I'm training with a veteran who's survived an IED blast. Not only am I keeping in shape, I'm helping another person reclaim an important part of herself. She's pushing me to be a better athlete and person. I finally see a successful return to the Warriors.

Nothing I say will erase the hurt I caused. I respect that you've moved on. You were the best thing that ever happened to me, and I was a fool to let you go. I put my desires ahead of you. I'm sorry.

Anyway, I need to get to sleep. I'm sure my new trainer has a full day planned. Feel free to call me anytime. I'll always make time to talk.

Love you forever,

Micah.

Before he could second guess his instincts, he clicked the trash icon, then shut down his laptop. That email would join the rest he'd written to Cassidy and deleted.

Not wanting to dwell on lost love any longer, he stripped down and climbed into bed. The memories of his day spent with Alice brightened his mood. Wonder what she scheduled for tomorrow? He could handle anything she dished out and would make sure she suffered right along with him. Even after one day, he noticed a change in her confidence. He'd build her up as he continued working on himself. Teamwork. And right now, he wouldn't trade Alice as his partner for any player or trainer in the league.

Chapter Six

The next morning at six a.m., Alice knocked on Micah's door. "Rise and shine. Time to go to work." She rolled her neck, working out the cracks and tight muscles.

"Go away," he yelled from inside the room. "It's still dark."

Why would a lack of light keep them from a workout? She used to feel best after an active early morning. "Get dressed and meet me downstairs. You've got five minutes. After that, I'm busting down the door."

A thud sounded from inside the room. Maybe a well-aimed shoe hitting the wall? No need to stick around and witness more of his grumpy attitude. Alice went downstairs and poured herself a cup of strong coffee. Thankfully, someone else was awake early and started the brew. She stood by the window and stared off into the dark.

Being pulled from his warm bed, Micah would no doubt be grumpy. She could handle grumpy. Though once he learned her schedule for today, his mood would sour even more.

As she waited, a tall, well-built man entered the gathering room—the guy who'd sat beside her at the first group therapy session. The one who'd put into words what everyone else here believed. She held no animosity, and her anger over the situation was long gone. Her mind was too focused on other things, like the guy hopefully now awake upstairs.

The veteran slowly approached, shoulders hunched. "Hey." He stuffed both hands in his pants pockets. "I wanted to apologize…you know…for being a jerk the other day…and presuming you'd been sexually assaulted."

"That's not why I'm here." She purposefully softened her voice, wanting to convey empathy and understanding. He reminded her of many of the men she'd served with—men with big hearts who at times lacked discernment.

"I know now you were injured in combat." He raised his gaze to meet hers. "Until recently, women weren't allowed in combat roles. Before meeting you, I never knew about the Cultural Support Team and how y'all were used on Special Ops missions."

An unexpected lump of emotion clogged her throat. She personally didn't need anyone's approval or accolades, but hearing the respect behind his words meant a lot. She understood the importance of speaking up. Educating others about her experiences helped grow appreciation of her team's contributions. "The CST is a group of extraordinary women."

"Why did you volunteer to join?" He sat on the arm of the chair across from her. "Not many people, especially women, can keep up with the Special Forces, Rangers, and SEALs."

Her pride bristled at his last comment. Still standing, she studied him with sharp judgement. He looked to be in his late thirties or early forties. In her opinion, his interest seemed sincere, so she'd give him the benefit of the doubt. "Before the Joint Special Operations Command created the Cultural Support Teams, a few women had been tapped by individual Special Ops units to ride along on missions. The unit commanders brought female soldiers to search and communicate with the local women and children. The military big-shots finally acknowledged the need and trained a group of selected women soldiers to attach to teams as support members."

He nodded and crossed his arms over his chest, showing forearms covered in tattoos. "Attaching you as support personnel is how command got around the 'no women in combat' rule. You still were sent out in combat missions though, right?"

Memories of riding in a Humvee over dusty, bumpy roads made her grin. Grouped together in a tight space, the team would distract from the discomfort by telling stories and jokes. What she wouldn't give for one more day living on the edge. "I had to fire my weapon on a few occasions, but most of the time, my role was peace keeping. Before the ban was lifted, the CST program was the only way women could see combat, so many of us ran with the opportunity." An intense rivalry existed within the group of women during training and selection, as well as a deep bond. They relied on each other while they collectively broke the military's glass ceiling, clearing the way for even greater changes.

He glanced at his feet, which tapped against the carpeted floor. "I don't want to pry, but I saw you walk with a slight limp. How were you injured?"

Out of the corner of her eye, she noticed Micah descend the stairs. Instead of coming toward her, he turned and went into the kitchen. Meaning she'd lost her excuse to avoid talking about a very uncomfortable memory. Maybe for the best. She inhaled deeply, then let it out. *You can do this.* "I was on a village stabilization mission with my A-team. We were securing the compound when an IED exploded. My wounds eventually healed, but two good men lost their lives."

Sorrow burned her throat, and tears filled her eyes. She'd been too injured to attend their funerals. While she lay in bed, hooked up to a morphine drip, two of her brothers were lowered into the ground. They'd saved her life by pushing her out of the way and using their bodies as shields. How could she ever repay that level of sacrifice?

"I'm sorry." He wiped a tear from his eye. "I watched men I cared about die, too. It's part of the reason why I'm having problems adjusting to civilian life."

The remaining frost in her heart melted. She stepped forward and rested a hand on his. "Both of us have witnessed things we can't forget. The only thing we can do is live well for those who will never come home."

Another tear glistened in the corner of his eye. "Thanks, Sergeant, for your time." He saluted, turned on his heel, and walked away.

After a few seconds, Micah appeared in the doorway from the kitchen. "I didn't want to interrupt."

"Thanks...I think." Alice strode to him, her leg aching in protest.

"I overheard your story. You're quite a woman, Alice." He blew across the top of the mug in his hand, causing the rising steam to ripple. "Breaking into a pack of alpha males and earning their respect had to be tough."

On her first mission, no one had respected her. She'd been so scared, she puked before boarding the truck. "I am tough. Keep that in mind as I work you today." He actually grinned, like a naughty schoolboy.

"Whatever you dish out, sister, I can take." He took a sip of coffee. "Bring it on."

A challenge—music to her ears.

They started with a run to warm up. After huffing for one mile, Alice dropped back and let Micah take off alone. He could run the remaining two in the same time she walked back to the gym.

As she strolled across the field, she took deep breaths, appreciating her blessings. The sun peeked over the eastern horizon, bringing the promise of a good day. A few early birds flew overhead, chattering into the breeze, which riffled through her damp hair.

Even though she struggled with the process of regaining her fitness, she loved the hit of endorphins after athletic exertion. Since her injury, she'd been too self-conscious to go inside a gym. Her body couldn't achieve what her mind wanted, and her physical pain often left her in tears.

Granted, she was only starting day two. Not at the point of pushing herself overly hard, but she felt motivated to work toward the next level. Maybe someday, she'd feel strong enough to get back to regular work-outs. If so, she might gain back enough confidence to pursue more challenges.

When Micah finally joined her at the gym, he wasn't even winded.

"Okay, what's next?" Grinning, he stood before her and rolled his shoulders.

She studied the Warrior trainer's workout schedule, which seemed safe—too safe. In her opinion, Micah needed a challenge. He had to find his confidence again. Not the surface kind he had in spades, but the private assurance that resided deep in one's heart. "I have some ideas that are a bit untraditional. Follow me." After tossing him a water bottle, she led him outside and over to a large storage building. Last night, she'd requested a few items from Storm, which he'd set out for her.

Once at their destination, Micah bent at the waist to stretch his hamstrings. "What crazy ideas did you dream up last night?"

She chewed on her lower lip—a bad habit that appeared whenever she was unsure. "See that tractor tire?" Alice pointed. "Flip it end over end until you reach the fence."

He shrugged. "You got it."

Surprised by his agreeability, she stepped aside and watched him go to work. After a few awkward attempts, he found a good rhythm.

Grunting, he covered the fifty yards and let the tire fall back to the ground. He returned to where she stood, took a drink of water, and then squirted a stream at her. "Your turn."

Laughing, she swatted away the offending water bottle. "Not today. This morning's workout is all you." A sledgehammer rested against a nearby building's wall. She lifted it by the handle and brought it to him. "Now, go beat the sass out of the tire."

After wiping his sweaty face with the hand towel

tucked in the waistband of his shorts, he took another long drink. "What do you have against tires…and me?"

Dripping with sweat, he grew more handsome. She had to find something to boost her Micah immunity. Could she find a vitamin supplement for an unwanted attraction? "This exercise is excellent for your shoulders and core. I'll do a few to demonstrate." Once standing by the tire, she lined up the head of the hammer with the thickest part of the rubber sidewall. She adjusted her grip on the handle, lifted the sledgehammer over her head, and swung downward. The shock from its impact reverberated through her body. "Use your hips for more power."

He accepted the hammer and went to work. "A good stress reliever," he huffed out between strikes.

"Do ten more, then stop for a break." She wouldn't overtax him to the point he'd become susceptible to another injury. How ironic she wished to strengthen and improve the performance of her favorite football team's rival quarterback.

A beeping sounded from the pocket of his shorts.

Irritation made her grit her teeth. Did he bring his cell phone? Allowing the mind to disconnect from all distractions was an important part of training. His focus should stay on the here and now.

Micah set the sledgehammer on the ground and reached a hand into his pocket.

"Don't you dare answer that call." Glaring, she pointed at the offending object.

He pulled out his phone and looked at the screen. "I have to."

Her temper spiked. "Let it go to voicemail," she yelled. "Call him back later."

"Not a him…it's a her." With his back facing Alice, he lifted the phone to his ear.

Stung by anger and a touch of jealousy, she lifted the sledgehammer and tossed it over by the storage building. If he wanted to continue, he'd have to search her out. Otherwise, she was done for the day. Micah's priority was obviously not on training or her. She needed to remember his world rotated in a different solar system. In the end, they only have a short time together. She was a temporary teammate and a temporary friend. The fight she'd felt earlier evaporated. Now might be a good time to walk away.

****

"Hello." Micah's voice cracked as he answered the call.

"Hey, there," Cassidy said on the other end. "Are you still in Texas?"

"Checking up on me?" If so, he'd take her call as a sign she still cared. "I'm still at the retreat and having a good time." He had Alice to thank for his enjoyment.

"I'm glad, Micah." She cleared her throat. "Are you staying clean?"

True to the past, she continued to distrust his commitment to sobriety. He balled a hand into a fist and batted his thigh. "Trust me, I've kept too busy to get into trouble. I've started working-out in preparation for training camp. One of the veterans here is acting as my trainer."

"That's wonderful. You have your own, personal drill sergeant. I hope he's not pushing you too hard. If you hurt yourself, you'll need the pain pills again."

At the memory of intense pain which eased in the hazy bliss of a high, he shivered. "Don't worry. Alice was a sergeant in the Army. She worked in Intelligence and then with Special Operations. I trust her. She'll make sure I toe the line." Micah glanced over his shoulder in search of Alice and realized she was no longer in view. *Darn.* He should have respected her wishes and let the call go to voicemail.

"You have a woman training you?" She heaved out a breath. "You're a professional athlete. Why put yourself in the hands of a woman with no experience training?"

Instinctively, he grew defensive for Alice. But yesterday morning, he'd asked himself the same question. Though after they worked together, he'd realized the most important part of the equation was that Alice benefited from their arrangement. Her face glowed every time she broke into a sweat. "I'm fine. Don't worry. How's your trip?"

"The trip has been a success, but I'm ready to go home. Ray's been in an awful mood lately." The line buzzed in silence for two seconds. "I'm sorry. I'm sure you don't want to hear about my relationship troubles."

Right. A crushing sensation settled in his chest. The last thing he wanted was a reminder Cassidy dated his former friend. "You can always talk to me, no matter what." A loud noise sounded on the other end of the line.

"I have to go. It's getting late here. Call me when you get home, and maybe we can meet up for lunch or something."

His stomach buzzed with a nervous excitement at the thought of seeing her again. "Sure, I'll be in touch. Bye." A click signaled the call disconnected. His heart squeezed with regret.

The memory of their last big fight replayed in his mind. A month after his knee injury, he'd taken a lot more pain medication than prescribed. The pills were the one thing making him feel good. At the time, everything else in his life sucked. He wouldn't play for the remainder of the season and was stuck on the sidelines. Week after week, he watched his team move on without him. Slowly, he sank into a depression.

One evening, Cassidy found a handful of pill bottles he'd stashed under the bed. He lost his temper, told her to mind her own business, and that he needed the medication to function. The illegality of his actions wasn't important.

She gave him an ultimatum, and he was too drunk and high to do anything but let her leave. After she was gone, he would have self-destructed if not for several of his teammates' tough love and intervention.

Right now, he needed another butt kicking. He'd been a fool to answer Cassidy's call while working with Alice. He should find her and apologize. After a thirty-minute search, he found her hanging out inside the sheep pen, petting one of the evil beasts. The sheep looked like putty in her hands, but he wasn't fooled. He refused to go inside and risk an attack by either the sheep or Alice.

"You're finished?" Keeping her gaze lowered to the ground, she knelt on the grass and soon surrounded by four ewes.

A small, gray lamb bleated at Micah before leaping over to Alice.

Even the lamb was ticked at his behavior. "I'm finished. The call was from my ex-girlfriend."

"I figured." She wrapped an arm around the body

of the lamb, stroking its wooly side. "You still in love with her?"

Alice's bluntness no longer surprised him. Actually, he found her honesty refreshing. "Cassidy broke up with me at a very low point in my life. We still have some unresolved issues."

She snorted. "Why waste your time and energy on someone who ran when you needed her most?"

Ignoring the sarcasm in her voice, Micah rested a forearm on top of one of the fence posts. "Back then, I was drunk and high most of the time. I couldn't play and took out my frustration on the people closest to me. She did what most people would do."

Alice stood and faced him. "Just because most people would do something doesn't mean leaving was the right thing."

How could he respond? The destruction of their relationship had been his fault, but he didn't have the energy to argue the point. His addiction and his behavior were the catalyst—and he'd learned to take responsibility for both. "Here's my phone. No more distractions. Promise." Smiling, he extended his palm with the device resting on top.

Alice exited the sheep pen and closed the gate securely behind her, and then marched to where he stood. "You think you can get anything you want with that flashy smile?" She rolled her eyes. "Hate to break it to you, buster, but I'm immune to your charms."

Was he in danger of losing his legendary charm? He stepped closer, until they were only inches apart. "I've never encountered a woman who could resist me."

Alice's eyes sparkled, and she grinned. "Let me

introduce you to the first. I spent years working alongside all shapes and sizes of men, but the one thing they had in common was the idea of being God's gift to women. You, my friend, are only one of many." She pushed an index finger into his chest.

"Being lumped in with every other guy you know hurts. You've wounded my male pride." He pressed his palm on his heart and staggered backward.

Alice angled her head and studied him. "I will admit I find one thing that makes you unique."

"Yeah?" He arched his eyebrows and fought back a grin. "What's that? Extraordinary good looks? Great hair? The ability to grow a full beard within two days?"

"You don't stink after you exercise. For some reason, you can look totally gross and sweaty but still smell good." Leaning in, she inhaled and smiled. "Yup…as fresh as a raindrop."

"I've been complimented a lot, but that's a new one." She smelled pretty great, too, but he decided to keep that little tidbit to himself.

Alice gripped his phone in her hand. "Let's get back to work. Go over to your friend the tractor tire and flip it back to the shed."

"Whatever you say, coach." Relief washed over him. *She hasn't given up on me.*

The tire lay where he left it, waiting for him. He crouched down and set his feet. Each flip caused his quads and glutes to burn. The return trip was uphill, and the increasing effort strained his resolve to finish.

Up ahead, Alice waited, hands set on her hips.

No calls of encouragement. No yells for him to push through the pain. She simply waited patiently, like she had faith he'd succeed. Did she really believe in him? Or only see him as everyone else did—a lost soul in need of redirection?

When he completed the final flip, he sank onto the damp grass and sprawled out. The cool moisture of the morning dew seeped through his shirt and shorts. "I need a break."

"How does your knee feel?" She glanced at his surgical scar.

"Fine. I'd tell you if it hurts." He set his hands behind his head and gazed up at the white clouds floating above in the blue sky.

"Don't get too comfortable. I have a few more exercises for this morning." She gently kicked his hip.

"When do you lace up for a workout?" He rolled onto his side and gazed upward. With the sun shining behind her head, she looked angelic. *Ha—I know better.*

"After lunch, I'll join you for some time in the gym. I'll even let you pick a few exercises for me to complete." Alice grinned down at him.

"I like that idea." He slowly stood. The air had grown warmer, which meant Alice would soon change out of her yoga pants and into shorts—an exciting prospect. She might be embarrassed about her scars, but he thought she had the longest, prettiest legs he'd ever seen.

Without a doubt, he was very eager for their afternoon session. He'd rack his brain for good payback exercises for her. Or maybe he'd let her off easy, and they could hang out and talk for the rest of the afternoon. Either way, he was game.

Chapter Seven

Alice liked Dr. Colleen Thompson as a person, but she did not enjoy sitting in the doctor's spacious office and talking about feelings. Despite her internal protests, she rested in a leather chair, ready to begin her therapy session. She steadied her nerves and smoothed out her worry.

"Since I just have you for two weeks, we'll only scratch the surface of some deep issues." Colleen rested a hand on the arm of her chair.

"I don't expect miracles." Alice inhaled a deep breath, then let it out slowly. Life had taught her to be a realist. "I expect my mental health will improve naturally over time."

"Time does heal, but only if you release what's weighing you down." After removing her black-rimmed glasses, Colleen rested them on her lap.

"My body will never be the same as before the explosion." She absentmindedly rubbed her right knee. A tingling sensation ran along the back portion of her leg. "I can't physically do what I used to."

Colleen leaned forward. "I'm talking about your mind…and your soul. After everything you've been through, psychological side effects are natural."

"I'm not depressed." She wrapped both arms around her body. After all she'd survived, since early childhood on, she'd never lost herself. But over the last year, she'd come very close. If she didn't start down a new path soon, she might stay trapped in the center of a frightening maze.

"Depression is one way the brain deals with trauma. Insomnia and anger are others. Many times, symptoms are not cut and dry." She folded her hands. "What I see in you, Alice, is a profound grief for the people you've lost, as well as for your stolen future. You've fought for so many years, which is a hard attitude to set aside now that you're out of the military."

"So, I should act like sugar and spice and everything nice in order to fit into polite society?" *Ha, no way.* Even as a child, she hadn't possessed those qualities. She'd never been the sweet girl her mother and father wished for.

Colleen smiled. "Don't lose your fighting spirit, just redirect it. You've spent your adult life pushing boundaries. You're a woman who loves a challenge. Use the fire inside to forge a new life." She stood and paced in front of her chair. "You've accomplished amazing things in your life, like climb onboard a chopper with a team of Green Berets, so I know you have the potential to do anything you want. Stay open to unexpected possibilities."

Going with the flow was not really her style. "I'm a control freak. Letting go won't come naturally." She lowered her gaze to her feet. In the past, she set her sights on a goal and did not quit until she accomplished it. Nothing distracted her. Now, her focus remained elusive, like she chased a purpose she couldn't see.

"Take working with Micah, for example. I'm sure in a million years, you didn't see yourself training a pro athlete. How is training going, by the way?" Colleen sat again and crossed her legs.

"Good...so far." Honestly, working with Micah was great. While she pushed him, he pushed right back. Too bad their time together had an expiration date. Sadness welled at the thought of saying goodbye.

"They'd hoped the arrangement would be good for you both." Colleen's wide smile sparkled in her blue eyes.

"Might be one of Heath's better schemes." Definitely better than any he'd had while deployed.

"Heath had the help of Storm and Reagan Harrison." Colleen laughed. "The three of them have been conspiring since the moment both of you agreed to come."

"Figures. I guess the fact we sat next to one another was no accident." She shook her head. Why would three busy men have wasted so much time bringing Micah and her together?

"Heath made sure your flight transferred in Jacksonville, and you spent time together on the plane coming here. He thinks of himself as a regular matchmaker."

She almost laughed out loud. How could anyone consider hooking her up with Micah a good idea? Maybe putting Heath in another headlock would teach him a lesson in minding his own business? "Heath is wasting his efforts. Micah and I are friends, but that's the extent of our relationship." She paused for dramatic effect. "Forever."

"And why's that?" Colleen gazed down and wrote on her notepad.

Whenever Colleen jotted notes during their sessions, Alice's nerves fluttered. She wanted to lean forward and peek, needing to know what the doctor thought but wasn't saying. "Micah has other things on his mind, like getting back on the football field. Plus, he still has a broken heart and likely in love with his ex-girlfriend. Most importantly, I wouldn't become romantically involved with anyone. At least, not seriously."

She hovered the pen over the paper and glanced up. "You're not open to finding love?"

A person couldn't find something she's not searching for. "I'm not a big believer. In my mind, marriage doesn't make sense. No offense, because you seem happy with Storm."

"Falling in love isn't logical." Colleen's expression softened. "Do you see a point in your future when you'd be open to marriage and a family?"

"Staying single means I live how I choose. I don't answer to someone else." Hadn't her mother done appalling things in order to make her husband happy? She'd stood by quietly while he married away their daughters to perverts. Nausea churned at the memories. "In regards to Micah"—Alice fought to keep her emotions from sounding in her voice—"he treats me like a sister. Same as how most guys treat me."

Colleen set both pen and paper on the side table. "You've put up a tall wall, one only a very strong and determined person could scale."

Very perceptive, Doc. Alice crossed her arms. "I wouldn't want anything less."

Smiling, Colleen nodded. "I'll inform Heath his plan has failed. He'll be very disappointed."

"You leave Heath to me." She pointed at her chest, having learned from past experience how to deal with the man. "He treats me like a kid, and it's time he learns I can take care of myself."

"Heath only cares about you." Colleen reached across and patted her hand. "He wants you to find happiness."

Alice's happiness would never be wrapped in a man—even a handsome man with an arm like a rocket and a charming smile able to melt ice. The cost of love—giving away her independence—was too high.

****

Within the privacy of his room, Micah ended the call from his agent. The reporter and photographer would be here tomorrow for a one-on-one interview, then capture photographs of Micah in action—a caring volunteer helping to improve the lives of veterans.

Once the interview concluded, Micah wished to head home. Officially, training camp was three months away, but the Warriors started mini-camps soon. He wanted to be in Timber Lake as soon as possible to train in the team's facility. Stepping inside the stadium would do wonders for his mental well-being.

Realizing when he left the retreat, he'd leave Alice as well, he struggled to maintain his upbeat mood. Every morning, he looked forward to their training sessions and the down time spent together afterward.

He'd miss their verbal jousting. No one else, not even the guys on his football team, had a mouth like Alice. Likely because hers was so incredibly pretty.

After a brief search, he located Alice. She stood outside on the patio, surrounded by several men. An irrational jealousy flared. Normally, she kept the male veterans at arm's length. Until now, he'd enjoyed her almost exclusive attention. Apparently, not anymore.

Micah approached the gathering but remained a few steps away, not wanting to draw attention from Alice. Right now, no one cared about Micah Palmer, football star. All the men were totally captivated by her.

Alice stood perfectly straight, hands on hips. "I was in a small, dark room, surrounded by scared women, and I had to search them all," she said to the group. "The first woman approached and lifted her *burka* to her knees, revealing the hairiest legs I've ever seen. I instructed her to lower the *burka* so I could administer a pat-down. As I worked up the left leg, I felt something long and very hard."

Deep-throated laughter filled the air.

Alice laughed, too. "I thought, 'either this lady is hiding a gun, or I'm searching a man and he's very happy to see me.' "

"Was it a dude?" asked the dark-haired guy standing to her right.

"A dude with an AK-47 rifle." She nodded. "He ran off before I put everything together but didn't get far. The soldiers stationed outside the hut captured him before he pulled his weapon." Alice lifted her glass and took a long drink, leaving small droplets of water on her lower lip.

Micah's pulse sky-rocketed.

"Good thing you were along to search the women." The short, stout man standing across the way folded his arms over his body and shifted his weight between widespread legs. "He would have blended in and gotten away."

Micah studied Alice. Her eyes glittered in the late afternoon light. His chest ached with missing her, and he hadn't left the retreat yet. He should do something special in appreciation for her efforts over the past week. Due to her persistence and drive, he once again felt like the kid he'd been, discovering the joy of sports.

He left Alice's group and searched the grounds for Storm, finally finding him with his daughter, who played on the swing set in their backyard. A wood fence separated the retreat from Storm and Colleen's house. Someday, he'd like to have similar tranquil and happy life. "Hey, man," Micah said. "I have a favor to ask."

Storm set a giggling Harper on the swing. "Let's hear it."

His heart raced. Suddenly, he transformed to an insecure boy about to ask a father's permission to date his daughter. "I want to take out Alice tonight for a nice dinner in thanks for working with me."

"What do you need?" He pushed his daughter.

Harper kicked her feet and squealed.

Micah grinned, a reflection of the glee on the little girl's face. A simple activity done with a loved one created so much joy. "Transportation, for one, and the name of a nice restaurant." Liberty Ridge, the closest town, likely wouldn't have many options due to its small population. But a few nice places must be around for a guy taking out a girl. Not that he was asking Alice on a date. Romance was the last thing on his mind. An attractive image of Alice as she worked out earlier today floated into his mind, and his body warmed. Okay, maybe a few brain cells were hijacked.

"You can take my truck." Storm tipped his head toward the garage. "I don't need it for the rest of the night. The Desert Rose is a nice restaurant in Liberty Ridge." His gazed fixed on Micah. "Are you interested in her...romantically?"

"No." Beads of perspiration formed on his brow. "Alice is a friend and sees me as the annoying brother type. I want to show my appreciation."

"I highly discourage you from putting the moves on her." Storm lifted his daughter from the swing, who then took off chasing the dog. "Alice has a lot of obstacles to overcome. I'd hate to see the addition of a broken heart."

Why did Storm think he had to play protector of her heart? In Micah's opinion, Alice was more than capable of taking care of herself. "I'd never do anything to hurt her. Besides, just as I said...to her I'm like an annoying brother."

As Storm strode toward the house, he waved for Micah to follow. "I'll get the truck keys."

With transportation secure, he sought out Alice with the expectation of convincing her to join him tonight. He found her talking with four other veterans. When she saw him approach, she gifted him with a breathtaking smile.

She waved goodbye to the other guys and came to stand beside him. "I was wondering where you ran off to. What did your agent say?"

"The interview's tomorrow. It's not that big of a deal." She didn't need to know how much he had riding on the interview's success. Without fan support, he'd struggle to return next season. "I made arrangements to take you out to dinner tonight. In thanks for training me."

Alice's smile faded. "You don't need to thank me. I'm sure my training hasn't been that life altering." For a brief moment, she watched as a couple strode hand in hand down the hiking path. She blinked before returning her gaze to him.

"Don't sell yourself short. You're a great trainer. You know how hard to push people without caving to their complaining." He blew out a breath. "Anyway, Storm loaned me his truck. I'll go shower and change. Let's meet in an hour." Jogging away, he hoped not to give her a chance to say no.

After showering and dressing in record time, he paced the floor in his little room, restless and edgy. His stomach twisted into knots, and his palms were damp. Tonight wasn't a date. He and Alice were friends. A friend who happened to be a woman—a very attractive woman.

Stop. Thinking about her looks is not helping.

When he descended the stairs, he found Alice standing before the fireplace in the gathering room. She didn't notice him and continued staring into the flames. Her cheeks glowed with the reflected color from the fire—a golden kiss on smooth silk.

On the last step, the board creaked, and she turned to face him.

She appeared melancholy, despite her weak smile. He wished to glimpse inside her mind and understand everything that shaped her into who she was today. Even after spending a week together, she was still such a mystery. One he deeply desired to solve before they went their separate ways.

****

Alice broke off eye contact with Micah and glanced back into the flames. Painful memories surfaced in her mind at the worst moments. Like now, right before leaving for a nice dinner out with a friend.

She'd been enjoying the warmth of the fireplace when the faces of the men who'd died in the IED blast appeared. Their screams echoed in her head, and she put her hands over her ears to block them out.

Why had they died instead of her? She walked the earth alone while their families lived without their loved ones. The unfairness of the loss made her want to scream. The IED should have taken her. She should have been the one returned to the US in a flag-draped casket.

"You ready to go?" Micah walked toward her, hands resting on his hips.

The sound of his voice broke through her reverie. "Yes." She followed him outside to Storm's old pick-up truck, which he'd parked on the circular driveway close to the main building's front door.

After he made sure she was seated, he strode around the hood of the truck and climbed inside. The truck rumbled to life, and she bit back a laugh. "I'll guess this hunk of Detroit metal is a step down from what you're used to driving."

He shifted into Drive. The truck jerked forward before stalling. "I don't care if the truck was built in the 1940s. All I asked for was something that wouldn't get us killed." Turning the key again, he shifted into Drive and stepped on the gas.

"We'll be fine. I've ridden in vehicles in worse shape. At least no one's shooting at us." The ghost sounds of gunshots rang in her head, and she turned to gaze out the window, needing the reminder she was in Texas, not in a faraway desert. On the other side of the road, a wide stretch of prairie covered the rolling landscape. In the distance, a herd of dark cattle congregated around a large mesquite tree.

"Thanks for the reassurance." Wearing a smirk, he tapped on the steering wheel to the beat of the country song playing on the radio. "I have an idea. Let's play two truths and a lie. You go first."

His childlike grin got her laughing. "Okay." His playful mood served as an effective distraction from her dark thoughts. "I'm game. Are we keeping score?"

"Of course." His hand slapped the steering wheel. "Winner gets to sleep in tomorrow."

She rolled her eyes. "I don't sleep in."

"But I do." Micah glanced quickly at her and winked. "Or at least I did. If I win, you let me sleep in. If you win, you can wake me up at five instead of six."

Terms she could live with. "Fine. Let's do this. Five rounds. I'll keep score. Good luck." Rubbing together her hands, she racked her brain for something guaranteed to trip him up. No excuses, she had to win. "Okay…I wanted to be an Olympic swimmer when I was younger. My favorite gun is a Beretta M9. I once hiked forty miles along the Appalachian Trail."

"You're lying about hiking the Appalachian Trail." Grinning, he nodded. "I'm right, aren't I?"

Did he doubt she could physically accomplish the feat? "You are wrong. A friend and I hiked the Appalachian Trail three years ago. The Beretta M9 is my favorite, but I didn't swim in a pool until I was seventeen." That hot summer day, with the smell of chlorine filling her nostrils, was one of her favorite memories.

"I was just warming up." Micah cracked his knuckles before quickly returning his hands to the steering wheel. "I was born in Hawaii. I grew up in

Clearwater, Florida. I played baseball in high school, earning All-State as shortstop."

"You weren't born in Hawaii." She was confident about her pick. Well, for the most part.

Micah huffed out a breath. "Right. I was born and grew up in Florida, and I was one of the state's top shortstops. Football won my devotion in the end, though." He glanced her way. "Your turn."

Alice tossed away any facts about her childhood on the compound. "I enlisted in the Army when I was eighteen. I was in the ROTC program in college. I earned my Bachelor's degree from the University of South Carolina."

Micah scratched his chin and remained silent, considering his options. "That's a tough one. You weren't in the ROTC."

"You're right." *Darn.* If she didn't get the next one correct, they'd be tied.

"I was selected during the second round of the NFL draft. I was a backup quarterback my first season with the Warriors. Until last season, I've never missed a game."

She mulled over her choices. She'd heard on a sports show he'd been a backup his first season. So, she was left with a fifty-fifty shot to answer correctly. "I'll guess the lie is you were drafted in the second round."

"I went during the first round." His chest swelled. "I was hot stuff."

She snorted a laugh. Just because she agreed didn't mean he needed to know. "If you're finished being modest, I'd like a turn. I wear a size nine shoe. My favorite movie is *GI Jane*. I've never been to a shopping mall."

"You don't seem like the shopping mall type, and you're basically GI Jane, so I'd say your lie is your shoe size is a nine."

"Wrong." Contentment settled her anxiety like a good rain over dust. Time spent with Micah had that effect. She'd laughed more in the past few days then she had in almost a year. "My favorite movie is *Gone with the Wind.*"

"I don't believe you." He kept his head facing straight ahead, but his narrowed gaze shifted toward her.

"Why? A soldier can't like movies other than shoot-'em-up ones?" Actually, even while enlisted, she avoided any shows that featured combat or war. Instead, she watched soap operas like an addict and read historical romances. The ones with men wearing kilts on the covers were her favorite. "*Gone with the Wind* is a classic. Scarlett and Rhett were two messed-up, selfish people, who ended up being perfect for each other. Unfortunately, they were too stubborn to acknowledge the truth until too late. I cheer for flawed characters."

"Like real people." Micah sighed. "Do you like tragedy with all your love stories?"

"I don't see tragedy but life. I don't believe anyone is guaranteed a happy ever after." Not in a romantic sense because some weren't searching for love. People like her.

"I hope you're not right, but I'm still holding out hope." Micah turned the dial on the radio. "My turn. Since we're talking movies…my favorite is *The Godfather*. I have one sister. I spent eight weeks in an inpatient treatment facility for drug dependence."

Micah's voice broke as he spoke the last word.

His pain hit her like a blow to the heart. "Micah." She rested a hand on his tense forearm. "Don't be ashamed you sought help."

He remained silent and quickly wiped at the corner of his right eye.

"Okay." She cleared her throat, fighting back tears herself. How could she communicate her respect for his journey from addiction then fight for redemption on the football field? Maybe someday, she'd share her thoughts, but right now, they were supposed to be having fun. "You don't have a sister."

"You're good at this." He gave a weak smile. "I'm an only child. The guy I consider my brother is not one related by blood."

"Jamal, right?" The darkness faded from his expression, and the light sparkling in his brown eyes warmed her heart. Remove the pro-athlete ego and she saw a little boy who simply wanted acceptance.

"Yes. His dad was my father figure growing up. I'll forever be grateful for their family."

"You better get the next one right, because I'm winning, three to one." She'd give him an easy one. "I used to be a fitness fanatic. My first Special Ops mission was with Heath's team. I hate hip hop."

"Oh, come on. The lie is you hate hip hop. You always have that type of music blasting in the gym." Micah braked for a stop sign and flipped the right turn blinker.

"Correct." She turned up the volume of the radio and sang along. How many months had passed since she'd felt so light and free? Happiness had always been encased in a bubble—easily destroyed. She'd learned to enjoy the gift of contentment, however short lived.

Her body held a physical lightness. At the same time, she sensed her roots searching for solid and secure ground. Day by day, she learned to accept her new reality. Her life would never be as before. How long until she was healed enough to fully move on?

She watched out the window as they pulled into town. Liberty Ridge had a cute, historic downtown area, filled with little shops and restaurants. Small towns were preferable to large cities. The constant noise of high population areas—car horns, people yelling, the growl of truck engines—grated on her nerves. She liked the quiet of the retreat. Without distraction, she could actually reflect and plan for her next step.

Micah turned onto the town's main street. He parked the rickety truck on the street, in front of The Desert Rose restaurant, then exited to open her door. "We can finish our game over dinner." Taking her hand, he helped steady her as she stepped out.

They entered the restaurant and were led to a table set toward the rear. Once seated, she watched as a few fans approached Micah, asking for selfies.

He agreed with a smile, but afterward turned his attention fully back to Alice.

She found herself drawn to his attractive aura but continued to battle any romantic feelings. Micah simply made her happy, and for a long time, nothing or no one else had.

Their server approached the table and took their drink orders.

"I believe it's your turn." Alice studied her surroundings. The Desert Rose restaurant was quaint and charming, and the menu appeared impressive for a small town. They specialized in locally sourced meat and produce, some from the organic farm partnered with the retreat.

"Get ready for a tough one." He grinned from across the table. "I don't like chocolate. My middle name is Francis. I own an engagement ring that's still sitting in my dresser at home."

Despite the smile on his face, she saw the pain etched in his eyes, which caused her own heart to ache. He'd loved his ex-girlfriend deeply enough to wish to marry her. She took a deep breath. "The lie is that you don't like chocolate. Everyone likes chocolate."

"I'm a freak then because I don't like chocolate. The lie is my middle name isn't Francis, its James." He accepted a tall glass of sweet tea from the server.

Once their server left, Alice's curiosity overpowered the warning in her head. "Were you engaged?" What kind of woman would have left a man like Micah when he needed her most?

He stirred his tea with the straw, causing the ice cubes to spin like a whirlpool in his glass. "Cassidy and I were together for two years, and our relationship had grown serious. Once I became addicted to pain pills, I wasn't the same. I didn't see the changes, because I was too blind to my own needs. When Cassidy threatened to break up, I purchased a diamond ring, thinking if we were engaged, she'd stick around."

"But she didn't." Alice clenched her hand around the cold glass set on the table.

"We had a fight, and she said things I didn't want to hear. She walked out, and I didn't stop her." He brushed a hand down his face. "After I got clean, I realized the extent of the damage I'd done. By that time, Cassidy had moved on with her life…without me."

"Have you moved on?" Jealousy snarled like a protective dog inside her chest. She was no relationship expert, but even she could tell he held on to a dream. Maybe guilt held him hostage, or he really did love her that deeply. Either way, he needed to let go.

"Let's just say my feelings are complicated." He sighed. "The destruction of our relationship is my fault."

Her quick temper wouldn't allow his statement to go unchallenged. She leaned in. "And she gets none of the blame? She left you when you needed her the most?"

"I don't blame her for walking away from the pain I caused her." Micah dropped his head, gazing at the glossy wood tabletop.

"Well, I do." If Cassidy had been with Micah for two years prior to his injury, she should have known him well enough to realize he was worthy of another chance. Alice pressed together her lips, stopping further comment. No use beating the point to death.

Their server approached and set two bowls full of lettuce topped with colorful, fresh vegetables on the table.

After they ordered their meals, Alice dug in, starting with the tomatoes, her favorite.

"I believe the score is three to two." Micah raised a full fork to his lips. "You're in the lead. Final round."

"Okay." She considered what truths she'd admit. "I've been engaged. I've been to five of the seven continents. I used to run a mile in five minutes flat."

"After seeing you run, I'd guess the last one is a lie." Micah grinned. "Just kidding. I'll say you haven't been to five continents."

She narrowed her eyes at his running comment, but a corner of her mouth twitched with humor. Her favorite friendships were ones of playfulness and teasing. "I've never been engaged."

"How come someone hasn't snagged you yet, Alice?" He rested his forearms on the table and leaned in.

"I'm not a relationship kind of girl." Shaking her head, she broke eye contact and glanced away toward the front windows of the restaurant. Outside, the sky had grown darker, rain clouds blocking out the setting sun. "I have no interest in marriage. I don't believe most people can commit to forever and mean it."

"Wow." Micah lowered his eyebrows. "Haven't you read stories of wonderful marriages that have lasted decades? What about your parents?"

Her parents were the last people she'd ever look to for marriage advice. "I would never combine the words wonderful and marriage to describe my parents." Thoughts of her family sickened her stomach. Not good while dining out. She anticipated her steak too much to risk losing her appetite. "Back to our game. You realize you have no chance of winning, right?"

"I still get my last turn." He poked at a mushroom with his fork. "I love playing football in the snow. My favorite month is September. I have six toes on my left foot."

Her belly hurt from laughing. "I've seen your feet. You don't have an extra toe. Which means I called your lie, and you're waking up at five a.m. tomorrow morning."

"Oh well." He shrugged. "At least I got to know you better. I consider that knowledge a win."

If one day she'd ever settle down, her partner would be a man like Micah—funny, confident but not condescending, and easy on the eyes. Though she'd committed to never handing over control of her life to anyone. No matter how perfect he might seem.

Chapter Eight

The next morning, Alice barged into his room at five a.m. "Wakey, wakey, sunshine. Dream time is over."

With a huff, Micah shoved his head underneath his pillow, hoping he was in a bad dream. Nope. As she yanked off the blanket, a cold shock of air invaded his warm cocoon. Good thing he'd worn shorts to bed.

"Come on, Micah. We had a deal."

"No sane person is awake this early," he grumbled.

"I never claimed to be sane."

Alice's warm fingers wrapped around his ankles. The good feeling only lasted a second until she tightened her grip. "Okay, I'll get up." Yawning, he closed his eyes.

"Micah!"

He laughed. "You have no mercy."

Thirty minutes later, he lay on the gym floor, tasked with fifty sit-ups. He fought not to stare at Alice's backside while she jogged on the treadmill. Micah traveled his gaze down to the smooth length of her thigh, to the indentation behind her knee, before lowering it over the gentle arch of her calf.

His sleepy brain had trouble focusing on anything else. Her little spandex shorts didn't help. The motion of her body was mesmerizing. Not mesmerizing—hypnotizing. If someone asked him to bark, he probably would. She must have sensed his gaze, because she hit the pause button on the treadmill and glanced over her shoulder. Caught like a little boy peeking early at the Christmas presents, he lowered his head.

"You're done already?" Her eyebrows arched high on her ivory forehead.

"Not yet." He huffed in and out with exaggeration. "I needed a break."

"Just keep your eyes down and focus on your form." Still scowling, she restarted the treadmill.

How had she detected his stare? Maybe she had another pair of eyes hidden underneath her dark brown ponytail.

While he executed his sit-ups, he peeked over at his hard-nosed trainer—only this time in short intervals so not to get caught. Once finished, he stood and stretched his arms overhead.

Alice's next directive—head outside.

The sun had begun its morning routine, rising slowly over the horizon. He faced east, and the warm light bathed his face. Texas sure knew how to do sunrises. And to think, he would have missed each one if Alice hadn't forced him out of bed before dawn.

"Catch," she hollered before flinging a football.

He caught it one-handed and breathed a sigh of relief. Holding a football felt like a missing limb had been reattached—the weight familiar and comforting. Micah tossed the ball back and forth from hand to hand, enjoying the bumpy texture of the leather on his palms.

"I'll play receiver." She took off at a jog. "Give me a head start, about thirty yards, and then let it rip."

"Sweet." He spun the football on the tip of his finger. "Giddy up, girl, let's go."

While she dialed up her speed, he waited until she turned and raised her hands. Stepping back, he cocked his throwing arm and launched the ball, which arched high in the air—a spiral of pure beauty.

Alice's gaze followed the ball, and she ran to keep pace with its descent. The ball spiraled straight into her outstretched arms. Sounds of hooting and hollering echoed across the field. Alice ran over and tossed him the ball. "Again, but this time don't put so much *umph* behind the pass. I can't run that fast."

They repeated the exercise until Alice tired. By that time, a group of veterans had assembled off to the side, watching the show.

"Who wants to go next?" Micah asked the small crowd. Immediately, several men stepped forward. "You." He pointed to a man with an orange baseball cap. "Do you know how to run a slant route?"

"Sure, man. I played football back in the day." The guy took off with speed.

Micah tossed an easy pass with little heat. Not like the ones he'd launched at Alice. He'd put fire behind those throws, and she'd caught all but three. A real shame the Warriors couldn't sign her for next season.

The veterans took turns fielding passes until his arm tired. A welcome feeling, though, like the muscles in his arm and shoulder had woken from hibernation, hungry to feed.

"This action is great," sounded a male voice. "Hi, I'm Vince Tretter, reporter for Sports USA. Nice to get good footage right off the bat."

Micah absentmindedly shook the man's offered hand. Why was the sports reporter here already? His agent said he wouldn't arrive until the afternoon.

"Thanks for coming down. I wasn't expecting you so early."

"We moved up our schedule since I'm flying to Seattle tonight for a sit-down with their rising star, Marco Rydle. Let's find somewhere quiet to set up for your interview."

He noticed Alice walking away. "That's fine, just give me a minute." Micah ran to catch up. "Hey, how about you stick around? I'd feel better with you there, you know, for moral support."

She blinked several times, then shook her head. "You've done hundreds of these interviews. You'll be fine. Come find me when you're done."

His body hummed with nerves, but male ego kept him quiet about how deeply he wanted her presence during the interview. Alice was better than any anti-anxiety drug. He had no choice but to carry on without her. This interview would pave the way for game day, when he'd step back on the field as a winner. "Alice," he called out before she was out of earshot. "Thanks for this morning. I had fun."

Her wide smile lit up her face. "I thought so, too. Now get back to the reporter and show him you're ready to reclaim your number one quarterback rating."

With the rise of confidence at her words of encouragement, he went to do just that. After all the struggles and heartache, failure was not an option.

****

Desiring to stay away from the reporter and cameraman, Alice returned to her cabin for a shower. Micah didn't need her hanging around to prove he was one-hundred-percent the man and athlete he'd been before the injury. Sure, his last season had been a wash and his behavior off the field stole all the media attention. The man she observed now was determined and strong. Nothing would stand in his way.

After entering her cabin, she grabbed her phone. She had a missed call and voicemail from her cousin. Kate was the only family she acknowledged. When Alice had needed her most, Kate helped her escape the sect.

When Alice discovered she'd been promised into marriage, she knew the time had come to leave. If she didn't, she'd be trapped with a husband and eventually children. At sixteen years old, she wouldn't allow herself to be shackled for the rest of her life.

She snuck out a letter to Kate, who'd successfully escaped a few years earlier and resided in Santa Fe. Kate made arrangements for Alice to hide at a safe house until she drove over and picked her up.

For two years, Alice lived with her older cousin, enrolled in a public high school, and attempted to live a normal life. She owed everything good in her life to Kate. While sitting on the bed, she listened to the voicemail.

"Hey. I hope you're enjoying the retreat. I got a letter from inside and need to talk to you ASAP. Call me back. Bye." A beep sounded, ending the message.

Why would Kate need her help? Her cousin usually handled sect member runaways on her own. She hit Dial.

Kate picked up on the second ring. "I'm so glad to hear from you. I was worried you'd be too busy and not check your phone."

"I'm never too busy for you." She smiled at the sound of a familiar voice. "What's up?"

"My mom sent me a message from your half-sister, Maddy. She needs help getting out."

Struggling for breath, Alice sat in stunned silence. Her half-sister, Maddy, had only been a baby when she'd left—a little girl with dark curly hair and an infectious laugh. How many siblings did she have these days? When she'd fled, twenty children lived in the household.

"Alice?" Kate paused. "You still there?"

She shook her head and straightened her posture. "I'm still here. What do you need from me?"

"Maddy plans to run very soon. As soon as it's safe. She'll stay at the safe house in Flagstaff until I can get her. But I have to find someplace for her to live."

"And that's why you called me?" A chilly uneasiness spread across her skin. "Because you want me to take her in?"

"Roger and I have only been married for a few months. He wants some time just for the two of us, and I agree. You're out of the Army now, and Maddy's your sister."

Her heart beat at an abnormally rapid pace. *Take a deep breath. They can't hurt you.* "You know how I feel about getting pulled back into the family."

"Alice, this girl is inexperienced and scared…just like you when you ran. Think about it, okay? That's all I'm asking. Maddy is fifteen. She's not a young child who needs a lot of care."

No sense arguing, at least not yet. "I'll consider it, but don't get your hopes up. I divorced myself from my family a long time ago."

"From what my mom said in her letter, Maddy is strong and very smart," Kate said. "Remind you of anyone?"

"I said I'd think about taking her." Alice pictured a younger version of herself, ready to do anything to escape the fate of a child bride. Her rising empathy left her with a deep desire to stop the sect from inflicting more damage. "Why don't you go to the police? What they're doing is a crime."

A long sigh sounded from the other end. "I've gone to the police. All I get is the standard response of 'there is nothing we can do, ma'am.' "

"They won't even try?" She balled a fist in anger.

"Try what? A raid? You saw what happened in Waco. No one wants to touch our old sect with a ten-foot pole."

Maybe someday, Alice would fight the battle to bring the cult leaders to justice. Not today, though. Simply thinking about them made her stomach ache. "I have one more week at the retreat. I'll get in touch when I'm home."

"Just promise you'll seriously consider taking Maddy," Kate pleaded. "Okay?"

She lowered onto the bed and lay back, staring up at the clapboard ceiling. "Yes. I promise."

"I'm holding you to it." Kate laughed. "Enjoy the rest of the retreat. Talk to you later."

Alice said goodbye and ended the call. A chill ran over her skin, like a ghost had entered the room. Not a ghost—evil memories of her mother being struck again and again by her father, and of heated arguments between her father's wives over the smallest things.

A few good times were scattered in between the pain. Her favorite was the feeling of leaving the house after her chores were completed, knowing she could run free the rest of the day. She'd play catch with her brothers then race them to the dried creek bed. Moments of happiness had found her, which ended the second her foot hit the house's door tread.

Still lying on the bed, Alice closed her eyes. She wouldn't go back home, not even in her mind. But then, she pictured Maddy, a girl she barely knew. A girl who needed rescuing from the very hole Alice had escaped.

With their shared, horrible upbringing, how would she say no?

****

Inside a small room in the retreat's main building, Micah took a few deep breaths while the cameraman clipped the microphone on his shirt collar. He sat on an upholstered armchair while Vince sat on its twin across the way. His nerves were tight enough for someone to play him like a guitar. He already knew the reporter, Vince Tretter, from previous interviews. The guy was usually a marshmallow, tossing out easy questions. Hopefully, Vince wouldn't decide today he wanted to transform into a hard-hitting reporter.

"Okay." Vince cleared his throat. "Let's get going. I have a noon flight to catch."

Thanks for verifying where I rank in importance. Micah pasted a smile on his face. "Yes. I have other obligations, as well."

Vince waved a finger at the cameraman to begin. "Micah, you struggled last year. First, the season-ending injury, and then reports of opioid addiction. You've also earned a reputation as the life of the party. When did you decide to change direction?"

He adjusted his mental armor. Reminders of his mistakes and failures wouldn't shake his confidence. "I struggled watching the game I love from the sidelines. In constant pain, I grew frustrated. Admittedly, I acted unbecoming of a professional athlete. I'm lucky to have several teammates who are also good friends. They convinced me to seek help."

"It's been reported you recently were in rehab. Is that true?" Vince maintained eye contact.

The constant prying into his life never became easier to bear. His brain screamed to remain silent. "All I'll say is now I'm totally clean and healthy."

"Why are you spending a portion of your remaining free time volunteering at the Liberty Veterans' Retreat?"

A similar question to what he'd asked himself before arriving. Through his time here, he'd discovered the answer. "The services offered, both physical and mental, are important. Our veterans have sacrificed a lot in service to our country, and my time here is my small way of saying thanks."

"How have the men at the retreat reacted to your presence?" Vince adjusted the wire-rim glasses on the bridge of his short nose.

Instantly, Alice's face came to mind. "The veterans are not only men. Women vets can experience the same issues as their male counterparts."

"I didn't mean to imply anything different." Vince's smile faded.

He straightened in his chair. "A member of the Cultural Support Team is at the retreat. She's been in combat alongside Special Operations teams in Afghanistan." Instead of droning on about himself, he'd take the opportunity to tell the world about Alice and the other brave and amazing women like her. He tipped his head and smiled. "During a mission, she was seriously injured by an IED." Micah said a prayer Alice wouldn't murder him for talking about her situation on national TV.

"A very compelling story." Vince glanced down at his notes. "I'd like to know your expectations for the upcoming season. What can the fans expect when you first run onto the field?"

In his head, he played the scenario—standing in the stadium tunnel while waiting for the team to be announced, and then running out on the field. He could almost hear the hometown crowd yelling his name. "Warrior fans should know I'm healed and ready to play. I'll give training camp my full and undivided attention. The Micah Palmer who led the team to the Super Bowl is back."

"Rumors abound that the head coach will hold try-outs during training camp for the starting quarterback position…you against Garrett Kantra." Vince raised his eyebrows. "Your back-up performed strong at the end of last season. How concerned are you Kantra will win the starting job?"

Micah's vision swam with stars, and he pushed down his temper. He'd concede Kantra had a few wins under his belt from last season, but a short run of success didn't make him a serious threat. "I have no problem proving myself on the practice field. I'm not concerned."

"Good." Vince nodded. "When we arrived this morning, we noticed you tossing passes behind the retreat building. Your arm looks good. What have you been doing for rehab during the off-season?"

He thought of Alice, who'd made training exciting

again. "While my knee healed, I focused on strengthening my arm. Right now, I'm working with an excellent trainer. She'll have me more than ready for training camp."

"She?" His well-trimmed eyebrows rose up his forehead. "You're working with a female trainer?"

"Yes." Warmth flooded Micah's face. Don't blush during a national sport's interview. "She is the best."

After a few more questions, Vince shut off his mic. "That's a wrap." He stood and extended his hand. "You did great. Really great. We'll get the interview posted online within the next few days. I'll send your agent the details."

"Thanks for coming down." He stood and shook Vince's offered hand. Positive publicity paved the road for his return trip to the top.

"My pleasure. Good luck, and I'll see you again at training camp." With his back toward Micah, Vince tucked his notes into the briefcase sitting on the floor.

Anxious to leave behind the interview, he unclipped his microphone and shook hands with the cameraman before making his exit. He didn't get far before running into Storm, who stood in the middle of the hallway, as immovable as a brick wall.

"Are you leaving?" Scowling, Storm raised his chin.

Micah crossed an arm over his chest, unwilling to yield. "My agent will arrive soon then we'll decide my next step."

Storm stepped forward. "And you'll do whatever he tells you?"

"No, but I'll take his advice into consideration. To be honest, I'm not doing much here besides training.

I've met all the guys, taken pictures together, and played some ball. What more can I do?" He remembered the sheep and shuddered. Best not to ask an open-ended question.

"What about Alice?" Storm turned his head to gaze out the window to his left. "Don't you believe you're a benefit to her healing?"

Micah followed Storm's gaze and immediately noticed Alice still tossing around the football with the guys. "She didn't come to the retreat to train me for the football season. If I leave, she can focus on her own recovery, not mine."

Storm narrowed his eyes. "When she's working with you, she's doing the best thing for her recovery."

Micah opened his mouth to dispute but then snapped it shut. Was Alice benefiting that greatly from training him? Her self-esteem had improved, but she might find other activities here more beneficial. "I care about her, but if my agent tells me it's time to go, then I need to consider the possibility. I hope you understand, man."

"If you leave now, you won't hurt anyone with the exception of Alice." Storm stepped aside to allow Micah to pass. "Think about that, man, when you're packing your bags."

With shoulders slumped, he continued walking down the hallway, then stepped outside. The shouts of laughter coming from Alice and the other vets struck his heart. What if spending so much time with him delayed her recovery? Instead of bonding with fellow veterans, she was stuck training him. He glanced across the lawn at Alice tossing the football with a few fellow veterans. If she had a choice, would she rather be with them or him?

Would leaving now be best for them both? Or were his own self-interests regarding his career clouding his judgment?

Deep down, he understood whatever his next move, he'd hold tight to Alice's fighting spirit, even if he'd have to let her go.

Chapter Nine

"How did the interview go?" Alice asked while she ate lunch with Micah. She munched on a turkey sandwich on rye—*yum*. "The reporter wasn't here for very long."

"The interview went well. Vince had another meeting scheduled in Seattle for later today. I guess I'm no longer a top news story." Micah shrugged and took a bite of his sandwich.

He'd secured the top spot in her mind. She needed to lift his spirits. "Don't worry. You've been out of the spotlight. Once you're making touchdowns again, the reporters will beat down your door."

"Thanks for the vote of confidence." One corner of his mouth lifted with a grin.

Given his sullen mood, she had a hard time reading him. Instead of his usual behavior of leaning back in his chair and rocking like a hyperactive grade school student, he sat hunched over with a clenched jaw—a stark difference from the man she'd left earlier. The interview must not have gone as well as he wanted her to believe. "Is your agent still coming today?"

"He'll be here soon. Our meeting might take awhile so don't plan training for the rest of the day." He lifted his glass of water and took a long drink.

Her concern switched to frustration. With the interview and news footage under his belt, he might decide his time volunteering at the Liberty Veterans' Retreat had come to an end. Imagining him leaving left a bitter taste in her mouth. Alice knew they'd soon head off in different directions. Likely, she'd never see him again. The sudden flood of sadness made her want to cry.

"Don't worry about training." She dipped a potato chip in the pool of ketchup on her plate, a taste she'd acquired during deployment. "Colleen asked for my help planning the Easter egg hunt for this coming Saturday. Storm and Colleen invited the town to the farm for a party. Heath will dress up as the Easter bunny, which I personally can't wait to see."

"Sounds like fun."

His tone stayed flat and lifeless, and his gaze focused on the table. "Is everything all right?" She reached across and rested a hand on his arm. The Micah she knew only grew sullen about two things—concerns about football and Cassidy.

The muscles in his arm flexed, but he didn't pull away. "Returning to football feels real now. I'm getting a lot of pressure to succeed straight out of the gate. The team, the fans, the media…they're all looking for me to again lead the Warriors into the playoffs. Plus, my backup poses a real threat. He's hungry for a chance to knock me out of the starting position."

She didn't need superpowers to sense the stress and tension rolling off him. "No one knows the future, Micah. Failure is always an option when we push ourselves to the edge." She'd picked herself up after many failures, brushed off the dust of defeat, and jumped back to work—with the glaring exception of her latest fall. "Take one day at a time. Focus on what you're doing today. Don't worry about the future."

Micah placed a large hand over hers. "How about I take you with me?" He chuckled. "You can be my own personal cheerleader."

His hand was calloused and rough, but warm. "Ha…you know I'd look horrible in those skimpy uniforms."

"I think you'd look pretty great." Micah opened his mouth before a loud voice interrupted their conversation.

"Micah." His voice boomed.

A well-dressed man walked toward them. Expensive suit, stylish haircut, shoes so shiny they could be used as mirrors—must be Micah's agent.

"What's in this southern air? You look great." The man approached the table and came to a stop.

Smiling, Micah stood and shook his hand.

Alice needed a quick getaway. She didn't belong in the realm of professional athletes, with the multimillion dollar contracts and endorsement deals—Micah's world. He didn't belong with her, doing sit-ups, weightlifting exercises, and jogging around the retreat. How could she be upset at Micah's eagerness to jump on the first flight out of here? But the rationalization was her brain talking. Her heart still broke, knowing the time had likely come to say goodbye.

****

After returning Alice's wave as she walked away, Micah engaged in several minutes of small talk with Carl, then suggested a tour of the retreat grounds, suddenly very anxious to conclude their business. The talk of media coverage and good press made him feel like a phony. His stomach clenched. Nothing would help him recover more than stepping onto the field and playing solid games. All the interviews and press releases were just white noise.

"I spoke with Vince." Carl walked with his hands stuffed in the pockets of his black dress slacks. "He liked the coverage they got of you playing football with the veterans. The story he'll run is a good start. We need more, though, and soon. I'll contact some of the other national sports news outlets and scheduled more interviews once you're back in Timber Lake."

Frustration burned at the assumption he remained frozen at the starting gate. "I feel better than I have in a long time. Since coming here, I've lost all desire for the false high of pills. Trust me, I'm ready to fully commit to playing my best next season." He glanced at his agent and wondered if Carl still believed in Micah's ability to win.

"I'm glad to hear of your commitment. Before your injury, you were a media darling and unstoppable on the field. But since then, people question your dedication to the game."

"I understand why." The statement left him even more determined to change their minds. "I have three years left on my contract with the Warriors and intend to spend every day proving I'm the best."

Wearing a wide smile, Carl patted him on the back. "Are you ready to fly this coop and start working-out in Timber Lake? I talked to the Warriors' trainers, and they're anxious to get their hands on you."

Not as enticing of a prospect as he'd initially thought. "I've committed myself for two weeks at the retreat. I still have one more before I'll return to Timber Lake."

"You're not obligated to stay." Carl halted, faced Micah, and then glanced at his watch. "You got what you needed. The press will eat up the story of you volunteering with veterans. You have nothing more to gain by hanging around."

Even if Micah spoke about his training with Alice, he'd never get Carl to understand what he received from Alice was more than athletic conditioning. Carl didn't appreciate the value of human connection, only the money those humans added to his bank account. Micah benefited from working with Alice—and his most surprising improvement—humility.

"I booked you a flight out of Austin for tonight." Carl led the way back to the main building. "You can spend a few days at your home in Tampa, get your affairs together, and then go to Timber Lake and start training."

His mouth went dry. He needed to squeeze out a few more days with Alice. "I feel I should stay and finish my commitment. Spending time helping others is just as valuable as working toward my own goals. Plus, the press could find out I left my volunteering early."

"For other people, yes." Carl scowled and rubbed at the back of his neck. "You're paid a lot of money to play football. When you said you were totally committed to your return, was that a load of bull?"

Pressure built in his chest, and he felt his heart stretch and twist. Carl was right. He should prepare to move back to Timber Lake and begin work-outs with the team. But a loud voice in his head scolded that leaving right now was a huge mistake.

Maybe Alice would be glad to get rid of him. She could focus on her own needs instead of babysitting him. Micah stopped at the wooden steps leading up to the main building's back porch. "I would never do anything to screw up my return to football. Give me some time to get my things together."

A smile animated Carl's face, which gleamed with sweat. "I'll wait inside and make a few calls. We leave in one hour."

Was leaving with Carl a mistake? Only one person would tell him the unfiltered truth, whether he wanted to hear it or not. Which meant he needed to find Alice before he packed his bags.

****

Instead of waiting in the quiet, small cabin, Alice wandered over by the sheep pen. She sat with the sheep for about thirty minutes before Micah found her. He strode across the grass wearing a grim expression, causing her mood to plummet.

A chorus of unfriendly bleats greeted him. How long did sheep hold a grudge? Probably just as long as the man who'd unsuccessfully attempted to shear them.

"I looked all over for you." He stood on the other side of the fence rail, resting a forearm on a post.

"Well, you found me." *Why go through all the trouble only to tell me you're leaving?*

"I'm flying to Tampa tonight. After I pack up what I need from my apartment there, I'll move to Timber Lake and start training with the team's staff." He paused, then exhaled a heavy sigh. "Carl is my agent, and I trust he has my best interests at heart. That is…if he has a heart." His joke fell flat, and his smile faded.

Humor would not win him any points. Alice didn't crack a smile. "Obviously, he's looking out for your career. Your big contracts are how he gets paid."

Micah ran a hand over the overgrown stubble on his jaw. "Your training has really helped me. We haven't known each other very long, but I consider you a good friend."

She bore her gaze into him. If only she could shoot laser beams from her eyes. "You're running away."

Micah pushed off the rail posts. "I'm not running away. I'm going home…where I should be."

"When you're with me, you're just Micah. You were a regular guy, no fame and glory, and being regular scares you." She jumped to her feet and climbed between the fence posts to stand on the other side.

He threw up his hands and huffed out a breath. "You honestly think I can't live without fame?"

"At the retreat, you came to terms with who you are on the inside…the man away from football. To be honest, I'll miss our time together." Alice refused to get all mushy and sentimental, but she wanted him to recognize the change in him. They'd had fun. Now, she'd move on.

He raked a hand through his dark hair. "Once I'm gone, you can focus on what you want instead of on me."

But what if you are what I want? Her pulse quickened. "If you honestly think it's best to leave, then get on the plane and don't look back."

He stepped toward her, arms crossed and chin raised. "You're being unfair."

"Really?" She moved closer. What nerve. "You made a two-week commitment to work at the retreat. Now, you secured good press, and you're on the next exiting plane." Micah moved so close, she saw every tiny freckle dotting his nose.

He gritted his teeth before one side of his mouth twitched with a grin. "You are the most infuriating woman I've ever met."

"Thanks. I'll take that as a compliment." She mirrored Micah's slow grin. The man always tossed cold water on her temper with his easy smile.

"I want to continue what we've started, but too many people count on me." He reached across and tugged on her ponytail. "Not only my agent, but my teammates, the team owners, and the fans."

"And what about you?" Alice touched a fingertip to his chest, tapping over his heart. "You'll be no good to anyone if you don't take care of yourself." Being so close jumbled her brain. She stepped backward, away from his body heat. "Whether you leave or stay, make the decision best for your wellbeing."

Micah reached out and held her hand.

His touch jolted her, from her fingertips all the way up her arm, straight to her heart. His hand, which dwarfed her own, forged a connection she wouldn't acknowledge as real. She'd never fall for a man who couldn't return her feeling. Her painful past had hardened her to flights of fancy.

"I'm sorry, Alice, if I've disappointed you." His shoulders slumped. "Meeting you is one of the best things that's ever happened."

"Then I guess this is goodbye." Alice slipped her hand out of his grasp and instantly missed his touch. "See you on TV." She strode away before he caught a glimpse of her pain. Tears flooded her eyes and blurred her vision. She'd told him to do what was best for himself, and if that meant leaving her and the retreat, then so be it. Though her conviction didn't soften the blow.

An hour later, she stood outside her cabin and watched a black luxury car drive away, dust kicking up from under its tires. Her eyes stung with unshed tears, and she cleared her throat to dislodge the lump of emotion. Well, Micah was gone. Guess she'd spend her remaining days helping with the farm and attending group therapy. No more gym sessions filled with hard work and laughter. No more runs, side by side, with the man who'd rebuilt a part of her confidence.

For the first time since the IED incident, she'd felt a sense of purpose. She was actually doing something useful, instead of sitting around in her little apartment in South Carolina, wondering how she'd spend the rest of her life.

Noticing the time, she cringed. Her session with Colleen started in fifteen minutes—more facing subjects too painful to discuss.

Despite attempts to block him from her mind, she thought back to Micah's goodbye, and her heart burned with resentment. How could he pack his things and leave? Had she been wrong in believing he was different?

As she walked across the yard to the main house, she felt a tap on her shoulder. Alice jumped, and her heart crashed into her ribcage with a startled jolt. Moving totally by instinct, she grabbed the offending arm and twisted. With her other arm, she elbowed the person in the ribs, causing him to grunt before dropping to the ground. She glanced down to see the prostrate form of Micah.

"What was that for?" He groaned. "I thought you'd be happy I stayed."

"Oh my…" she choked out. "I didn't know it was you. Never sneak up on a soldier." Alice knelt beside him and brushed a hand over his head. "I'm sorry, Micah."

He rested on his side. "I think you broke a rib." Tears formed in his eyes.

He'd only recovered from one injury. Now, with a shot from her elbow, she'd dealt him another setback. If he couldn't start training camp, she'd be at fault. "Where is the pain? Should I call an ambulance? I can't believe I just hurt you."

Huffing out a laugh, he wrapped his arms across his chest. "I'm fine, Alice. Don't call 911."

She had a strong desire to erase the grin off his face. Instead, she rolled him over with her foot so he gazed upward as she towered over him. "Someone will have to dial 911 after I'm done with you."

"Please be merciful." He pressed his hands together like in prayer. "I'm staying…which means I'm all yours for the next week, whether you want me or not."

Had he really chosen staying over following the advice of his agent? Happiness and relief shimmered inside her chest. She shouldn't be so incredibly overjoyed at one more week.

Alice hated depending on Micah to light up her otherwise dull life. She hated being dependent on anyone besides herself, because experience had taught her well. Her best defense was complete independence.

When she left the retreat, she'd go back to being independent. For now, she'd enjoy every minute of what little time she had with him. In seven more days, they'd say goodbye again—permanently. How would she deal with the loss then? As she continued to emotionally grow closer, wouldn't the pain be even greater?

Chapter Ten

"What are we doing in a barn?" Micah glanced around at his surroundings. Back at the retreat, Alice instructed him to pack a change of clothes before driving over to True Horizon Ranch in Storm's old truck. Once they'd arrived, he followed her into the red-painted barn, still wary of her plans.

When he'd made the decision to stay and complete his volunteer commitment, he'd suffered an ear-full from his agent. Carl reprimanded him for wasting precious time playing a do-gooder when he should be totally focused on his career. But Micah didn't see his time at the retreat as a waste and he'd argued the point to some length. After only one week, he felt an internal shift. Each day he awoke more balanced. He walked a tightrope and needed to complete his journey instead of jumping off midway, risking a hard fall.

Alice pointed to the ceiling of the barn, which hovered about thirty feet above. A thick rope hung from one of the sturdy rafters, its frayed end resting on the straw-strewn floor. "Climb the rope all the way to the top."

He didn't hesitate but jumped and clung to the rope, swaying back and forth like a monkey. Arms straining with effort, he ascended about ten feet before conceding and returning to the ground. His breath came out hard and fast. "No way can I get to the top."

"Sure." She stood with wide-spread legs and hands on hips. "Just stand still long enough to listen to my instructions."

"Fine. I'm all ears." She smiled another devastating smile, making him want her as more than a friend. A temptation he wouldn't entertain because Alice was— well, Alice. Another woman still ruled his heart. Although, lately, he thought of Cassidy less often.

"First, wrap your foot around the rope." She took hold of the rope, lifted a knee, and then twirled the rope around her foot like a vine. Lifting herself up, she was now about two feet above the ground, with her left foot resting on top of the other. "See, now I can use my legs to grab and step up. My arms are only to steady myself as I climb." She demonstrated a few more reps before sliding down. "I used to love climbing rope. Now, I can't go more than four or five feet."

"You'll get there again." Micah imitated Alice's foot wrap but failed.

Grinning, she reached down and encircled his foot with the rope.

He pushed off with his legs and moved upward. Once he found a productive rhythm, he progressed easily to the top, then smacked the ceiling beam with a hand before slowly descending. "What a rush." When he hit the ground, he took several seconds to catch his breath and let his legs stop trembling.

"I'm glad you had fun because I want you to repeat the exercise ten more times."

"If I do, then you need to go up once." Only fair to push her while she pushed him. "Prove you still got it."

She flicked her gaze toward the roof and grinned. "Sure, if you make it to the top all ten reps."

"No problem." He winked, not doubting he possessed the strength to get the job done.

By his fifth rep, he could barely feel the muscles in his legs and shoulders. A jolting pain zipped down the back of his right thigh and into his calf. "I need a break." He huffed and sank to the ground. He'd dreamed about a roll in the hay, but not like this. Micah was so exhausted he couldn't complete one more trip up, let alone five.

But if he didn't, then Alice was off the hook. Standing on shaky legs, he picked out the straw stuck in his hair and stood before the rope. He struggled through each pull upward but charged through the pain, finishing his assignment from the world's most sadistic trainer. "Your turn, sister." He gulped down water. "Show me what ya got."

She wiped her palms on her T-shirt.

That particular one happened to be Micah's favorite. The tight fabric showed off her curves. Again, he forced out thoughts about her attractiveness. *Get a grip, man.*

Alice moved slowly up the rope until she was about three-quarters of the way to the top, then she conceded and shimmied down. "Ugh. I was so close. My legs turned into a bowl of pudding."

With a wide smile, he licked his lips. "Chocolate pudding? My favorite."

"If I had the energy, I'd poke you in the ribs." Alice lowered herself to sit cross-legged on the floor and blew out a long breath.

The sounds of various animals filled the barn. A black dog darted inside, then ran to her, pushing his muzzle into her hand.

"Hey, Shadow. How've you been?" She snuggled the dog's head.

Next, Heath entered, strolling toward them down the main aisle of the barn. "How'd the rope work?"

Alice patted the ground, and the dog sat beside her. "The rope works fine. Me...not so much. I didn't make it to the top."

"You told me the set-up was for Micah." Heath glanced at Micah, wiggled his eyebrows, and smirked.

She snorted. "Micah negotiated a deal. The only way I could get him to finish his reps was to agree to give the rope a shot."

Micah grinned. Not the only way, simply the most effective.

"So, did he make it to the top or wimp out?" Heath asked.

The comment ruffled his male pride. Micah stepped toward Alice and cleared his throat. "You realize I'm here, right?"

"I see you." She laughed. "Micah did very well. He climbed to the top eleven times. Next session, I'll show him how to complete the exercise without using his legs."

"Oh no." Micah held up his hands in protest. "I'm training to play football, not live in the jungle."

"Never hurts to be prepared, man." Heath turned his attention to Alice. "Are you still staying for dinner? Grace invited Colleen and Storm, too."

She nodded. "We'd love to stay for dinner. What time should we be changed and ready?"

"Grace told me six." As Heath walked away, he glanced over his shoulder. "If you want some privacy, I can close the barn doors. Under the right circumstances, a dark barn and straw are very romantic."

Sounded nice. Like if Alice was Micah's girlfriend instead of his trainer. Micah shot a sideways glance, judging her reaction to Heath's teasing.

Alice hopped onto her feet, her cheeks turned hot pink. "Get back here, Heath, and I'll wipe that grin off your face."

"No can do, warrior princess." Heath stepped outside, and his body was swallowed by the bright sunlight. "Catch you later."

"Don't listen to half the things coming out of his mouth." With a low groan, she shook her head.

"Romantic, huh?" Smiling, Micah reclined on the soft hay covering the ground. He crossed his ankles and slipped both hands under his head. "The man does have a point."

Within three steps, she stood over him .

Looking every bit a warrior princess. He flinched.

"I guarantee you'll find no romance in here." Alice reached down and pulled him upright. "Break time's over. Let's get back to work."

Now standing, he shook out his exhausted legs. Too bad. After the work-out she'd already put him through, he wouldn't mind spending the rest of the time with her wrapped in his arms. Not a good idea, since they'd be going their separate ways in less than a week.

****

As Alice stepped out of the shower to dry off, she took a moment to enjoy the sound of the rain shower pattering the window. After spending a few hours with Micah in the barn, she accepted Grace's offer to use a guest room to clean up. Dressed in her underwear and bra, she sat on the bed and lifted her leg, studying the crisscross of scars. The backside of her right calf had seen the worst damage, with skin covered in bumpy scar tissue—ugly to look at, repulsive to the touch.

In a flash, she was propelled back to the scene—a chaotic yard outside a compound in rural Afghanistan—women screaming and kids crying. Several team members were unaccounted for. Her goal was to contain the women and children, herding them into an interior room to keep them safe. But no one listened to either her or her interpreter.

Without warning, an eerie stillness settled over the yard.

Seconds later, Alice was pushed to the ground. A loud explosion burst her eardrums, and a bright flash blinded her. Initially, she felt no pain, only confusion. She didn't realize she'd been hit until she saw a soldier ripping apart the leg of her pants and field treating her injuries. Like a bystander, Alice observed while he worked on her leg. She felt nothing, like he touched someone else until suddenly agony ripped through her body, sending waves of sharp pain. She barely remembered being carried to the medevac chopper. Was she dying? Unconsciousness faded her vision before she arrived at the base hospital.

The fact she survived was a miracle. But what purpose did good fortune serve? Until now, she'd wasted her second chance by hiding from the world and feeling sorry for herself. She promised herself to change the direction of her life.

After taking one last glimpse at her scars, she pulled up her jeans and buttoned the waistband. How could anyone find her legs attractive? How embarrassing she wore shorts around Micah.

She exited her room to find him waiting in the hall. He'd showered and changed, his athletic frame showcased in a pale green button-down shirt and jeans. He reached in her direction to take her arm, and his broad shoulders stretched his shirt while the muscles in his forearms flexed. Standing close, he had several inches on her. Micah was tall, probably six-three, and moved with a grace uncommon for a man of his height and build.

"They're waiting for us downstairs." He hooked an arm through hers. "I didn't want to face the squad alone."

His touch sent sparks of pleasure over her skin. "What are you afraid of, Mr. Football?"

Micah stopped at the top of the stairs. "If you haven't noticed, the two men downstairs are very protective of you."

"I don't understand what you mean?" Why would anyone, let alone Heath and Storm, feel the need to protect her? Especially from Micah?

"They want to make sure I'm behaving as a man of honor." He patted her hand. "I've reassured them we're friends. You're like a sister to me."

His platonic sentiment sent disappointment spiraling into her gut. A sister was what he'd always consider her, which was good, of course. She wouldn't want any romantic misunderstanding to ruin their friendship. "Heath has known me for a long time. Now, he's gotten into his head that his mission is to look after me. He never would have suggested we work together if he thought you'd put the moves on me."

"How did he know I wouldn't put the moves on you?" Micah winked, then motioned for her to go ahead of him down the stairs.

I wish. She chuckled. "I was in the service for eleven years, so I've been 'one of the guys' for a long time. Men see me as a buddy, not someone they'd take home for a fun time." When she descended the stairs, she saw Heath standing by the entryway to the dining room.

"Who's taking you home for a fun time?" He glanced up at Micah and scowled.

"No one, which is my point." She cringed at the truth behind her teasing words. Someday, would she desire a change in her romantic status?

"Don't count yourself out of the game, yet, Lipstick." Heath gave her an amused grin. "Now, let's go eat."

Alice seated herself between Micah and Grace. The scents of tomato sauce and seasoned potatoes caused her stomach to growl in anticipation. While the food and conversation filled the room, she enjoyed getting to know Colleen outside the therapy office. She watched Grace act as their hostess and care for little John with ease. Heath lucked out in finding a loving and patient partner.

"So, where's Harper?" She twirled long strands of linguini onto her fork, wrangling all the dangling ends. The food was warm and delicious.

"She's at home with Storm's mom." Colleen touched Storm's arm. "She wasn't feeling very well."

"I hope she gets better soon. Your farm is the perfect place to raise children. She's a lucky girl." Alice noticed Colleen's smile had faded.

Storm patted his wife's hand. "Yes, it is. We plan to have another child someday, just not as soon as we hoped."

"I lost a pregnancy not that long ago." Colleen's blue eyes glistened with tears. "We're waiting a few more months before we try again."

"I'm sorry." Having never experienced pregnancy herself, Alice wasn't sure what else to say. Absentmindedly, she placed a hand over her middle. How would she feel having another life grow inside her? She'd never given much thought to motherhood. But what about now? Her commitment to the Army had finished. The rest of her life was a blank slate. Would a child fill the void?

Another person would never make her whole. She'd only find fulfillment on her own. Then, perhaps, she'd allow another into her heart. Although now, she'd grown afraid she might never find her life's dream.

****

The next morning, Micah sat at the kitchen table in the main building. After reading the latest text from his agent, he shook his head.

—Warrior media relations requests an interview for local TV. Since you're hiding out in TX, I didn't know what date to tell them. They'll probably do a sit down with Garrett Kantra instead—

A clear overreaction. Micah would leave on Sunday—in only three more days. Meanwhile, Carl should find another athlete to micro-manage.

—I'll be back in Timber Lake by April 20 for team workouts. Schedule the interview any time after that—

At the thought about jumping back into the spotlight, he tensed with nerves. What if he'd lost the talent that made him a force on the field? Playing football was his life. Without fame and money, he'd never win back Cassidy. She wasn't the type of woman who'd be content with an average man. After she'd broken up with him, she'd started a relationship with another professional athlete.

If Micah Palmer had been a regular guy with a regular job, Cassidy wouldn't have given him a second look.

Alice stood at the counter, elbow deep in buckets of color. She'd been tasked with dying eggs for the farm's Easter festival. She glanced over at him and raised an eyebrow. "What's wrong?"

The air in the kitchen smelled of vinegar mixed with the scent of fresh bread the cooks baked earlier. "Nothing. Carl texted again. The man's driving me crazy."

"He'll get you back soon enough. Right now, I need you to put the colored eggs in the fridge." She pointed to the open containers filled with eggs stained every color of the rainbow.

Alice looked very enticing today. Tendrils of brown hair escaped the rubber band at the back of her neck and swirled around her flushed face. She hid her long legs behind yoga pants—really a shame. He noticed she'd worn pants the last two days, making him really miss her tight shorts.

"Storm asked if I'd clean-up the animal pens. He wants to open them for a petting zoo." Micah gathered the egg cartons and safely placed them in the stainless steel refrigerator. "Would you mind helping me? I can't speak for the pigs and chickens, but I already know how the sheep feel about me."

She wiped her hands on a large white towel. "I probably can be persuaded, but only if we hit the gym later."

"How is your leg feeling with the increased exercise?" He noticed her limp wasn't as pronounced and credited the improvement to the strength she'd built.

"My leg hates me, but I don't care." She shrugged. "The rest of my body loves the activity. I've spent almost a year either laying in a bed or sitting on my rear."

He allowed his gaze to roam down to that part of her anatomy then mentally kicked himself. His feelings for her had to stay locked in the friend zone. "It's warm outside. Go change and I'll meet you by the barns."

"What I'm wearing is fine." She waved a hand over her hot-pink T-shirt and black yoga pants.

"You'll get too hot." Micah straightened his posture so he had a height advantage on her. "Go change into shorts."

"No." With a scowl, Alice crossed her arms.

"Why not?"

"Because I don't want to." She turned her focus to the eggs on the counter, facing her back toward Micah.

Was she feeling self-conscious again about her scars? "I don't care about your scars. No one here does."

She shook her head. "Trust me, no one wants to be reminded of what an IED can do."

"What about the guys walking around on prosthetic legs? Should they cover up, too?" He rested a hand on her shoulder and spun her to face him, not allowing her to hide.

Her expression softened, and she lowered her shoulders. "No, a prosthetic leg is different."

"How?" Micah folded his arms over his chest. "Keeping a part of yourself shut away is not helping you heal. Your scars are part of what makes you amazing. I think so…and so do the rest of the guys here."

She wiped at the corner of her eye with her shirt sleeve. "Being blown up isn't amazing."

Losing the battle with his self-control, he pulled her into a hug. "Alice, I can't possibly understand what you endured this past year. Just know I think the world of you and admire every single scar on your body." He almost called her beautiful but bit his tongue. A micro-thin line of restraint stretched between them…one he couldn't cross.

She rested her head on his shoulder. After a deep breath, she stiffened, stepped out of his embrace, and straightened her back. "Fine. I'll go change." Before she exited the kitchen, she stopped and turned her head. "Thanks, Micah. You're a great friend."

After she left, he let the word friend hang in the air. Friend didn't feel strong enough. He wished for another word in the English language that better described what she meant to him.

Chapter Eleven

As she made her way across The Bunny Pit, she carefully stepped around tiny balls of fluff that hopped around her feet.

Kids screamed with delight while madly dashing around the enclosure in an attempt to pick up a rabbit. For their part, the rabbits didn't mind the attention, as long as a few food pellets were held inside the little hands.

Four-year-old Harper Thompson guided little John Carter around the animal enclosure, petting anything within arm's reach. Storm and Heath stood outside the fence, watching their children, wearing wide smiles.

Alice waved at the men before making her escape out of the Bunny Pit and toward the relative safety of the food tent. Inside, the spicy scents of Alex Murray's cooking made her mouth water. She bought a bowl of pasta primavera, then found a quiet spot to sit and eat.

For being the first gathering of this magnitude, Thompson's Easter Festival was a hit. Families from all over the area had come for food, games, a petting zoo, and a chance to let their kids run around and burn off energy. She'd heard Heath would make an appearance as the Easter Bunny soon, something she greatly anticipated. Her assigned task was managing the colored egg hunt, which wouldn't start for another hour.

All the veterans currently staying at the retreat had

been tapped to help, which lifted everyone's spirits. Who wouldn't be positively affected by seeing the happy faces of children? Keeping freedom secure in order to enjoy times like the festival was the reason most went into the military.

Alice savored her first bite of pasta and moaned out a sigh of bliss. The taste of ripe tomato, basil, zucchini, and parmesan cheese danced on her tongue. The next bites were just as delicious. Out of the corner of her eye, she saw Micah enter the tent.

He walked over to join her. "I've looked all over for you." He slouched in the chair. "I need a break."

She glanced at him and smiled. He looked hot and tired—his hair disheveled and sexy. "You're not used to playing football with people who only reach your waist. Kids are a lot of work."

"They're crazy…like a pack of wild animals—and they never get tired. I've probably thrown two hundred passes in the last hour alone." He rotated his neck, producing several cracks.

"Poor guy." She rested her fork in the bowl and rubbed his right shoulder. "Did the local reporter at least get pictures for the paper? Maybe the national media will pick up the story? I can see the headline now—*Former MVP Quarterback Micah Palmer Turned Coach of Pee-Wee Football Team.*"

"You're not funny." He grinned. "I hope my attendance brought in more people, even though I'm not as big of a celebrity as I was a year ago."

"We're in Texas, where people worship the game of football. Storm and Colleen are very grateful for the extra attention you're bringing." In truth, she knew the word of Micah Palmer's presence had spread around town, and many people had come to the festival to meet him. He was still hot stuff, whether he thought so or not. Once the season started, he'd have no trouble regaining top-tier status.

"I'm glad I stayed." Micah lounged in his chair and rested his hands behind his head. "I've had a really good time. I can't believe we're both leaving tomorrow."

A depressing thought. Her stomach sank. "Back to the real world." For her, leaving meant heading back into the unknown. When she'd agreed to come to the retreat, she'd made a deal with herself that she'd start making decisions about her future. Well, time was almost up, and she still had no better idea now than when she'd first arrived. Colleen had done her best to help Alice focus on goal setting, with journaling and long talks. The IED had not only injured her body but also some of her hunger for life.

Heath approached, walking slowly while holding the hand of little John, who hopped along with a carrot hanging out of his mouth. "Alice," Heath called out. "You have a visitor."

He must have mixed her up with someone who knew more than a handful of people here. "Who?" She squinted, looking around.

"She says she's your cousin. I found her over by the retreat's main building." Heath swooped up his son before he hopped too far away. "She's waiting there."

Kate? Apprehension and worry snaked in her gut. Her being here made no sense. Not when Alice was leaving tomorrow. "Thanks, Heath. I'll go find her." She walked at a quick pace in search of Kate, feeling the earth shift as her two worlds collided.

****

Micah stayed behind with Heath, watching Alice take off like the law was on her heels. "She didn't look happy about her cousin's visit."

Heath adjusted his hold on John. "Probably just took her by surprise."

"What do you know about her family?" Micah walked to the trash can and tossed away the empty bowl she'd left behind. "Alice doesn't talk about them."

"And you think I'd betray her confidence?" Heath scowled.

"I want to understand what makes her tick." Had anyone figured out that riddle yet? Probably not.

"When we served together, Alice never talked about her family. Her cousin flew out to Walter Reed to visit after she'd been injured." Heath dodged his son's chubby fists, which grasped at clumps of his beard. "She was the only family to come."

"What kind of parent would ignore their critically injured child, even if they'd had a falling out?" He imagined Alice recovering at the military hospital, alone, without the care and support of loved ones. Anger burned. Had the lack of familial care formed the hard shell she'd encased herself in now?

"Sorry, I can't be of more help, man." He shrugged. "Parts of Alice have always been a mystery. Maybe she'll trust you enough to share, if you ask her nicely."

He'd already discovered the win-more-bees-with-honey tactic didn't work. Alice responded to strength and honesty equal to what she possessed. "I've already asked. She shot me down fast."

Heath handed over the squirming toddler to Grace

when she approached. "Maybe her cousin can provide some insight."

"Thanks." Micah glanced in the direction of the main house and didn't see Alice. Where had she run off to?

"Good luck. I better go put on my Easter Bunny costume. The eager masses await." He pointed to the crowd of kids gathered nearby and smirked.

Micah almost searched for Alice, but better sense prevailed. She'd want privacy with her cousin. The colored egg hunt would start soon so she wouldn't be gone long. He'd wait for her return, hopefully with her cousin in tow, and be gifted a glimpse into Alice's life.

What would the glimpse show? Inside his head, he knew he shouldn't care so much about a woman he'd only known for two weeks. His heart was still with Cassidy, right? Or had his affection slyly shifted allegiance? He had so many unanswered questions, and time was running out.

****

Alice saw Kate standing alone under a mesquite tree. The sparkle in her cousin's blue eyes told Alice she was doing well. Longing and emotion hit her like a blow to the chest at the sight of the only family member she remained close to. "What are you doing here?"

"I've been trying to reach you, but you haven't called me back." Kate wrapped her in a quick hug.

A few missed calls didn't warrant a long car ride. Something must be wrong. "I'm sorry. I've been so busy and thought we could catch up once I got home tomorrow."

Kate pointed to the crowds in the distance. "What's going on? Looks like I picked a good day to come."

Her cousin's voice sounded with forced cheer, which worried her more. "Why are you here?"

Kate chewed on her lower lip. "Maddy ran."

A combination of relief and worry filled her stomach. "Is she safe?"

"Yes." Kate rested a hand on Alice's arm and squeezed. "Don't worry. I picked her up a few days ago from the safe house."

Alice narrowed her eyes and stared down at her cousin. Kate might be five years older, but Alice beat her in height by six inches. "What are you not telling me?"

"Okay, well, first of all…Maddy is here." Kate blew out a breath. "She's so excited to meet you, and I figured you were geographically closer now than after you flew home. If you got to know her, you'd be convinced to take her in."

Alice felt the earth tip under her feet, and her vision swam. "You're kidding me, right? Please tell me you did not spring a half-sister on me?"

"That's not all." She returned to biting her lower lip.

Taking a deep breath, Alice closed her eyes. No need to panic. She trusted Kate. At least she'd trusted her before today. "What else?"

"Your half-brother, Joshua, is here, too." Kate took a step backward.

With quivering knees, Alice lowered herself onto the grass and rested her head in her hands. The memory of a toddler with blond curls came to mind. The last time she'd seen Joshua, he'd been two years old. "Why bring them here?"

Kate sat beside her, cross-legged. "Maddy and

Joshua are your family. I know you'd rather pretend they don't exist, but I'm sorry, they do. They need you, Alice. Think about their welfare before you turn your back."

Guilt piled on to her already-anxious heart. "I didn't agree to take Maddy, let alone Joshua. My own life is a mess. I can't be responsible for two people who will need special care and attention."

"Who better than you to help them heal?" Kate gently held her hand. "Just meet them then I'll take them back to my house. But they can't stay with me for very long."

Alice glanced up at whomever yelled her name.

Micah halted about twenty feet away. "The egg hunt is starting soon. Do you want me to do anything to help?"

She shook her head. "I'll be right there."

Across the distance, he sent her a smile.

"I'm in charge of the egg hunt. Take Maddy and Joshua over to the festival and let them have some fun." She reached into her pocket and pulled out a twenty. "For food. As soon as I'm finished, I'll find you."

Kate accepted the cash. "I'm sorry to rock your world, Alice, but I can't manage the sect runaways alone anymore. I need to focus on my marriage and my husband."

Remembering everything Kate had done to save her from hell, she choked back tears. "You know how much I love you. If you say you need me, then I'll help." Deep down, she hoped what she could offer was enough. She'd never consider herself mother material for a couple of teenagers, even if they were related. But she had a funny feeling a substitute mother was exactly what Kate, Maddy, and Joshua expected of her. If that was the case, they'd leave very disappointed.

****

Micah watched as Alice and Easter Bunny Heath gathered all the kids together for the egg hunt. He wondered who the kids were more in awe of, the guy in the rabbit suit or a smiling Alice. The tough girl had a soft side, and he loved seeing it in action.

With the release of a mass of little ones, the air filled with their laughter. About fifty children ran in zig-zag patterns in search of hidden eggs.

He let his gaze drift from the children to Alice, who strolled hand-in-hand with a little girl as they searched for eggs. A tall woman standing off to the side stole his attention. At second glance, he saw she wasn't a woman but a teenage girl, who looked very much like Alice.

Was that Alice's cousin? He should go over and introduce himself. While he made small talk, he could learn more about Alice's family history, taking advantage of the fact she was currently distracted.

As he approached, he was surprised by the striking resemblance. Not only did they share a leggy height, they had the same brown hair and hazel eyes, and even their stance was similar. "Hi, there. You must be Alice Liddell's cousin."

At the sound of his voice, the girl jumped, and her gaze darted to the ground. "I'm her sister," she mumbled.

A sister? An interesting development. "It's a pleasure to meet you. I'm Micah, Alice's friend. What's your name?"

The girl raised her head, but her gaze scanned the

ground. "Maddy."

"I'm sure Alice is happy you came for a visit." Honestly, he wasn't so sure about Alice's excitement at unexpected guests, but he'd keep her potential anxiety to himself.

"We surprised her." Her voice cracked as she spoke.

He opened his mouth but was cut-off by the arrival of a teenage boy.

"What are you doing with my sister?" He stood at Maddy's side, arms crossed over his tall, lanky body, wearing a scowl.

First a cousin, then a sister *and* a brother. Alice's family was popping out of the ground like ants. Micah relaxed his posture and folded his hands behind his back to appear as unthreatening as possible. "I'm a friend of Alice's," Micah said. "I didn't know she had a brother and sister."

The teenage boy loosened his fists and let his hands fall to his sides. "She has lots of siblings. Our cousin, Kate, brought us out to introduce us. We're hoping Alice will let us live with her."

Stunned, Micah could have been knocked to the ground with a brush of a feather. The mystery of Alice's family grew deeper. Another visitor approached, and her broad smile made her appear friendlier. With bright blue eyes and auburn hair, she didn't look like either teenager. He recognized something familiar in her eyes—a flash of pride very similar to Alice.

"Hi." She extended a hand to Micah. "I'm Kate Simon. Alice is my cousin."

"Micah Palmer." He shook her small hand. "Nice

to meet you all. Alice should be finished with the egg hunt shortly."

"Our arrival was a bit of a surprise," Kate said with a laugh. "Alice was never one for surprises."

"You came on a great day, with the Easter festival going on." Now was Micah's chance to learn about Alice's family and her past. He better not waste the short window of opportunity. "Do you all live in the area?"

Kate glanced over at Alice, who was still occupied with the egg hunt. "Has she told you anything about her family?"

"A little." He stretched the truth. Guilt pricked his conscience, an uncomfortable awareness he tried to brush off.

"Our family has a complicated history. Alice has had no contact with her parents in a very long time. Maddy and Joshua have decided to follow in Alice's footsteps and leave the fold, so to speak."

Micah noticed Maddy's hands shaking. Then Joshua wrapped an arm around her shoulder. "Is there anything I can do to help?"

Kate shook her head. "Thanks. Their situation is something Alice and I have to deal with." She smiled at Micah before turning her attention to her young wards. "Come on, let's get something to eat while we wait."

"Nice to meet you, Mr. Palmer." Joshua nodded before resting a hand on his sister's back and leading her away.

Maddy's gaze stayed focused on her shoes as they walked.

While he contemplated Joshua's intense over-protectiveness toward Maddy, Micah returned to studying Alice. She must have felt his gaze, because she looked over.

A flock of children surrounded her, all showing off their finds. Inside their hands, they held colorful eggs and treats.

He considered all the obstacles she'd overcome, and his pride in her grew. Tomorrow, he'd say goodbye. Dread ached in the back of his throat. How would he get on a plane bound for home, knowing she'd no longer be a part of his life?

Chapter Twelve

As Alice watched her cousin, brother, and sister approach, she felt her insides seize into a gnarled mess. She still couldn't believe Kate drove eight hours to introduce her to Maddy and Joshua—all in hopes Alice would be overtaken with sibling love and agree to take them in.

She studied the tall girl next to Kate, and a small portion of her apprehension dissolved. Looking at her little sister was like gazing into a mirror, back to when she'd first escaped the sect. Not only was Maddy's appearance identical to Alice's, she perceived the same heart-wrenching, scared aura—similar to a hunted fox having just escaped the hounds.

"Alice, meet Maddy and Joshua." Kate squeezed her hand and smiled.

Joshua's hovering beside his younger sister reassured Alice that Maddy would be well cared for, regardless of who ended up housing them. She led them to a picnic table, away from the crowd.

"It's important you get to know each other and know you're not alone." Kate held Maddy's hand. "You three share more than a father. You share the same hopes and dreams for a better life." She glanced at Alice. "I wanted Joshua and Maddy to see how successful you've become."

Alice didn't consider herself successful, not after

her injury and departure from the Army. Though before, she'd taken the world by storm. If she'd fought for what she wanted before, why couldn't she again? "I can't believe you drove from New Mexico for a day trip."

"We'll do some sightseeing on the way home." Kate folded her hands and rested them on the picnic table. "Remember how you felt when you first got out, Alice? The world was scary, as well as exciting. The sect taught us to regard life on the outside as evil." She pressed her lips together. "Really, the sect was the devil's playground."

Recalling left her gut churning. She'd spent the last sixteen years trying to forget. Now, memories served as footsteps stirring silt on the bottom of a lake.

"Father told us over and over that if we stepped foot outside the compound, people would kidnap and kill us." Joshua furrowed his brow. "But I heard the stories about you and Kate, so I knew he wasn't being truthful."

"Our father is a liar." The word father tasted bitter on Alice's tongue.

"I know." Joshua peered at his sister sitting beside him. "See, Maddy met with Leader Joseph. He said she'd marry Harlow Wilcox in three months."

At the mention of Harlow's name, Alice cringed. Back when she was still part of the sect, Mr. Wilcox had a reputation for beating his wives. Surely, he hadn't mellowed over time. More likely, he'd grown crankier and more aggressive in his old age.

Kate's mouth drooped. "Joshua made arrangements for Maddy to run. At the last minute, he decided to go with her."

He straightened his back. "I couldn't send her out into the world alone. I had to protect her."

Her younger brother's loyalty amazed her. None of her older brothers ever showed concern for any of the girls in the family. They saw women as objects, just like they'd been taught. Obviously, Joshua missed that lesson, which gave her a glimmer of hope that redemption could be found among her family. "I'm glad Maddy has someone like you to watch over her." Alice turned to her cousin. "Today is the last full day of the retreat. They asked for my help cleaning the grounds, and then we have some planned activities tonight. How long are you here?"

"We're heading back to Santa Fe today. Probably stop about half-way and stay in a motel for the night. I know you're busy, and we didn't want to disrupt your retreat. I thought since you were staying within driving distance, I'd bring Maddy and Joshua to meet you."

Alice needed clarity about Kate's intentions. Did she really still think Alice was in any position to take on two teenagers? Ones who'd need a lot of help acclimating to the outside world. "Kate, can I have a word with you in private?"

"Sure. Be right back, you two." Kate patted Maddy's hand before rising from the picnic table bench.

She guided Kate to a sunny spot on the lawn. Under the warm sunlight, Kate's hair glowed like backlit amber. "They seem like really great kids." Alice waited to speak until they were out of earshot. "I won't become their substitute mother. My own life is up in the air, and I can't take on responsibility for anyone else—especially not runaways from the sect."

"I only wanted a chance for y'all to connect. They were very excited to come today." Kate smiled.

In an attempt to dull the throbbing pain, Alice rubbed her eyes. "You are an angel, Kate, but I know you didn't travel so far for a simple introduction."

"Just think about taking them." Kate's blue eyes widened. "Remember how scared you were at first on the outside? They look up to you with almost god-like reverence. And I think your influence would be very good for Maddy. Underneath the frightened girl is the same strength I see in you."

"You're lucky I love you." Choking back tears, Alice hugged her petite cousin. "I promise to consider the possibility, but don't get your hopes up. Someone with a stable home can offer them more."

"No one is as good as you." After a quick squeeze, Kate took a step back. She tilted her head to look up at Alice. "Is it all right if we stay and enjoy the festival for a while longer before we go?"

"Of course." Alice walked with Kate to a waiting Joshua and Maddy. She took a seat by Maddy and studied the girl, wishing she could explain that the world outside offered unlimited potential—something she should remember herself. "Maddy, you're very lucky to have family who loves and cares for you. I'll work to arrange to see you again soon. Know you have nothing to fear. No one can hurt you."

For the first time, Maddy raised her gaze to meet Alice's, and her eyes glistened with tears. "How do you know for sure?"

She gently placed the palm of her hand on Maddy's warm cheek. "Because if they try, they'll have to deal with me." No matter what, she'd stay a part of the kids'

lives, meaning she just might end up taking them in.
****

Micah must have posed for a picture with almost everyone here, except the one person who mattered most. Still hidden from view, she was likely still at the retreat's main building, talking in private with her family.

A tap on the shoulder sent a jolt to his heart. He turned to see Heath's head sticking out of a white and purple bunny suit.

"Colleen asked if you'd take a picture with the Easter Bunny, which unfortunately is me." Heath rolled his eyes. "If I haven't been humiliated enough."

"A photo with me should boost your bunny ego." He laughed. "You've done the rabbit community proud today. What did they bribe you with to get you into that costume?"

He wiggled his eyebrows. "My wife did all the bribing, and I won't go into the details within earshot of young children." Heath's gaze followed Micah's to Alice, who now stood about fifty yards away. "Do you care about her?"

Across the distance, he watched Alice, and his body flickered with an electrically charged attraction. He would not allow their relationship to be ruined by romantic entanglements. "Alice's friendship means a lot." Micah worked to keep his true feelings out of his voice, speaking each word in a flat tone. "I hope, after tomorrow, we'll find a way to stay in touch."

"Is that all you want…to stay in touch?" Scowling, Heath set his bunny head on the grass.

He shook his head. "These past two weeks have been great, but our time's up. Alice will focus on her future, and I'll support her in whatever she decides." She'd done so much to help him return to the core of why he played football. The debt he owed her would be hard to repay, especially living a thousand miles apart.

"Working with you has been the best thing for her recovery." He set a furry hand on Micah's shoulder. "You've given her a sense of purpose again. I'm afraid when she gets back home, she'll be alone and fall back into depression."

He pressed a hand over his heart to compress the ache. "I won't let that happen."

"She loved serving in the military and now a promising career was taken away. She was…still is…devastated." Heath let out a long breath. "Anyway, I don't want to see her get hurt. Just understand she has an entire team of government-trained killers who'd do anything to protect her. And I mean anything."

The corners of Heath's mouth twitched in a grin, but Micah detected a serious undertone in his voice. He swallowed hard. "I'd never hurt her. It's good you watch out for her, but she can take care of herself."

"Yes, but we're a team. We watch out for each other." Heath picked up the bunny head and pointed to the photographer. "Come on. Let's take a picture so I can change out of this ridiculous costume."

As they stood side by side to take the picture, Micah swiped a floppy bunny ear off his face. He glanced at Alice, who approached at a slow, relaxed pace surrounded by her family.

Over the past few days, he'd devised a plan to keep Alice in his life. He was convinced she'd benefit from the arrangement as much as he. Only one question hung in the air like a hovering sword before its lethal descent.

Would she agree?

****

The next morning, Alice awoke with a startle to a crack of thunder. She rubbed her eyes to remove the memory of her nightmare. She'd dreamt she was a teenager, running across a desert field in the dark, cloudless night. The sliver of the moon gave little light. The trek was long and scary. In the distance, she heard the bark of her father's dogs. He was away on a trip, and she hoped no one would get out of bed to find out why the dogs were all worked up.

Dressed in little more than a cotton nightgown and old tennis shoes, she walked for miles. The cold wind turned her skin to ice before finally going numb. Pebbles collected inside her shoes, and every so often, she'd stop and shake them out.

If she was caught by anyone from the sect, then her punishment would be severe. No threat, though, would stop her from fleeing. Alice would rather die in the desert than be married against her will.

Now sitting in bed, Alice wrapped a blanket around her shoulders to protect her skin against the sudden chill. After thirteen plus years, she could recount every minute of her journey from the sect compound to the safe house. The fear in Maddy's eyes transported her back to a time when she'd woken every morning terrified her father would find her.

She showered under a stream of hot water, which didn't dispel her unease. A chill nestled inside her core. After dressing, she dashed through the rain to the main house. Breakfast should be waiting, and although she didn't have an appetite for food, she got a flutter of excitement at seeing Micah. Maybe some verbal jousting with her favorite quarterback over bacon and eggs would help clear her mind.

This morning was their last breakfast together. Later, Micah would leave for the airport. She'd pack and head out a short time later. When they said goodbye, she had no illusions she'd ever see Micah again. The thought soured her mood into a perfect reflection of the gloomy weather outside.

She found Micah standing with a plate outstretched in his hands, sweet talking the cook into a few more strips of bacon. "I need the extra protein." He grinned. "My trainer works me like a bull at a stud farm…Oh hi, Alice."

Laughing, she elbowed him in the ribs. "Very funny. I'm sure you'd prefer that type of exercise."

After accepting an offering of three strips of bacon from the amused cook, he shifted his gaze. "From what I hear, those boys don't actually see a lot of lady action, if you catch my drift."

"Please don't explain any further." Alice helped herself to pancakes, fresh fruit, and coffee then followed Micah to a table by the window.

They ate in silence. The only noise was the patter of rain against the glass. Ribbons of lightning flashed across the sky. Thunder rumbled over the fields, rolling in giant waves of deep vibrations and rattling the windows in their panes. How had her time here already come to an end? Two weeks didn't seem long enough. "You all packed?" she asked between sips of coffee.

He glanced out the window. "I wanted to get in one more run before we leave, but from the looks of the weather, I'd say we're out of luck."

Alice shrugged. "I don't mind running in the rain."

"The rain isn't what worries me." A clap of thunder punctuated Micah's sentence.

Nature appeared to be providing dramatic effect. "Good point." She wouldn't mind a solid run before sitting on a plane for a few hours but preferred not becoming a moving target for lightning.

Micah stabbed a strawberry with his fork then swirled it in the leftover syrup from his pancakes. "Will you finally tell me about your family reunion yesterday?"

"Nice try, but no. You met them, which is more than most." She wasn't embarrassed by her cousin, brother, and sister. Part of her wished she could brag about how strong and capable Maddy and Joshua seemed, and how Kate had rescued them. A few words of praise would lead to questions—ones with painful answers too private to share.

"They all seem really nice. I don't understand…"

Alice stole a strip of bacon off his plate and waved it at him. "Drop it, Micah. I don't talk about my family. I've told you that more than once."

"Fine. I'll drop the subject." He pulled his plate out of her reach. "I've had a great two weeks. I'm sad to see it come to an end."

Sad didn't even begin to cover her emotions over leaving. She carried in her chest a heavy weight of misery and disappointment. "I hope you find the transition back to professional football a little easier after working together."

From across the table, he watched her.

His dark eyes filled with something she couldn't read—worry, relief, concern?

Folding his hands and resting them on the wooden

tabletop, he leaned in. "Alice, what are your plans for after you return home?"

Good question. "I don't know." She raised her now-lukewarm mug of coffee and sipped. "I have a few opportunities, but nothing I'm excited about."

He leaned in closer across the table. "What would you say about the opportunity to work with a professional athlete, full-time, until the season starts?"

"Depends on who and where." Interesting prospect. A shimmer of anticipation danced across her skin. "I don't have any illusions about being a real trainer. I've only worked with you for less than two weeks and am in no physical condition to inspire anyone."

"The potential client told me he'd be lucky to work with you...a former combat soldier and all-around great lady." With waggling eyebrows, he reclined back in his chair. "If you accept the job, you'd need to relocate for a few months."

A change of scenery for a little while longer might do her some good. At the retreat, she'd been forced outside her comfort zone—a good reminder of how much she liked pushing boundaries, even if they were only her own. "Where is the athlete located?"

A grin pulled at the corner of his mouth. "He has a really nice house in Timber Lake, Wisconsin, with a guest house for your use. You'd be very well compensated."

The perpetual jokester. He obviously wasn't serious. Even so, she felt her pulse quicken. "I'm not moving in with you to be your personal babysitter."

"You wouldn't be my babysitter." He grinned. "You're the best trainer I've ever worked with."

She snorted in disbelief. Why did he feel the need

to tease right before they'd say goodbye?

"I'm serious." He reached across the table and took hold of both her hands. "When I return to Timber Lake, I'm reentering the world of professional football. Too many people want to pull me back into my old lifestyle. I need you in Timber Lake, by my side."

Maybe he was serious, but the idea still lacked merit. "You don't need me. I have no idea what a pro athlete needs in conditioning and exercise." Plus, he had a team of professionals at his disposal.

Micah squeezed her hands. "I'm not asking for you to be solely responsible for my training. You're separate from my football life, and that's why having you close is a good thing."

"You must have hit your head." Alice shook hers and glanced at their connected hands, causing a pulse of electricity to dart up her arm and into her heart like a bullet. "I'm a former soldier. I know how to accurately shoot and assemble a gun, parachute out of a plane, and survive in the wilderness. I'm not an athletic trainer. Micah, you can't be serious." The firm set of his lips and his tight jaw told her he was.

"Don't dismiss the idea. In the guest house, you'd have your own kitchen and living space. I only ask you to stay until training camp starts at the end of July. I'd pay you salary plus whatever you owe on the place you're renting in South Carolina."

Wow, he'd gone for the hard sell. Excitement boosted her endorphins, making her body buzz. Maybe her presence wasn't as much for the physical training but building his mental strength. Over the past two weeks, she'd witnessed a growth in him having nothing to do with the accuracy of his throw. He'd shed some of that million-dollar ego and replaced it with humble good humor. Likely, the calm environment of the retreat caused the internal change, but Alice couldn't help but think she might of have had an effect as well. Ready to consider his proposal, she blew out a breath. "Okay, tell me more."

"The guest house is new." His voice cracked, and he laughed. "It's across the backyard from my house. I have an in-ground pool and sauna. You can use one of my cars anytime you want."

"Are you selling a job or a relaxing vacation?" Honestly, what she'd appreciate was a little of both.

"We'd definitely make time for fun, but my goal is for you to keep me on track." He tapped a finger on the table. "The team trainers only have so much time to devote to me when I'm at the gym. You'd be around twenty-four/seven. My own personal Mickey Goldmill."

"Great." Alice rolled her eyes. "Now you think you're Rocky." She itched to accept his offer. Still, uncertainty kept her from saying yes. Was her hesitation really due to her deep and growing attraction to the football star?

"Look…I need to go up to my room to pack. My car is arriving soon to take me to the airport. I'll leave you alone to think about my offer." He stood. "I meant what I said, Alice, I need you in Timber Lake. When I come back downstairs, I hope you tell me you'll see me in two weeks." Micah disappeared up the stairs.

Was he really confident she'd accept his crazy proposal? If she followed him to Timber Lake, she'd have to remove all inappropriate thoughts of the quarterback with the sexy smile. Meaning she was once again relegated to buddy status. Why didn't men look at her as a desirable woman? Sure, she was not all sugar and spice, but some guys had to find a strong personality attractive.

Being Micah's personal trainer for a few months wouldn't lead to romantic problems. But when the time came to part ways, she might be left with a bruised heart. For a few months at least, she'd be spared the agony of sitting around her apartment, contemplating the meaning of the rest of her life.

So really—what did she have to lose?

Chapter Thirteen

For the thirtieth time in the past hour, Micah looked at the clock on the microwave. He still had sixty minutes before he left to pick up Alice from the Timber Lake airport. Restless nerves overran his normal cool confidence, which had nothing to do with the short drive to the airport and everything with seeing Alice again.

Two weeks ago, he'd said goodbye with every hope she wouldn't back out of their agreement. The steady stream of her shipping boxes arriving at his house served as proof she hadn't. He'd taken each one to his guest house for her to unpack once she arrived. He'd paid a crew to clean the little house until it shined. Her favorite foods were stocked in the kitchen. A few of his friends teased if he was preparing for a visit from royalty. For as much as impressing Alice meant to him, she might as well be the queen.

He opened the fridge to search for a snack when his phone rang. Cassidy's name flashed on the caller ID. Anxiety filled his chest, making breathing difficult. "Hi!"

"Hey, Micah. How have you been?"

Her voice sounded high-pitched and sweet. "I'm good…back in Timber Lake. I returned last week to focus on football full-time."

"Oh." She paused. "I planned on going to your

house in Tampa for a visit next weekend."

Internally, he sighed. Why now, after pushing him away for so long, was she reaching out? "I'm sorry I never told you. I've been busy with the move."

"Don't be sorry." She let out a breath. "You don't report to me anymore."

Of course he didn't. She was another man's girlfriend. Cassidy only cared if he'd stayed clean. If she'd been around for the past month, she'd seen regressing held no danger. "You could always come to Timber Lake, bring Ray, and stay for a few days. I'd be glad to see you again."

"Ray's out in LA for meetings with his agent, and I'm in New York working on next season's collection. Then I'm traveling to Miami for a few days. I thought if you were in Tampa, I would arrange a layover and see you."

As his heart squeezed with remorse, he hunched over the kitchen counter. If he hadn't put his addiction before her, she'd still be his.

His thoughts switched to Alice and her impending arrival, and the pain in his chest eased. Calm drifted over him like a cloud without threat of rain—the ones dotting a blue sky on a warm summer day. As a boy, he watched them transform into countless forms—just like Alice. As soon as he figured her out, she'd do something new, catching him off guard.

He returned his attention to the woman on the other end of the phone. "You're welcome here anytime, so don't be a stranger. I'll always value our friendship."

"What we had will never totally be over." A muffled noise sounded in the background. "I have to go, Micah. Talk to you again soon. Just remember to stay away from the pills. Okay?"

Did she think he couldn't show control—once an addict, always an addict? After everything he put her through, he couldn't blame her for doubting his sincerity. How many times had he denied abusing his pain management program? How many nights had she worried while he was out partying?

Too many.

After the call disconnected, he pressed the phone against his chest. No way to make up for the damage he'd done. He held out his phone and opened the photos, then scrolled down until he found one of them together. The photo was taken in New York when they'd attended the Sportsman of the Year award ceremony. When he'd won, he walked off stage like he was invincible. How far the mighty fall.

Micah zoomed in on the picture until only Cassidy's face filled the screen. She was beautiful, with full make-up and a hairstyle that had taken a stylist two hours to pull together. They'd almost been late because she called in a seamstress for last-minute alterations.

He imagined Alice on his arm instead. She likely wouldn't have needed the fuss and still looked gorgeous. Alice's beauty was one hundred percent natural. He could attest, since he'd seen her many times with no makeup and hair in a messy ponytail. If she'd ever agree to go as his date to an event, he knew he'd serve as her arm candy.

Lost in deep ruminations, he lost track of time. After checking his watch, he jumped with a shot of adrenaline. He should have left for the airport five minutes ago. *Shoot, please don't arrive early.* He grabbed his wallet and keys off the counter, then almost forgot to lock the door behind him on the way out to the garage.

The excitement over seeing Alice again scrambled his brain. Now, if he could arrive at the airport on time without getting into an accident, he might finally calm down.

****

Alice strode through an active and noisy airport terminal and found the escalator to take her down to the ground level. While she waited for her luggage to appear on the conveyor belt, she thought back to the first encounter with Micah Palmer. She hadn't been overly impressed with the star quarterback. Now, four weeks later, she'd arrived in Timber Lake to become his personal babysitter. He called her a trainer, but she knew the truth. Micah needed a firm hand to oversee his progress. Training camp was two months away, and he couldn't afford to regress into bad habits.

Her stay couldn't have come at a better time. Only four days ago, she'd been contacted by a General with the Special Operations Command. They'd spoken at length about a contract position offered at Fort Bragg. If she accepted, she'd help build training programs for women who volunteered for a combat role now that the ban was lifted.

After Alice ended the call with General Stetler, she was left with a head spinning with possibilities. Instead of obsessing about the decision while alone in her apartment, she'd keep busy working with Micah. During her two-month stay, she could gather details about the position and fully consider the opportunity.

Was working as an Army advisor the answer to her questions regarding her future? Could she handle working with soldiers while no longer being one herself?

Yawning, she located her suitcase and grabbed hold of the handle. Luckily, she'd shipped most of her things ahead of time, so she had only one small suitcase to retrieve. Looking around the terminal, she didn't see Micah and panicked. He'd planned to meet her at the baggage claim area, then take her home. Maybe he'd mixed up the day or time?

Alice pulled out her phone to retrieve his address from her Contacts. Guess she'd hire a cab. Micah must be too busy to remember her arrival.

At the sound of loud voices growing closer, she glanced up to see Micah, slowly working his way through a crowd. People surrounded him with cell phone cameras while others held out items for autographs. He sent her an apologetic-looking smile and slowly progressed toward her.

Eventually, the crowd dispersed, leaving her alone with the handsome man she hadn't gotten off her mind. Unfortunately, her attraction hadn't lessened. If anything, he made her body spark even hotter. Why did he have to be both gorgeous and nice?

"Sorry, I'm late." He reached down to take her suitcase.

"It's okay. My plane only arrived twenty minutes ago." Even though she was perfectly capable of managing her own luggage, she let him perform the small act of chivalry.

"You're lookin' good, Alice. I like the tan." He winked.

Heat pulsed up her neck and face. "I spent more time outdoors these last two weeks instead of locking myself away in my apartment. You'd be proud of me. I've been walking on the beach in shorts."

His gaze moved down to her jeans-covered legs.

She shivered and bumped him with her elbow. "Don't start. Wisconsin in May is colder than South Carolina and Texas. From what the pilot said, the temps are only in the fifties here."

"Plenty of time to get you back into shorts." Laughing, he motioned her forward. "Come on…let's go before I get mobbed again." Micah led her out of the small airport and to his truck. He opened the door, then tossed her suitcase on the rear bench.

"Your ride is an upgrade from Storm's truck." She ran a hand over the seat's smooth leather. "I like the new car smell instead of the fumes of burning motor oil."

"This sweet ride was part of a spokesman deal with a local car dealership. I added the aftermarket stereo system and running boards." He turned the key in the ignition. A deep rumble of the engine mixed with loud bass from the speakers.

While Micah drove, she visually soaked in her surroundings. The landscape passing by appeared fresh and green, ready to take on the summer heat to come. City buildings and homes gave way to a more rural setting. Large oak trees mixed with pine to create large, dense swaths of forest on the side of the road. After a twenty-minute drive, he pulled up to a wide gate.

As she passed through the gate and down the driveway, she took in the view of a two-story contemporary home with an abundance of windows overlooking the spacious yard. The house was beautiful but surprisingly unpretentious. Besides the security gate, she would never have guessed the residence belonged to a famous and wealthy athlete.

Micah parked in the driveway, shut off the engine, and turned to face her. "This is home for about seven months of the year. The guest house is around back. It's totally private. I built a small gym next to the pool area. Nothing fancy. Kind of like the one at the retreat."

He kept rambling, but she didn't want to interrupt. Obviously, his home held a lot of importance. If she had a pad this nice, it would mean a lot to her, too.

"So, anyway. I'll take you over to your new digs and get you settled." He opened the door and exited the truck. "Then I'll give you the grand tour."

His laughter held a hint of edginess, which made her wonder if he still wanted her here. Her stomach churned. What if he'd changed his mind but was too polite to tell her? Coming to stay with him might have been a mistake.

"Can you tell I'm really excited for you to be here?" Carrying her suitcase in one hand, he guided her with his other hand lightly resting on her low back along the stone pathway that wove behind his house. "You must be laughing at me on the inside." He glanced at her and grinned. "I'm just eager to hit the ground running. You know? Thanks for agreeing to come."

His constant stream of chatter finally cracked her reserve. As her laughter rolled, she held her stomach. "Did you have a truck load of sugar today?"

"No, why?" He opened the door to a little bungalow.

Silly guy. The house was dark until Micah flipped a switch. The cottage-style living room was simply lovely. Oversized and overstuffed furniture filled the small space. Pictures of colorful flower gardens hung on the white walls. If she had a knack for interior design, she'd decorate her apartment in the same style.

The front room opened to a sunny kitchen. She entered the room and spun, admiring the clean, fresh look of the cream tile floor, the brushed nickel, and the glass light fixture hanging over the bar-height counter.

Micah guided her to each of the two bedrooms, both with an attached bath. "I had the house stocked, but if you need anything else, let me know."

What more could she need? She grinned. "The house is perfect."

"Really?" The expression on his face relaxed.

"I wish I could show you the barracks I lived in while deployed. I'm able to sleep almost anywhere, but this little cottage is really great. Thanks, Micah." She reached over to give him a hug. The second his body stiffened against her, she realized her mistake. Horrified, she pulled back, her heart racing. The last thing she wanted was for him to think she was flirting. Even if her own body pulsed with electric currents at their brief contact, she'd never admit her attraction. The way his familiar smell made her brain tingle with a release of endorphins didn't matter. Micah would never see her as anything other than a friend.

"So, how about I give you some time to get unpacked and settled in?" He cleared his throat and stepped toward the door. "Come on over when you're finished. I'll leave the back patio door unlocked."

She watched as he strode across the lawn and disappeared behind a row of evergreen trees blocking the view of his house. Had she made her desire obvious with one simple hug?

After the retreat, once she been alone again in her apartment, she realized how strong her feelings had grown. During all her years of serving alongside men in the Army, she'd kept her heart securely closed off. She'd made a commitment to never trust her heart and soul to a man, no matter how wonderful he seemed. So, why had one pushed her so off balance that she second-guessed her own convictions?

Now, she was living in his guest house on his property. As they worked together to get him ready for the upcoming football season, she'd see him every day. While he focused on football, she'd work to keep things cool and casual between them. *Good luck.* The second she saw him at the airport, she'd known clearing him from her heart would be easier said than done.

****

Micah sat in the kitchen, watching out the glass patio doors for Alice. Why had his body reacted so strongly to an innocent hug? When they'd said goodbye at the retreat, he felt a spark, but something changed during their time apart. When their bodies touched a few minutes ago, he'd been hit in the heart by a lightning bolt.

But his heart was damaged and unavailable, behaving like a broken record that played the same name over and over again—Cassidy.

Additionally, Alice Liddell was too good for him. She was a combat veteran while he played a game for a living. She'd been willing to sacrifice her life in service to their country, and he hadn't even wanted to spend two weeks volunteering at a veterans' retreat. Yes, he had fame and a lot of money, but material things didn't make him worthy.

No matter how high he rose in the pro football ranks, deep down he remained the boy with both parents in jail, living with his grandma, and looking up to his best friend's dad for a role model. He'd come from nothing, and throwing a football was the only thing he'd ever been good at. A skill, which lucky for him, provided a very good living. But everything he'd worked so hard to achieve had almost been stripped away. Last year served as a wakeup call.

He'd faced a little adversity and turned to drugs in order to cope. The same vice that had put his parents in jail. He'd been no better than any other addict—only he had enough money to pay for the best treatment facilities.

Out of the corner of his vision, he saw Alice stepping onto the patio at the back of his house. He felt his heart skip, and for a moment, the incessant Cassidy tune halted. Alice's beauty drowned out all other sounds.

She slid open the door and stepped inside. "Hey. Hope I'm not interrupting."

Only several inappropriate thoughts. "No." He turned his gaze in search of something to distract his mind. "Let me show you around the house. My door is always open, whether I'm here or not. I'll get you a key."

"How do you know I won't go rummaging through your underwear drawer?" Her cheeks flushed pink. "I'm totally kidding, by the way."

"Whatever floats your boat." He winked and imagined his face was almost, if not more, red. "Let me show you around."

He spent the next hour showing her the house and grounds while sharing stories about the design and construction process. When he stepped into the gym, he noticed her eyes light up. "Like I said…the gym isn't much. Let me know if you think we need a piece of equipment. I'll get it delivered."

"Must be nice to be loaded." She brushed her fingers over the control panel of a high-end treadmill. "Anything you want, you go out and buy."

"Not anything." He pictured Cassidy walking out the door, then focused on Alice. Real love couldn't be bought.

"I'm sorry." Her smile faded. "I didn't mean to sound snotty. You've put together a nice space. What you have already should work."

He glanced at the clock on the wall. How was the time almost six already? "Since it's dinner time, I'll order delivery. What would you like to eat?"

"You have enough food in that tiny cottage kitchen to feed an army." She continued inspecting the weight machine set against the back wall. "I'll cook tonight."

"You sure?" His stomach growled for a home-cooked meal.

"I miss cooking for other people. Making dinner for one isn't much fun." Her gaze dropped to the floor. "How about you bring the wine?"

He understood the challenges of living alone. Having Alice stay with him would help ease the pain. He would enjoy her company for the next two months, even though he'd likely battle his growing fascination until the time came they said goodbye.

Chapter Fourteen

"When will I meet your grandma?" Alice watched Micah perform the last of his dead-weight pull-ups. Beads of sweat dripped down his bare back, and muscles rippled with his effort, causing her heart to beat an abnormally high rate. She wiped away the growing moisture from her brow.

"So, you want to talk about my family, but I can't ask about yours?" Micah grunted, then dropped down to the ground. "That's not fair."

Every day for the past week, Micah tried to ferret out information about her family. Yes, asking about his was only fair. "I'd like to meet the woman who raised you. What's wrong with that?"

"Nothing. She's a fantastic woman, who prefers not to travel to Wisconsin unless I can guarantee eighty-degree weather." He picked up a hand-towel from off the bench and wiped his face.

Outside, cold rain pounded the windows. May felt a lot like October. Alice didn't mind the temperatures, which made for pleasant running weather. Plus, she knew warming temps meant summer and the start of training camp, when she'd leave and head home.

"Tell me about the family who lived next door?" She wouldn't let the issue drop. "Will I at least get to meet your mysterious best friend?" His brown eyes sparkled.

"Like I said before, you spill something of your childhood, even a little, and I'll tell you more about mine. But until then, my lips are sealed." He ran a finger over his tightly pressed lips.

Fine. She'd submit to his demands—just a little. "My best friend growing up was named Margaret. She lived two houses down." Alice removed the rubber band from her ponytail and shook out her hair. "We used to play war against the boys. I was the general, and she was the soldier."

After finishing a drink from his water bottle, he laughed. "Why doesn't that arrangement surprise me? Did you and Margaret go to school together?"

"We were both homeschooled." She faced away so he couldn't see the flush on her skin. "That's all you're getting out of me today, buddy. Back to work."

"You're worse than the team trainers." He blew out a long breath. "At least they let me take breaks."

"You'll get a break when you've finished another rep of pushups." Alice turned back to the sight of Micah toweling off his upper body. *How am I becoming more attracted to him instead of less?* She'd scolded herself again that he was a friend, nothing more, but obviously her heart hadn't received the message.

After lying on the mat, he smoothly ran through a set of twenty pushups.

She placed a weighted bag across his shoulder blades. Impressively, he didn't lose form or speed.

After several grunts, he finished his task, removed the bag, and rolled onto his back, gazing up at her with a grin. "What's next?"

So far, her time in Timber Lake had been fun—a week full of early morning runs and late-night movies.

Alice was in charge of dinner, and Micah made omelets for breakfast. During his days at the Warrior's training facility, she busied herself with research on the new position she'd been offered.

She kept enough contacts with her CST sisters, both active and veteran, to gain an impression of what the Army expected of the female soldier training program. With the Army lifting the ban on women serving on the front lines, they created a striking need to ensure the female soldiers had equal training and opportunities as the men.

The six weeks of training she'd received as a CST had not been enough. The limited time had not adequately prepared her for the battlefield. Most of her training had been on-the-job, which was insufficient with lives on the line.

While she waited for Micah to finish jumping rope, she walked over to the wall and grabbed the pull-up bar. In another life, she could pound out pull-ups without breaking a sweat. Now, she struggled through each lift. But she wouldn't give up until she completed ten. Every muscle in her shoulders and arms burned so deeply, she feared she'd self-combust. Before the last pull-up, she paused and pictured the piece of paper tucked away in her diary—a note she'd scribbled to herself the night she ran away from the sect, which read—*Never Quit!*

After as far as she'd come, she refused to surrender.

****

Micah couldn't stop looking at the woman who sat beside him in the truck. Tonight, she looked like a super model. Her face glowed with natural beauty. She

171

pushed up the sleeves of her gray sweater, showing off the lean muscle in her forearms. As the intersection light turned green, he returned his gaze to the road. If he got into a car accident due to distracted driving, his public image wouldn't improve.

"Are you sure the Harrisons invited me?" Alice brushed her fingers through her hair. "Did you even tell them I'm coming?"

Tonight, she'd worn her hair down, and thick, brunette locks framed her face. "Yes, now stop worrying. Julie is the nicest person you'll ever meet, and Reagan is pleasant when he's not on the football field." Since the last two minutes had been non-stop commercials, he turned down the radio volume. "The only reason they invited us is because Julie found out you were staying with me." Micah glanced over at Alice, understanding exactly why Julie Ellis Harrison would want to meet her.

Julie's late husband had been Army Special Forces and was KIA while deployed to Afghanistan. While Alice hadn't served with her late-husband, she had served with Heath and understood the heartache of losing loved ones to war. Over the last six years, Julie remarried and rebuilt her life, but she held a special spot in her heart for her late husband along with anyone who'd served in the military.

Alice glanced at Micah in the driver's seat. "Was Reagan the one who finally convinced you to go to rehab?"

The memory of his life as an addict was like walking through a foggy swamp. An unpleasant journey, and he hated admitting failure. Though during rehab, he'd come to terms with his past, which was part of recovery. He learned opening up about uncomfortable subjects was a strike against his wall of guilt. Eventually, the divide would tumble down. "A number of my teammates tried to intervene. Reagan just didn't take no for an answer."

She glanced over and patted his arm. "And you finally reached a point where you were ready to listen?"

"At my lowest, I couldn't get out of bed without taking pills. I could only function when high. Because of my injury, I couldn't practice with the team, so I stood on the sidelines for every game and watched my backup play." At the time, Micah doubted whether he'd ever dominate the playing field like he had before the injury. That nagging doubt, along with the absent hit of adrenaline, made every game torture. He'd watched his team struggle without him. Men who he'd respected became frustrated with the team's lack of success. The high of the pain pills along with their mind-dulling effect helped him cope with the struggles. Unfortunately, those little pills also made his life worse—going from bad to debilitating.

"The Warriors are lucky to have you as their starting quarterback." Alice leaned over to change the radio to another station. "What's up with all these commercials?"

The scent of her perfume flooded his nose. What brand did she wear? She smelled so good, more spicy instead of floral. Maybe she wore a pheromone-based perfume that drove men crazy. Or more likely, everything about the woman stoked his desire.

He cleared his throat. "The starting position is not guaranteed. They're using my backup as leverage. Either I show up better than ever or watch once again from the sidelines."

"I saw Kantra play last season." Frowning, Alice shook her head. "You shouldn't worry."

"Thanks." Her vote of confidence meant a lot. "I can't wait for you to meet Reagan Harrison. You'll get an idea of what kinds of beasts line up against me across the line of scrimmage."

"Those huge beasts are why I'm helping you become quicker on your feet...so you can outrun the big meanies." Alice laughed. "Tomorrow, I'll get a paintball gun and use you as target practice. Fear of being shot should get you moving."

"I'm not serving as a human bulls-eye." Micah drove down a long, tree-lined driveway leading to the Harrison's house. Built on a five-acre site along Timber Lake, their home had been transformed from a bachelor pad to a family home. Reagan had been the gold standard for a single, professional athlete, until a widow and little boy stole his heart.

Walking alongside Alice to the front door, Micah tortured himself with the thought he'd likely be married to Cassidy by now, if he hadn't messed up. At times, he wanted to ask Alice's advice on how to win back his ex but never felt comfortable bringing up the subject. Not the right time, not the right place—not when his attraction to Alice grew every day.

Julie Harrison answered the door wearing a large smile. "Micah, I'm so happy to see you. You look healthy and strong." She squeezed his bicep. "You must have an excellent trainer." She turned her attention to Alice. "You're exactly how I'd pictured you...beautiful and fierce. You must be an amazing soldier to have fought alongside men like Heath and my late husband."

"I never had a chance to meet John, but he's a legend in the Special Forces community." Alice accepted Julie's hug. "I was privileged to serve next to some of the country's greatest soldiers."

Two little girls ran into the entryway, chasing one another and yelling back and forth. They skidded to a halt and stared wide-eyed at Alice.

"Hope and Avery, this is Alice Liddell. She's helping Micah get ready to play football with Daddy." Julie took hold of both girls' hands, placing one on either side.

"It's very nice to meet you." Alice smiled.

Reagan and Julie's girls were a couple of cuties. The older girl was a red-headed smaller version of Julie. The younger, Avery, wore her blonde hair in two braids and sported a dusting of freckles on her nose.

Micah helped Alice out of her coat, then hung both theirs in the hall closet. He'd spent enough time at the Harrison house to feel like family instead of a guest.

"Daddy said Micah didn't get rid of the ball fast enough, and he got clobbered by a big, fat lineman." Hope stepped away from her mother and stared at Alice. "And that's why he got hurt. Micah can't spend all day in the pocket 'cause guys like my dad will make him pay." The little redhead slapped her hands together.

The truth of her words didn't dull the sting over being called out by a child. He ruffled her curly hair. "I learned my lesson the hard way."

Alice chuckled. "Are you a big football fan?"

"Yes." Hope nodded her head. "I love to tackle my big brother, Aiden."

"Come on," Julie said to Alice and Micah. "Let's go out back. Reagan's warming up the grill."

Micah followed the women outside, and his heart tugged with surprising devotion. Alice deserved a completely wonderful future. Instead of worrying about his own career, he should focus on helping her figure out what challenge she'd tackle next. He knew her possibilities were limitless. She needed the confidence to go after a new goal, and he'd work day and night to help her succeed. Even if her success took her away when he still needed her so very much.

****

After dinner, Alice sat on the deck and watched bats swoop low over the lake as they indulged in their nightly buggy snack. The sun dipped until the orange ball disappeared underneath the water's surface. The evening air turned chilly, but a roaring fire made sitting outdoors pleasant.

The adults sat around the fire pit while the four Harrison children played flashlight tag on the lawn. The youngest, two-year-old RJ, stayed close to his older brother, Aiden. The game appeared to be boys against the girls.

"You want to go join?" Reagan looked at Micah, then pointed toward the kids.

If fun could be registered by decibels, their glee was off the charts.

Micah set down his bottle of soda on the small, tile-topped table next to his chair. "I'm game, but only if I'm on the girl's team. Looks like your daughters inherited your wife's speed."

All six-feet-four-inches of Reagan's muscular form rose and towered over Micah. Alice had to admit, the line-backer was a hunk—one who was happily married.

"I'll show you who's got the fast feet around here,"

Reagan said. "Come on. Let me see if you still have any fancy moves left."

When the two grown men joined the kids, the volume of shouts increased.

Alice scooted closer to the warmth of the fire. She held out her hands, heating her palms. "You have a lovely family. What's being married to an NFL player like?"

"Oh...it's crazy, fun, scary, and I love every minute." Julie gazed toward the backyard and her husband. "Reagan is so passionate about what he does both on and off the field. But I'll admit watching him play takes minutes off my life. I worry about him constantly."

"Micah's had a tough year. One wrong hit and done for the season." Alice looked over to see Micah being chased by two giggling girls, and her heart hitched. "He's done a great job of recovery."

"Thanks to you." Julie reached over and rested a hand on Alice's arm. "Before he left for the veterans' retreat, Micah was a mess. Not only had his addiction drained him physically, his emotional health was rocky. He fought the lure of a quick high all while nursing a broken heart."

At the thought of his struggles, her chest ached. "Now he's as good as new, if not better. Cassidy will want him back." She hoped the bitterness she felt saying Cassidy's name didn't sound in her voice.

Julie snorted a laugh. "Cassidy isn't good enough for him."

"Micah still loves her." She gritted her teeth. If she was truly his friend, she'd want to see him happy. If Cassidy made him happy, then she'd grin and deal with her own gloom from seeing him with another woman.

"The truth about people always shines through." Julie's smile faded. "Can I ask you a question, totally off the subject?"

"Anything."

"What was Afghanistan like? John talked about his experiences sometimes when he was home, but he didn't like to dwell on them for long. I always imagined what it was like for him…going out on dangerous missions and living in less-than-ideal conditions, away from his family. How did you deal with the difficult times?"

For her, the good moments heavily outweighed the bad. "Serving as a CST was the best experience of my life. I was finally fulfilling my purpose. Some of the men saw the CST women as taking away spots from guys they thought were needed more. When I was attached to Heath's ODA, he'd often go to bat for us and got me placed on missions." Her time on the combat support team had been like stepping from a black-and-white world into brilliant color. As a female soldier, many of the jobs that appealed to her were unavailable. She'd been marginalized because of her gender, but the CST program changed that. She'd seen more combat than some of her male counterparts. Now the experience was behind her, Alice couldn't imagine anything else would ever compare.

"John mentioned sometimes his ODA would bring along a female soldier because they needed someone who could communicate with the village women." Julie lifted her glass of white wine and took a sip. "He said the women would jump at the chance to head out on a mission. With all the intel they gathered, they had saved many lives."

"The formal program grew from a real need out in the field." The evening air was growing cooler, and Alice rubbed her hands in front of the fire. "I'll forever be grateful for the opportunity."

Julie's gaze drifted off into the distance. "John died doing what he loved, but the knowledge doesn't make me miss him any less. Don't get me wrong, I love Reagan and the life I've built with him. He was the man who pulled me back into the light. If not for his love, I don't know how I would have survived."

"I know John would be thankful for Reagan." Julie was a lucky woman to have been loved by two good men, proving to Alice healthy relationships were possible. Would one ever be possible for her? "Many of the men I served with would speak about how much they worried about their wives and kids if they were KIA. Everyone understood the risks, not only to their own lives but also the lives of their loved ones."

Julie wiped a glistening tear from the corner of her eye and sighed. "You are a wonderful woman, Alice. I hope Micah realizes how lucky he is to have you."

She was the lucky one—getting paid to babysit and work beside a professional athlete, who'd grown to be a very good friend. "He's where he needs to be physically to start training camp. I'm sure he'd be fine without me."

Over on the lawn, cheers and giggles sounded.

"Oh…he needs you for more than keeping his training program on track." Julie smiled. "And I'm growing more and more certain he's realizing that, too."

She glanced over to see the four kids pile on Reagan, and Micah doubled over with laughter. He looked her way, and his tender expression stopped her heart. Each day, she felt her heart slip further into loving him, despite the warning inside her head. Did he really need her or was Alice simply a short-term substitute for the woman he couldn't have?

Chapter Fifteen

Later that week, Micah exited the tunnel and stepped onto the grassy field at Warrior Stadium. Unlike game day, he strolled without the pressure to perform until he reached the fifty-yard line. Surrounding him were tens of thousands of unfilled seats. The chirping of birds echoed through the empty stadium. Four months had passed since he'd been here last. The final game he'd sat and watched from the sidelines.

As he imagined running onto the field for their first preseason game in less than three months, a nervous energy pulsed inside him. Would he hold the same command as before his injury? He'd been the team's leader and let down everyone. The Warriors had gone from Conference Champions to missing the playoffs. "What if I don't have what it takes to come back?" he whispered into the empty stadium.

"Son," a gruff voice sounded. "You've got a talent I've seen only a few times come through that tunnel."

Micah turned to the sight of a member of the grounds crew walking toward him, a man well past the normal age of retirement. "Mr. Turf, good to see you." He shook the older man's hand.

Mr. Turf was the nickname he'd been given by a few players back in the '70s, when he'd been promoted to Chief Groundskeeper, and the nickname stuck. "Nice to see you too, Micah. Been awful quiet around here these past few months. Can't wait until the start of the season."

"You and me both." He nodded.

"I hear you've been workin' hard." Mr. Turf waggled his gray eyebrows. "Got yourself a lady trainer staying at your house."

Micah laughed at the term "lady trainer" and wondered who else knew about Alice. Her training wasn't a secret, but he liked the idea of keeping her to himself. "Alice is great. She's not a typical professional trainer, which is what I need. She thinks outside the box and refuses to take no for an answer. I don't doubt her skills. I do doubt my own."

Mr. Turf exhaled a long breath. "You've had one tough year, kid. I'll give you that. I've seen many men who possessed great talent fail because they didn't have the mental toughness to succeed in the game. People make mistakes. They pull themselves back and move on." He lifted his gaze to meet Micah's. "You, son, need to have faith in yourself again, and have faith your team will stand behind you when you lead them onto the field. Have faith in your arm and its ability to work magic."

The kind words touched his heart. Not everyone had given up on him. He glanced down at his right arm and flexed his hand. "And what if I've lost the magic?"

"Then you embrace the other parts of your life. You are not defined by how well you play football, no matter what those pinheads in the media say." Mr. Turf chuckled. "A man can take pride in what's in his head and heart, as well." He pointed to Micah's chest. "That's what makes you special, son. No one honest will love you more because of your throwing arm or how many decimals in your contract."

"Thanks for the words of wisdom, Mr. T." Micah took one last look around the looming stadium. "When my career is all said and done, I want the records to say I gave my all on the field and enjoyed every minute."

"There may be hope for your generation yet." A deep laugh sounded from the old man. "Go home to your lady trainer and keep working hard. But don't forget to have a little fun…if you know what I mean."

With a wink, Mr. T left him standing alone. He had an appointment with Warrior's upper management, and then he could head home to his lady trainer for some fun. He was excited to discover what new torture Alice had invented for the day, despite the worry nipping at the back of his brain that his abilities wouldn't rise to her challenge.

****

"I call this course *Shock and Awe*." Alice glanced at Micah, who was not smiling. He crossed his arms securely over his chest and lifted his chin with obvious indignation. The man appeared ready to run.

Early that morning, when he'd been at the Warrior's offices for meetings, she recruited a local fitness club to help outfit his backyard. Before them lay an obstacle course of biblical proportions—tire runs, barrier wall, net climb, rope climb, and a log ladder made an impressive sight. The course itself didn't seem extremely intimidating. The extra challenge Alice planned earned Micah's protest.

"I am not letting you shoot at me while I'm maneuvering through a death trap. Do you want to kill me?" Micah huffed.

He acted like a stubborn child. "Stop being so overdramatic. I'll use a paintball rifle and be far enough away that you won't hurt too much if I'm accurate. But if you run fast, I won't hit you. I'm out of practice shooting at a moving target."

He snorted. "I saw how well you did at the firing range yesterday."

"I'm great with a stationary target. If you keep moving, you'll be fine." She looked over his clothing. She'd asked him to wear long pants and a long-sleeved shirt, just in case she got a hit. Since she was the shooter, she'd dressed in a camo tank top and cargo shorts—more appropriate for the sudden heat wave. The Wisconsin weather in May kept her guessing—chilly one day and hot the next.

"You'll be over there, right? On that rise by the trees?" Micah pointed to a spot about fifty yards away.

"Yes, but I'll have a clear view. Run through the course once without me shooting then do it for real." She was enjoying watching him squirm way too much.

Micah completed the course with ease, which was exactly why he needed the extra pressure of serving as target practice.

Alice took a prone position on the hill and raised the red flag over her head, giving Micah the signal to begin. She lifted the paintball rifle and gazed through the scope. He was all confident smiles until she took her first shot then his pleasant expression quickly dissolved. Her shot went wide, hitting the barrier wall beside him.

He glanced over his shoulder at the red splotch before shimmying up the wall.

She took aim and again pressed the trigger, sending

another paintball off target. Micah picked up his pace, making hitting him more difficult. She waited until he began the tire run before setting her sights on the last tire. If her timing was on, she'd hit him when he stepped onto the grass.

Steady, aim, fire. He must have heard the pop of the paintball rifle, because he moved his upper body and the shot missed. Micah had the nerve to glance over and grin.

As upset as she was for failing to hit him, she was proud of his instincts—exactly what she'd wanted to develop from the workout. When he held the ball, a quarterback should be aware at all times. On the field, Micah relied on all his senses, as well as pure instinct, to avoid being sacked or throw an interception. Now, he used those same skills to avoid becoming Alice's personal paint canvas. If she could sell him on the art market, she'd call her creation *Man in Motion.*

After another run-through, they took a water break under the shade of one of the oak trees dotting Micah's yard.

"I've got a bet for you." He sprawled on the grass, flushed and sweaty.

Still smelling good. How did he do that? "Oh yeah? What a shocker." She took a long drink, and the cold water ran smoothly down her parched throat. "You can't go to the bathroom without making a bet." With a straight face, he ignored her teasing.

"Every time I make it to the finish line without getting hit, you tell me one fact about your family."

"No." She shook her head. She almost admired his persistence, if it wasn't aimed in her direction.

"Oh, come on." Micah rose to a sitting position and

lightly punched her arm. "Why not? I'm putting my life on the line for your sick pleasure. All I'm asking is for fair play."

"I'm not doing this exercise for my sick pleasure." She whacked him on the bicep as payback.

Looking away, he sighed. "Then I'm not doing this anymore."

"Oh yes, you are." She worked to keep the humor out of her voice.

"Agree to my terms." He raised one dark eyebrow.

Alice wanted to grab her paintball gun and shoot him point blank in the back of the head. "You are a pain in the…"

"Now, now, Alice. Deep down, I know you love me." Micah's gaze shifted back onto her face.

She turned away and focused on the grass beneath her. His teasing had hit the truth. Ever since the retreat, she'd been falling in love with him. She understood her feelings would never mean anything to him, and he would never know how deeply she cared. Too many obstacles stood between them. Not only her own fears about committed relationships, but Micah's heart was still with his ex-girlfriend. No way in heaven or hell would she ever agree to share a man's heart with another woman. Not after she'd seen the damage done to her own mother and the other women in the sect.

In an attempt to ignore her crushed chest, Alice stood. "Okay. You win. But I'll do my best to hit you, so be prepared."

He rose to his feet and scanned her body, from her lower legs to her face. "If I get through unscathed, you better be ready to share. And not some insignificant detail. I want information with a bit of meat."

"You just worry about working the obstacle course." She rolled her eyes. "I will hit you this time."

Before she raised the red flag, Alice waited for Micah to get into position. The man moved as quick as a superhero and not in a straight line. She couldn't keep him in her scope. After letting off five missed shots, she worried he'd win. How had she been sucked into agreeing to his bet? Desperate to keep her personal history private, she poured all her focus into reviving the shooting skills she'd learned in the Army.

Micah finished without a spot of paint on his clothes and wearing a huge smile, meaning she was in so much trouble.

****

Micah raised his hands and jumped around like a champion. After four more times through the course, he'd only been hit once, earning him three facts about Alice and her family. "You ready to talk?" He hobbled alongside her toward his house. Not only did every muscle hurt, he ached to the bone. A dip in the hot tub sounded like a wonderful idea.

She walked with long strides, her paintball rifle slung over her shoulder. "Good grief, you're relentless…and nosey. Did anyone ever mention you're annoying?"

"My grandma." He laughed at the memory of Grandma becoming so flustered by his never-ending questions, she'd banish him to his room. "I have a curious mind. What's wrong with that?"

"Nothing, if your curiosity is directed at someone else." She shrugged one shoulder to adjust the gun-strap.

"Sorry, but you are the most fascinating person

I've ever met, plus the most secretive…an attractive combination." He found many more things about her attractive, from her pretty eyes to her great legs but kept those thoughts to himself.

"Can we at least cool down before starting the great inquisition? Maybe hop in the pool?"

Right on. Alice in a bathing suit was his favorite sight. The temps hadn't been warm enough to use the pool, but he'd seen her slip into the hot tub a few times, and the image of her in a sexy, black bikini now burned into his mind.

By the time he changed and returned outside, she swam laps. He took a running start and cannon-balled into the water.

"You just splashed half the water out of the pool." Alice swam over to the side and hung onto the edge.

"I'm done with the stall tactics, Alice. Time to pay up." He glided across the pool then stopped behind her and treaded water.

"Okay." She groaned. "I'm originally from northern Arizona but haven't been back since I was sixteen."

Good start. "Did you move with your family?"

"You don't get to ask the questions." The muscles in her jaw twitched.

He edged a little closer but remained silent.

"I ran away," she whispered.

He didn't find the information surprising. Alice was strong and independent, personality traits that might have put her in conflict with controlling parents. "Where did you go?"

"I lived with my cousin, Kate, until I was eighteen, and then I enlisted in the Army. I haven't seen or talked to my parents since I left."

"Do you miss them?"

"No." She bit out the reply. "And no more questions. Fact two… Joshua and Maddy are only two of many siblings."

"They are very nice, by the way." He'd liked the two teens and Kate when he'd briefly met them at the retreat. He'd also noted Alice's fierce protectiveness of all three.

"Yes, they are good people." A flash of a grin crossed Alice's face. "Fact three, and this information is all you're getting…Joshua and Maddy have asked to move in with me."

"What was your answer?" Micah asked, surprised by the news. What had caused the teens to seek a life away from their parent's home?

"I told them I'd think about it. I'm not made for motherhood, and Maddy especially will need someone with a nurturing spirit."

He disagreed. Alice might be harsh at times but never unkind, and he detected a gentle soul under her hard shell. "You'd make a wonderful mother, someday. You were great with the Harrison children."

"I've never been responsible for anyone but myself." She floated on her back and lightly kicked the water. "I've never even had a pet fish to care for."

"What about on missions? Don't tell me you only watched out for your own safety?"

"Of course not." Raising her chin, she huffed. "I was pulling security when I was injured by the IED."

"So, you have been responsible for the lives of others. Caring for Joshua and Maddy would be a little different but down to the core, the same concept." His heart pounded so hard, he could hear it reverberating in his eardrums. Being near Alice left him with the desire to pull her in and claim her with a kiss. The feeling grew too overwhelming, and he released his hold on the edge of the pool wall and dove underwater.

He couldn't confuse the deep bond of friendship with falling in love. If Alice knew the thoughts going through his mind, she'd pack up her suitcase and leave. And as he moved closer to the beginning of training camp, he'd be devastated without her.

"I said I'd think about it when I get home," she said once he resurfaced. "After all my crazy training ideas, I bet you can't wait for the day I'm out of your hair."

Micah's gut clenched. "I like you in my hair. It's never looked better."

A ringing sounded from under Alice's towel. She pulled herself out of the pool and strode over to grab her phone.

He studied the multitude of scars covering the right side of her body. They didn't detract from how smoking hot she looked in a bikini. Her scars were part of what made her special. The pain lingering from her injuries was the one thing he wished he had the ability to take away.

Alice lifted the phone to her ear. "Hello." After a brief silence, she lowered slowly onto the deck chair, her body stiffened, and her face paled. "Where did it happen? Yes, email me the details. I'll be there," she said. "Thanks for letting me know. Stay safe. Bye." When the call ended, Alice set down her phone and looked past Micah.

Her eyes looked flat and expressionless. "What's

the matter?" He exited the pool and sat on the chair beside her. "Who was that?"

"A friend who's still in the service. She called from a base overseas to tell me one of our CST sisters was KIA yesterday. Gail was on a mission, and the team came under fire. She took five bullets." A sob escaped her mouth.

"I'm so sorry." Meaningless words were not enough, but he had no idea what else to say. Her pain ripped through him. After a minute of crying, Alice pulled back her emotions.

"Her body will be flown back to the States for burial." She leaned forward and cupped her head in her hands. "I'll need time off to go to the funeral."

"Take all the time you need." He had no problem with her leaving but didn't want her going alone. "I'll come with you."

Straightening, she shook her head. "You don't have to do that. Gail's won't be my first military funeral."

He firmly held her hand, which felt like ice. "You've done so much for me. Let me do something for you."

"You don't have to…"

"I want to."

She lifted her gaze, and a single tear fell, landing on his hand covering hers. Micah used his thumb to wipe off the dampness from her cheek. Seeing her hurting gave rise to a fierce protectiveness—a feeling stronger than anything he'd ever felt. Unfortunately, his physical strength couldn't fight off her grief. He'd need to dig deeper. "I know you're capable of taking on the world, but what I'm saying is, from now on, you don't have to do it alone."

Chapter Sixteen

Even though his better judgment told him to let it go to voicemail, Micah answered the call, "Hey, Carl. What's up?"

"Organized Team Activities start tomorrow, and you're not going…that's what's up." Carl's raspy voice barked. "I hate that I need to say this, but missing OTAs is a huge mistake."

"I talked to Coach, and he excused me for the first two days." Micah rubbed his face to remove his irritation.

"I've hustled to secure a deal with a performance athletic gear company, but before they agree to invest millions of dollars, they want reassurances. You heading out of town right at the beginning of the training season hurts your case."

"I wish you and the media wouldn't take every single thing I do and twist it to question my commitment to football." He'd read the online TV news reports. Yes, he'd messed up last year, and the press loved to point out his faults. Despite Micah making huge changes in his life, he remained guarded. Even the slightest slip-up would be distorted as an epic failure.

"Those sharks wouldn't have jobs without dirt to report." Carl huffed. "I strongly suggest you reconsider leaving town tomorrow. Be at the team's training facility first thing in the morning."

"I won't stay here while Alice attends the funeral of a close friend alone. I'm going with her." He added a hard edge to his voice.

"When did Alice become your number one priority?" After a pause, Carl cleared his throat. "Are you in love with this girl?"

"She's a good friend and has helped me prepare for the season. Time for me to return the favor. Understand that without her, I wouldn't be at the level I'm at right now." His hand trembled as he held the phone. "Carl, I'm ready to lead the team, but I will take this trip first."

"Okay, I'll trust you know what you're doing. Mini-camp starts next week, and so help me, you better be there."

Micah ended the call, then sank onto the couch. Gazing out the picture windows overlooking his backyard, he stole a glimpse of Alice doing burpees on the small patio by the guest house. Leaving with her to attend the funeral was the right thing to do. His head and his heart stood firm.

Yesterday, when he'd spoken with the head coach about missing OTAs, Micah had been reassured his absence wouldn't be seen as neglect. Although, Kantra might see his absence as an opportunity. Last session, the Warrior's backup quarterback got a taste of life as the team's starter, and the experience left the young gun hungry for more.

His phone rang again. This time, Cassidy's name flashed on the screen. Micah glanced up at the sound of Alice entering through the patio door. He didn't feel like answering questions from Cassidy about his sobriety. One tongue-lashing today was more than enough. Pressing the button, he sent her call to voicemail, instantly easing the tightness in his chest. He'd connect with her another day. Right now, he'd focus on the positive—like the woman standing before him. Because in too short of time, she'd be gone, taking the best parts of him, like his heart.

****

When Alice stepped into the Kent, Ohio, high school auditorium for Gail Neely's memorial service, she reached out for the only thing keeping her from falling apart—Micah. His reassuring squeeze of her hand helped ease her growing panic. Her body didn't feel like her own anymore. Instead, she moved like an apparition, and her only line to reality was Micah. He served as her medium, and without his touch, she'd crumble.

In the past, she'd attended several military funerals. They'd always held a strange aura of disconnect, like the flag-draped casket couldn't possibly hold the larger-than-life person she knew.

Gail's funeral was different. She and Alice had been CST partners while attached to their Special Forces Team. They'd spent seven months living side by side, fighting an institution asserting their male counterparts as superior. They'd gone out together and risked their lives in service to their country. After Alice's injury, Gail stayed in Afghanistan to finish her deployment, then volunteered to return one more time.

She considered Gail a true sister in every sense of the word. Now, she'd sit through her memorial service, reliving their time together. Tomorrow, she'd attend the funeral of a woman too young to die and watch her husband say his final goodbye.

"Come on. Let's find a seat." Micah tugged her

hand.

She followed, barely aware of the people around her. As light and detached as her body felt, she could be a ghost.

He led her to an empty chair and held her elbow as she sat. "Are you feeling all right? You look pale."

"Yes." She tucked the back of her dark blue dress underneath her legs, then smoothed out the front draped over her lap. "The funeral doesn't seem real."

He rested an arm on the back of her seat. "Focus on getting through the next few hours, then I'll take you back to the hotel to relax."

Gazing around the auditorium, she saw faces of people she'd known in her other life—men and women who she hadn't seen in over a year. They were gathered together to honor Gail, whose body would be buried tomorrow.

Her breathing became fast and hard. Lights floated in her vision. A school band played the National Anthem, and the gathered crowd stood. Micah placed an arm around her waist to keep her steady. What would she have done without him?

When the emotional service was finished, she asked to leave immediately. She didn't have the emotional strength to speak to anyone, let alone have an articulate conversation.

After a ten-minute drive through Kent to their hotel, Micah checked them in.

Alice went into her room, sat on the bed, and stared at the wall. Memories of time with Gail spun through her mind like a movie reel. She remembered the late nights and early mornings spent together prepping for the next mission. And all the items they shared while deployed, from romance books to Gail's lilac-scented body lotion.

A knock pulled her back to reality. Slowly, she rose and opened the door.

Micah stood in the hall, wearing shorts and a T-shirt. Stepping into her room, he held out a pizza box. "Thought you might be hungry. I ordered one with banana peppers and sausage…your favorite."

"Thanks." The dull quality of her own voice disheartened her further.

Setting down the pizza on the little hotel table, he turned to face her. "Talk to me. Don't keep all your feelings bottled up."

For as long as she could remember, she locked away her emotions. She didn't talk about feelings, not even to the people she was closest to. But with Micah, for some reason, she wanted to peel back a layer and allow him a glimpse of her soul. "Gail was such a special person. I can't believe she's gone. This world doesn't know what a hero it's lost." She shuffled toward the bed and sat on the edge.

"Listening to the speeches today, I was totally in awe of what she accomplished. Then, I'd look at you and realize all the brave things she did, you did, too."

The bed shifted underneath her as he lowered beside her. Instead of inching away, she stayed fixed.

"They tried to kill you, and you survived," he whispered. "And I'm so glad you did."

When she met his gaze, she stopped breathing. Micah's face was close, and his lips only inches away. If she leaned slightly, she could take the kiss she'd wanted since the evening of the Star Wars movie marathon. Would reality live up to her fantasy? Only one way to find out.

She moved in, and he met her halfway. Their kiss blasted her apart like an explosive buried in the sand. So much better than she imagined.

He buried his hand in her loose hair and pulled her closer.

Every cell tingled with pleasure as his lips moved against her. Alice switched off her brain and simply enjoyed the sensations. The rough skin of his palm dragged down her bare arm and traveled lower, before his fingers found the hem of her skirt.

"Alice," he rasped. "We shouldn't…I'm sorry."

He halted their kiss with all the finesse of an overwhelmed teenager and pulled away. Still dazed, she blinked. "What do you mean sorry? Are you sorry we kissed?"

"No." He eased back a little farther. "You're emotionally vulnerable right now, and I don't want to do anything to destroy our friendship."

Her earlier elation turned sour in her gut. "Just say it. I'm no Cassidy." Pain flashed in his eyes, proving she was on target.

"That's not it."

Moving quickly and without grace, she untangled herself from him and stood. "I can't believe you're still hung up on a woman who walked out on you when you needed her most. You men are all the same."

Micah stood and faced her, arms crossed. "What's that supposed to mean?"

"That most of the time you're thinking with one part of your body and it's not your brain."

He stepped forward and ground his teeth. "If that was the case, then you wouldn't be wearing clothes right now."

The image his words created sent her heartbeat into overdrive. She swallowed any additional comment.

"We have something special." Micah reached out with both hands and rubbed the gooseflesh on her arms. "I don't want to do anything to ruin it."

Of course, he didn't want a romantic relationship—she was such a good friend. But keeping her heart too secluded to fall in love was what she wanted, right? Alice didn't do serious relationships. Hadn't she committed to remaining single? So, why did his rejection sting as sharp as shrapnel piercing her skin?

"Thanks, then, for not letting things go too far. I know sometimes I can be hard to resist." She forced a smile to mask her pain. "We were told over and over again during CST training to be careful around the guys, because they might find it difficult controlling their base instincts while serving alongside a woman. It became a running joke among us girls."

"I can understand the struggle." He opened the pizza box. "Come on. Let's eat before this gets cold."

"Do you still love her?" For some reason, she had to know. What if she tossed aside her marriage ban and pursued him? Would she even stand a chance? He rubbed a fist over tired-looking eyes.

"I don't know. Maybe I'm in love with the idea of her. Our relationship ended without much closure, and I still feel guilty about what I did to destroy her trust."

"You need to stop feeling guilty about the past. It's over. Move on." She picked up a slice of pizza and took a bite, comforted by the fact he knew her well enough to order her favorite pizza.

"Just like you're moving on." He narrowed his

eyes.

"I'm getting there. And we weren't talking about me. I'd like to meet your ex. See what she's made of." As she watched, he visibly paled.

"Probably not a good idea."

"Why?" She took another bite of pizza.

Micah didn't answer. Instead, he sat at the table and cracked open a bottle of water, then began eating.

With a month left of training, she would have to forget their supernova explosion of a kiss. Sure, she could fight for a real relationship, but what was the point? Why open her heart when he'd made his feelings clear that he wasn't interested?

Her head said the risk was too great. She needed to focus on her own future—like pursuing a new career path, and whether or not to take in her half-siblings. Weren't those decisions enough, without adding a heaping pile of love trouble?

But then she thought of Gail and how short life could be. Did she really want to make decisions based on fear? Would she arrive at the end of her life and regret not taking the chance? Gail had once told her she'd never regret taking the risk of being a CST.

No reward worth anything came without taking risks.

Love was definitely a risk. Did she have enough strength to let go and fall?

****

Micah paced in his hotel room, replaying the scene in his head. He was a fool. No, really. How could he have had the most amazing kiss with Alice, only to pull away?

The hurt look on Alice's face when he'd ended

things from going further nearly crushed him. He pressed a hand on his chest, which held a heart twisted between an old love and new possibilities.

Was his relationship with Alice now in jeopardy because he couldn't fight his growing attraction?

He raked a hand roughly through his hair. She was his best friend—the one he wanted to spend time with, even over the guys. She understood him. Not just as a football player but every multidimensional piece that made him a man. Feeling ill, he lay face down on the bed. He'd turned off his brain function for a few minutes and now possibly ruined his relationship with Alice.

The ringing of his phone jerked him out of his daze. Of course, Cassidy was calling. She'd called ten times over the past two days, and he'd declined every one. She probably feared he was holed up at home, as high as the Empire State Building. "Hey," he answered.

"Micah, why haven't you answered my calls? I'm starting to get worried."

Her breathy voice filled his ear. "Don't be. I had to leave town for a few days. I'm fine."

"Where are you? OTAs are starting followed by mini-camp."

Micah pinched the bridge of his nose, wishing he could remember how deeply he'd loved her. "A friend is attending a funeral, and I went along for moral support. Coach gave me the okay."

She huffed out a breath. "What friend?"

Her question hung in the air like a long pass, before dropping onto the ground with a thud. "Alice. A former teammate was killed in action. I need to be with her." He braced himself for her reaction.

"The woman who's staying with you? What's going on between you two?"

"Alice is my trainer. She's helped me a lot. I owe her."

"I'm coming to Timber Lake to check up on you."

What would Ray say about his girlfriend visiting her ex? Likely, he wouldn't be happy. Her announcement filled him with panic instead of joy. "I'm fine. Really. You have a business to run. Don't worry about me."

"I'll check my schedule and let you know." She sniffled. "I miss you."

His chest constricted. Did he miss her, too, or was his guilt keeping him tied to her? Lately, Cassidy had taken less space in his heart and mind. "I need to go. We have an early morning tomorrow and another long day. I'll talk to you when I get back home."

"Take care, Micah."

The call disconnected, and he fell back onto the bed. What if all the calls and concern masked the fact Cassidy wanted to get back together? She'd moved on very quickly after their break-up, finding solace in the arms of another professional football player. Ray and Micah had been close, until Ray swooped in to scavenge on the wreckage of his failed relationship.

His thoughts turned to the woman staying in the hotel room next door. Alice was as different from Cassidy as a cactus was from an orchid. One was tough and hearty, able to survive the harshest environment and still appear regal. The other was delicate and beautiful. A thing requiring nurturing in order to bloom.

Lately, he preferred the prickly over the pretty. And a sharp tongue that expected the best out of him instead of a gentle one that treated him like a failure.

Maybe if he could see Cassidy again and spend some time in conversation, he'd either get a second chance or finally find closure. Either way, he knew he couldn't stay in this emotional purgatory forever. With his hot kiss with Alice still burning on his lips, Micah vowed to resolve his feelings for Cassidy. Because if he ever kissed Alice again, he'd come to her with a completely faithful heart.

Chapter Seventeen

The next morning, Alice stood in the church vestibule, wondering how Gail could really be gone. She'd been twenty-nine-years old and in the prime of her life. After her last deployment, she'd planned to enter the public sector and return to college for her Master's Degree in Linguistics. Why had she been taken from the world when she had so much to offer?

Micah, who'd been her rock, remained at her side while she greeted a multitude of Army personnel she'd worked with in the past. Even General Stetler, who'd contacted her about the opportunity to train female combat soldiers, was in attendance. She noticed Micah stiffen when General Stetler mentioned her job offer, emphasizing how much the program needed her expertise.

Micah knew she only planned on staying until July, and honestly at this point, he didn't need her training. Maybe her leaving sooner than expected was for the best.

"Alice?"

A quiet voice sounded from behind. She spun to see a petite woman dressed in a formal Army uniform. "Mckenna. You're a sight for sore eyes." As she embraced her dear friend, Alice blinked against stinging tears. Seeing Mckenna brought a flood of memories—most comforting and familiar.

"I was granted leave to attend the funeral. I can't believe our Gail is gone." Mckenna looked into the church. "She was one of us."

Most in attendance were seated, and the funeral service was about to start. She stepped toward the entrance of the sanctuary. "Do you have time to talk after the internment?"

"Yes, definitely." Mckenna flicked a glance at Micah and smiled, her eyes widened. "Micah Palmer?"

"The one and only." Wearing a large smile, he reached out to shake Mckenna's hand.

"Mckenna Preston." She returned his smile. "I met Alice the first day of CST selection. She left quite an impression on the rest of us girls."

"I believe it." Micah clasped Alice's hand and squeezed. "A pleasure meeting you. Alice, we should take our seats." He escorted her to an open spot in a church pew.

Taking a seat, she breathed in deeply, attempting to steady her emotions. The pianists played "Abide With Me" while the Honor Guard carried a flag-draped casket down the center aisle. The service began with readings from Scripture Gail selected prior to her deployment. Two senior commanders of the Joint Special Forces Command spoke on Gail's military service and bravery. Sniffling, she accepted a tissue from Micah and dabbed at the corners of her eyes.

During the service, Alice expected Gail to walk into the church and explain the whole thing was a huge misunderstanding. She was still alive—still the beautiful, vibrant woman Alice held dear in her memories.

The service ended, and Gail's parents and husband

were escorted out of the church.

When Alice stood, her legs wavered and her knees buckled.

Micah embraced her waist, keeping her from falling. As she exited the church to join the rest of the funeral procession, he held her steady.

The attendees gathered behind the horse-drawn hearse. Trumpets sounded, and Gail's casket was slid in through the back for the final leg of her journey.

She followed the carriage for the short walk to the cemetery. At the show of people lining the street, emotion overwhelmed her and tears flooded her eyes. Elderly veterans stood beside young children while they paid their respects to a local hero who'd died in service to their country.

A year ago, people might have come to see her flag-covered casket. Instead, she was alive, a survivor with a scarred body and soul. Why had war taken Gail and not her? Choking back a sob, she wrapped her arms around her waist. She could think of no good reason why she'd been gifted with her life—a gift Gail had been denied.

At the cemetery, the pastor spoke words meant to comfort, which did little to distil her grief. The pain in her chest sharpened, and she struggled to breathe. When the service was over, Alice walked away in silence with Micah at her side.

As he stepped onto the pavement, Micah pulled her into his arms. "I can't imagine how hard today has been for you."

She clung on to the lapels of his suit coat like he was the only thing real in the middle of a nightmare. With a sharp inhale, she took in his familiar, masculine scent and became wrapped in soothing comfort. "Thank you for being with me. I don't know what I would have done without you."

"I'm glad you can lean on me, if only for a few hours. Do you want some time to talk with your friend?" He wiped off a tear from her cheek with a thumb.

Looking behind her, Alice saw Mckenna standing several feet away. She took a steadying breath. "Yes, if you don't mind."

"Of course not. I have a few calls to make. I'll walk back to the church and wait in the car. Take all the time you need." He kissed her forehead, lingering before letting go.

The ache in her chest deepened while she watched him stride down the narrow wooden path back to the church and disappear from view before heading toward Mckenna.

"You've got a keeper." Mckenna pointed to the spot where Micah disappeared into the trees. "And a football player, too. Hot stuff. I heard a rumor you were training a pro athlete, but I didn't know you'd hooked up."

"He's only a friend." Another crack opened in her already wounded heart. "Come on…I noticed a bench over by the river. Let's sit a while and catch up."

With her right leg throbbing, Alice lowered to the bench and stared over the slow-moving water. Birds filled the air with movement and sound. The little cemetery used the best of nature to create a peaceful space for reflection.

"You look really good," Mckenna said. "Are you happy?"

Good question. What did happiness feel like? She thought of eating breakfast with Micah and smiled. "I'm finding out who I am now, after leaving the Army. I'm searching for my purpose."

"You're so gifted and strong, and I believe your future will be great. Just give yourself more time to heal."

"What about you?" She admired Mckenna's dark blue skirt and jacket, shiny black pumps, and the badges and service ribbons decorating her jacket. Not long ago, she'd dressed in a similar uniform. Whenever she donned the symbols of her rank, she always felt deep pride. "How many more years will you give to the Army?"

"Michael wants me out after this enlistment expires. He wants to start a family. We've waited for six years, and he's been supportive of my military career." Mckenna lost her smile. "I was preparing to attend Ranger School, but after a lot of thought, I've decided to separate from the military next year."

"You'd want to put yourself through Ranger School?" Alice's reaction was a mixture of awe and apprehension. Women were now allowed to chase the elusive Ranger tab, but training and selection were brutal processes for either gender.

She straightened her posture. "I wanted to try. When I told Michael, he threatened to file for divorce. He's watched me leave too many times, fearing I won't come home alive."

Anger gave way to reason. "Getting into Ranger School is a long shot. Then, you'd have to complete the phases and graduate. I understand he's worried about you and wants to start a family, but threatening divorce is not cool."

"Ever since I went out on my first mission as a CST, I've held a fire inside me to see what more I can accomplish. Dousing that level of drive is hard."

She swatted at a bug on her arm. A hot fire had lit on her first day of CST selection. If she hadn't been injured in the IED blast and forced to retire, would she be contemplating Ranger School?

"Will you ever settle down?" Mckenna asked. "Get married and start making cute little Palmer babies?"

She rolled her eyes, and heat bloomed in her cheeks. "I told you, Micah and I are friends. Once he starts training camp, I'm heading home. And you know how I feel about marriage."

"I'd hoped time would change your negative attitude about committed relationships." A small leaf blew in the breeze and landed on top of Mckenna's tightly wrapped blonde bun. She brushed it off before returning her attention to Alice. "Don't keep your heart closed off to love."

"My trust issues go too deep to ever change." Alice trusted Micah with everything but her heart. Though, he did have a special talent for chipping away her defenses. Would he ever get past her barriers to catch a glimpse of the person she kept hidden inside—a scared little girl, a misfit, a woman who'd become paralyzed from an uncertain future?

Someday, she'd find the courage to stop running and fight for what she wanted. Deep down, she knew Micah would never love her as much as she did him. Destiny had played cruelly with her heart. Perhaps, the time had come to pick up her sword and do battle, ensuring the future she desired. Whether her future included a certain pro-football quarterback or not still remained to be seen.

****

Back home, Micah pressed the button for the gate and waited for the metal uprights to slide open, before he drove his truck down the driveway and into the garage. "Alice, we're home." He tapped the shoulder of the woman sleeping next to him.

She groaned and rubbed her eyes. "Did I fall asleep?"

"About one minute after we left the airport parking lot." Leaving his suitcase, he pulled hers out of the back seat and waited for her to exit. He took his sunglasses off the brim of his baseball cap and placed them onto his nose, needing to protect his eyes from the low hanging sun. A warm breeze brushed against his skin, hinting at the promise of warmer weather to come.

"You don't have to walk me to the guesthouse, but of course you probably won't listen." She raised her arms overhead and stretched.

"Nope." He shook his head. "I'm as thick headed as they come."

After depositing Alice and her suitcase in the guesthouse, he lingered at the front door. "If you're not too tired, how about joining me by the pool? I'll have some Chinese food delivered and open a bottle of wine."

She yawned then smiled. "Wow, you know how to charm a lady…Chow Mien and Chianti."

"And good company." He winked. "Unless you're sick of me." *Hope not*. He'd never grow tired of her.

"Let me change, and I'll be right out." She shuffled down the hallway to her bedroom.

With a smile, he closed the front door and headed to his house.

Thirty minutes later, he raised a pair of chopsticks filled with noodles and placed the delicious goodness into his mouth. The sun had already set, and the landscaping lights reflecting on the pool water made the air sparkle. Micah couldn't explain the magical sensation floating in the evening air. Maybe, he was overtired from the funeral service and plane ride home. Something buzzed past his ear, causing him to jump in his seat.

"What was that all about?" Alice laughed while twirling her chopsticks in the bowl of saucy noodles set on the table.

"Must have been a fairy." He wiggled his eyebrows, enjoying her contented look.

"A fairy?" Her brows arched over wide eyes.

"Like in kiddie cartoons. They sprinkle pixie dust and then you can fly."

She gazed down at her meal. "I have no idea what you're talking about."

"Didn't you watch movies about fairies growing up?"

"We weren't allowed to watch movies or television." Alice shifted in her seat. "No books, other than the Bible, were allowed."

Wow. Shock stole his reply. She'd shared something personal without bets or bribery. *Keep cool and don't come off as overly curious.* An extremely difficult task given he wanted to ask her a hundred questions. "Is your family very religious?"

She snorted. "Yes, but the god they worshipped was very human." Taking another sip of wine, she relaxed her shoulders. "I already told you I ran away. I never mentioned why."

He scooted to the edge of his chair, hands clasped on his lap. "I understand a rough childhood. Every once in a while, a reporter digs up the fact my parents have been in and out of jail my entire life." He spotted the corners of her lips in a sad-looking smile.

"My father should be in jail." She paused. "If I share my story, Micah, you might think differently of me."

He doubted anything she'd say would diminish her value. "You can trust me." Brushing a hand over her arm, he swore to work every day to prove worthy of her confidence.

"I was born into a polygamist household in northern Arizona." She rubbed her hands down her face and let out a long exhale. "We were part of a small sect. Our homes were isolated to keep out law enforcement. Women were treated like property and girls married off at a young age. My cousin, Kate, ran away before her wedding at the age of sixteen. When I was told I'd be given in marriage to a man as his fourth wife, I snuck out a note to Kate, asking for her help to escape."

His stomach sickened. "I've heard about polygamist communities. You were a child and shouldn't be ashamed." No wonder she kept her past private and distrusted committed relationships. The pieces began coming together.

"The men in the community were very good at managing the law. All of the children had birth certificates and Social Security numbers so their parents could receive government benefits. The sect wanted no government interference in their lifestyle. I broke into my father's safe and stole my paperwork. Kate made arrangements for me to get picked up about ten miles outside the compound. I stayed at a safe house until she could collect me."

He swallowed hard against the urge to throw up his meal. Young Alice, on the run from her family—the people who should have protected her. "So instead of marrying, you left."

"I wouldn't be forced to live like my mother and older sisters. One night, when my father was away, I snuck out. I walked for miles, afraid if I was caught, I'd be dragged home and beaten. But they didn't find me." Her chin lifted, and her eyes shone with tears. "I lived with Kate until I turned eighteen, then joined the Army."

And he had thought his opinion of her couldn't get any higher. What an amazing woman. "Did you go to the police?"

"Kate has, but the cops won't do anything. For me, speaking with the police means dredging up memories from my past I'd rather forget."

Images of a very skittish teenage girl and her overprotective brother came to mind. "Maddy and Joshua ran away from the same type of situation?"

"Maddy had been promised to a very evil man. She needed to escape, and Joshua wouldn't let her leave alone. You already know they've asked to move in with me. I haven't decided yet what's best." She lifted her glass of wine and took a long drink.

"Who better to be their role model?" Micah pulled his chair closer.

"I'm afraid I'll let them down." She spun her glass between the palms of her hands.

"Yes, you'd be taking a chance. Allowing them to live with you could be a positive change...the purpose you've been searching for." And a purpose that held the potential to keep her close.

"I need to figure out my own life first."

"You can go on the adventure together. I'm not saying you should or shouldn't take your siblings, but I can see how deeply you struggle with your past. Maybe connecting with your siblings is one step in the healing process."

"My upbringing really messed me up." She pressed her lips together and paused. "I had no role models for healthy relationships. In my world, men were evil creatures who used women to clean their homes and breed, which is why I don't believe in marriage, at least for myself. I don't want either Maddy or Joshua to mirror my cynicism."

Micah lowered his gaze, his chest gripping with pain. "Not every man is like the men you grew up with, Alice. Don't write off the whole gender because of a few parasites."

"I know good men exist. I served alongside many, and you have become one of my closest friends." She rested a hand on his knee. "But to make a commitment for forever...I can't do it."

With the contact, warmth spread through him. "Can't or won't?"

She shivered. "Doesn't really matter."

"Maybe someday you will." He reached down to take her hand, but she pulled away. How could he ask for more when his heart still held feelings for another woman? He imagined as a child of a polygamist, complete fidelity was the only gift she'd accept.

"It's been a long day." She blew out a breath. "I'm turning in for the night." As she stood, she winced and rubbed her right leg. "Thanks for listening. Hopefully, you're not too weirded-out by my past."

Needing to convey his respect, he rose to face her. "I'm glad you confided in me. I'm here for you…anytime you need to talk." A sting of longing hit his heart. Alice was as close to perfect as a woman could get. The intense push and pull of attraction between them jumbled his normally very stable judgment. A loud section of his heart asked—what if?

Cassidy's ever-present ghost hovered along the edges of his consciousness. Very soon, he'd deal with the destruction triggered when their relationship ended and free his emotions. Only then could he move on.

Chapter Eighteen

Micah twisted the throttle and rocketed down the road. He flew like a black bird, only he kept two wheels on the ground. The new black motorcycle underneath him rumbled. He couldn't wait to show Alice his latest toy.

After pulling up to his security gate, he punched in the code and drove down the driveway. He revved the engine a few more times before turning it off. Where was Alice? She wasn't in the backyard, and he noticed no movement by the guest house. The car he'd left for her use was still parked. "Yo, Alice," he yelled at the empty space.

Only birds chirped in reply.

With his helmet in hand, he walked to the guest house and knocked on the door. Footsteps sounded before the door flew open.

"What?" She stood blocking the entrance, arms crossed.

"I was wondering where you were. I've got something to show you." He grinned so large his cheeks ached.

She dropped her gaze to the motorcycle helmet then frowned. "Seriously? Do you have a death wish?"

Leaning against the door frame, he turned on the charm. "I've always wanted one. Come out and play. We can take a drive out to the lake."

"I'm not your girlfriend, Micah. Go find someone else to ride behind you." She started to close the door.

Kicking out his foot, he stopped it from latching and swung the door open again. "What's the matter? I didn't see you this morning when I left for the training facility. Now you're crabby." She'd even skipped their usual breakfast together. Was she embarrassed about what she'd told him last night?

"I just don't feel good…okay." With a sigh, she stepped aside to allow him in. "Why would you take such a risk? Especially after you lost a season due to injury."

The room was dark and the blinds were closed. "I've devoted my life to football and when the game was taken away, I became lost. I don't want to be that person again. I want to enjoy life. Every part." He raised a hand to touch Alice's arm.

She jerked away. "I'm glad you want to expand your life, but I'm not in a good place mentally right now to go on a motorcycle ride. I'm still bummed from the funeral, I guess." Alice walked into the small kitchen and sat at the table in front of her laptop.

How could he brighten her spirits? "What have you been doing all day?" He lowered onto the chair across from her. "Do you want to go for a run later?"

"I've been researching Army civilian positions." Her gaze stayed fixed on her computer. "And I ran earlier."

Three strikes and you're out. Defeat weighed heavily on his shoulders. Maybe now wasn't the time to bring up that Cassidy was coming. Likely, she wouldn't take the news well. His ex-girlfriend called earlier, stating she'd arrive tomorrow afternoon for a visit.

Initially, he wanted to say no but then thought a face-to-face conversation was exactly what they needed.

After a minute of silence, Alice looked up. "Yes?"

Growing frustrated and concerned, he slid back the chair and pounded a fist on the table. "Why are you shutting me out? Last night, I thought…well, that you were finally comfortable confiding in me. Today, you're acting like you don't want me around. What's going on, Alice?"

She flinched. "You don't owe me anything, you know. You must have other people to hang out with."

"I'm hanging with some of my teammates in the weight room, but I'll see their ugly mugs almost every day for the next five months. I only get you for another five weeks." The memory of their hot kiss floated inside his head, warming his body and troubling his mind. "Is your mood about what happened in the hotel? Our kiss?"

"*Pfttt*, you think I'm still hung up on that? It wasn't that good." A small smile curved her lips.

"Ha, admit it." He leaned in, grinning. "Kissing me was that good."

"Okay." She shrugged. "You kiss respectably. I don't take rejection well."

"I didn't reject you." He needed a shovel to help dig him out of the sinkhole he created. "I don't want anything to ruin our…"

"Yeah, I know…our friendship." Alice rolled her eyes. "You value my friendship too much to damage it by a little hanky-panky."

Why was she being so difficult? "You're not fair. You can't be mad at me for prizing your friendship."

"I'm not mad, Micah. I've had a rough couple

days, and I'm over emotional. Go ride your motorcycle and don't worry about me." She waved her hand toward the door.

He worried about her more than himself. He'd rather see her face light up with a smile than throw a touchdown. "As unlikely as getting a country singer to stop writing songs about break-ups." Again, he fought the overwhelming urge to pull her into his arms and kiss her until neither could breathe. "Come on." He reached for her hand and gave it a tug. "Come riding with me."

Her gaze moved back to the computer. "I'm sorry, Micah, but I'm just not in the right frame of mind."

Disappointment instantly ruined his mood. He didn't want to go riding by himself. What was the point if he couldn't feel Alice sitting behind him with her arms wrapped around his waist? "Then I'll put away the bike for the night. You want to have dinner together, or are you too emotional to eat, too?"

As she jerked up her head, she grinned. "I'll make dinner. Give me another hour to kick myself out of my funk."

How would he survive after she left? Judging from the conversation he'd overheard with the Army General, she had a great opportunity training female soldiers. He'd never stand in the way of her going after a career perfectly suited for her strengths. But the thought of her leaving depressed him. He just wished the future she desired was a little closer to Timber Lake, and to him.

****

The next afternoon, Alice studied her training plan before setting the clipboard on the shelf placed at the rear of the gym. She'd set an aggressive workout pace, and Micah performed better than she expected. With a smile, she watched him finish with ease a rep of push-ups. At the sound of a car engine, she looked up to see a red sports car stop at the side of the house. A tall blonde shimmied out and without hesitation, she walked over and entered the gym.

Micah jumped to his feet and scurried past Alice to greet their guest.

Watching him kiss the woman's cheek, Alice grew nauseous. She wished for a backdoor in the small gym so she could disappear. A minute earlier, when the gate buzzer sounded during their workout, he'd acted very jittery. Like he'd known his ex-girlfriend, whom she recognized from a photograph in Micah's house, was coming for a visit and hadn't had the guts to tell Alice.

She faced the other direction and collected her sweatshirt hung on the wall. She didn't want to witness their reunion. While she pulled her sweatshirt over her head, she heard Micah clear his throat. She rolled back her shoulders and straightened her spine, then turned to face Micah.

"Alice, I want to introduce you to Cassidy." He shifted from one foot to the other.

"Nice to meet you." Alice extended a hand, which hovered for several seconds until the gesture was reciprocated.

"Micah told me you're doing wonders with his training." She looked at Alice, then shifted her gaze to Micah and smiled.

"He's been working hard." So, she finally met the woman Micah couldn't get over. Sure, she was pretty, with delicate features and a curvy frame. Gorgeous actually. Jealousy poked and prodded her confidence. Stop, she ordered herself.

"Do you mind if we take a break?" He stood on wide-spread legs, shifting his weight from one to the other.

Today was the first time he'd ever asked to stop early. "You don't need my permission." He was the million-dollar athlete. In reality, she was simply his employee. "Go ahead. We're finished for the day."

For several seconds, Micah didn't move or speak. "Are you sure?"

"Yes." Emphasizing her point, she walked over to the sound system with pulse racing and turned off the music.

"Okay. I'll see you later." After another long look at Alice, he guided Cassidy to the door, a hand resting on her lower back.

The punching bag hanging from the ceiling would make a good vessel for her emotions. She stripped off her sweatshirt and poured out her hurt, pounding the bag over and over, until the muscles in her arms screamed for mercy.

In another month, she'd move home, and hopefully, leave behind her heartbreak.

****

Admittedly, Micah was a coward. Every time he wanted to tell Alice about Cassidy's visit, he couldn't push the words past his lips. Cassidy was only staying two days and not at his house. He'd made reservations at the nicest hotel in town, which hadn't made her happy. She asked to stay with him, and he couldn't understand why. Was she concerned about his health, or did she want him back?

Once he'd got Cassidy settled on the comfortable sofa in the great room, he poured a glass of wine and grabbed a sports drink for himself. He handed her the wine and sat. "I'm clean and sober. I stay home every night. I don't know when the last time I went to a party."

"Are you hanging around home because of the woman staying in your guesthouse?" Cassidy pointed toward the patio doors. "Don't get me wrong, I'm glad you've cleaned up, but I'm wondering if you've substituted one dependency with another. Maybe Alice leaving would be for the best."

"I disagree." A spike in his pulse warned him to take a deep breath and relax. Shouldn't she be happy he'd given up partying, no matter the reason?

"Micah." She exhaled a long breath. "Ray and I aren't together anymore. Our relationship grew unhappy." She traced a finger down his forearm. "I want to give us another chance."

Those special words. He'd wished for this moment since the day she'd left. Inhaling, he filled his nose with the scent of her familiar perfume. He waited for the trumpets and angel songs, but nothing. So, why didn't he pull her close and seal the deal?

"You're not saying anything." Cassidy chewed on her lower lip and studied him. After a few seconds, she rested a palm against his cheek.

He closed his eyes, gauging the feel of her hand on his skin. Without the spark of love he'd once experienced with her touch, he understood the implication. "I don't know what to say. After everything that's happened, do you really want to give me another chance?"

221

"I can tell you're different. You're healthy and ready to play."

A success again. "I'll be a star, not the guy standing on the sidelines wearing a Warrior sweatshirt."

She leaned forward. "I still love you. I never stopped loving you."

Her warm breath caressed his skin. He let her wrap her arms around his neck, waiting for the passion to reignite. The uneasy feeling in his gut advertised deep down, he no longer desired a reconnection. Finally, he broke away and lifted her hands off his shoulders. "I still care about you, but what we shared together is over."

Her cheeks flushed pink. "I want you."

The statement should have sent him soaring. Instead, his feet were firmly planted on solid ground. He couldn't meet her gaze, so he stared at the wall, which held a framed photograph of the moment he'd been handed the MVP trophy two years ago. "You want what we had. I'm not the same man."

She pressed a hand against his cheek and turned his face toward her. "I don't believe it."

Three months ago, he'd given the world for this moment. But he'd changed. With Alice, he'd been gifted with a glimpse of an authentic romantic relationship. "Please don't be angry. Our past will distort a future together. You are better off moving on."

Wearing a frown, Cassidy grabbed her purse and stood. "Maybe it's best that I leave."

"Don't." He shot to his feet. "Let me take you out to dinner so we can catch up."

"All right." She huffed. "But you need to shower first. You stink."

Funny, Alice thought he smelled good after working out. He left Cassidy to cool her heels while he went upstairs to clean up.

Under the spray of water, he grew more certain he'd done the right thing. Cassidy had been his first love, but she needed to bask in the brightness of a star. He would have married her if he hadn't messed up, but since their break-up, his outlook had changed. He wanted an identity outside of football. Yes, he loved football with a passion, but the game wouldn't rule his life. He wanted Alice sitting behind him on his new motorcycle, riding into the sunset. He wanted to build a family with a woman who'd stand by his side, no matter how well he threw a ball.

Realization pounded him like a sledgehammer. He wanted Alice. Micah set his hands on the warm tile in the shower for support, remembering all the times she'd stated she'd never commit to a serious romance. If he was to win Alice's heart, he'd need to play the game of his life.

****

Alice had just turned out the lights in the gym when Cassidy entered. She peered out the front window for Micah, who was nowhere in sight. In her physically exhausted state, she could summon nothing but apathy toward Micah's ex. "I can turn everything back on if you want to work out."

"I'm not exactly dressed for the gym." She pointed to her high heels and short skirt. "We need to talk."

Wonderful. "I'm all ears."

"I don't know what's going on between you two, but Micah seems really different." She scanned the gym, moving her gaze along the equipment before returning it to Alice. "He has a team of professional trainers at his disposal, which leads me to ask…why are you here?"

She met her piercing gaze, remembering Micah loved this woman. Cassidy didn't know Alice and likely watched out for a man she cared for. "He asked me to train him for the football season. Nothing else is happening between us, so whatever changes you perceive in him have nothing to do with me."

"He's vulnerable right now, along with being rich and famous." Cassidy crossed her arms.

"Look." She checked her temper. "Micah asked me to stay here and work with him, and that's what I'm doing. I'm not seducing him."

Her blue eyes widened. "But you're in love with him."

"And why are my feelings your business?" Muscles tense, she focused on keeping a neutral expression. Was her affection for Micah so obvious? She opened the door and waved Cassidy outside. "Micah's relationship with you is none of my concern, and I won't interfere. He's a good person, and I value his friendship more than anything." No way would she get catty over a man—even a great one like Micah.

Leaving Cassidy standing outside the gym, Alice strode to the guesthouse and hurried inside, fighting the sting of tears. Her eyes and throat burned. Were Micah and Cassidy close to reconciling?

She brushed off the worry and hurt. Didn't she prefer living without too many personal entanglements? Accepting her brother and sister into her life was one thing. Micah was different. If she let him in, then he had the power to destroy her heart. Micah getting back together with Cassidy was what he wanted. She'd walk away while making a clean break. Though she understood, she'd likely break in the process.

****

The next day, Micah woke early and headed to the Warrior's facilities for the first day of minicamp. First, he had a meeting with the team's General Manager. The position of starting quarterback would remain open until after training camp. If Micah played at the same level he had before his injury, he'd secure the position. If not, then Kantra had a shot at taking over.

After the meeting concluded, Micah left the GM's office with a strange sense of calm. Despite the General Manager's reservations, he had no doubt he'd stand behind the offensive line on game day. Not Kantra. After a trip to the locker room to change, he joined the team on the field. Returning onto the practice field with the guys felt really good, even if only for low intensity drills.

His arm never felt stronger, and his passes were both long and accurate. After wiping sweat off his brow, he stutter-stepped backward and released the ball, which arched through the air and into the hands of his favorite wide receiver.

Micah accepted the handoff and ran to gain momentum. As he cocked his arm to throw, he winced at pain shooting through his knee. He carefully lowered to the ground. Shaking his head in disbelief, he suppressed growing panic. A few easy passes shouldn't cause another knee injury. Not when he'd worked hard to strengthen it.

The team's medical staff ran out to where he sat. "Can you extend your leg?" a trainer asked.

Micah followed their instruction until another shock of pain burst from his knee. He sucked in a breath through clenched teeth. *No, not another injury. Not now.*

One of the medical staff pressed fingers into the outer portion of his knee joint and studied the area. "Don't worry. The tendon might be tender from overuse. We'll take you for an MRI to verify the pain is nothing serious."

Micah accepted help to stand. If the pain was something serious, he'd deal with the repercussions. Until then, he'd remain calm or at least try to hold himself together.

A trainer stood beside him, supporting some of his weight as they walked toward the entrance of the building. "Your knee has been through a lot of trauma. Like I said, don't panic until the doctor gives you something to panic about."

Kantra grinned at Micah before running out to claim the quarterback spot on the field.

Once inside, he let his discomfort show on his face. "Someone go to the locker room and get my phone." He needed to text Alice.

One of the assistants ran off. Three minutes later, he arrived at the MRI room and breathlessly handed Micah his phone.

He pulled up Alice's name in his texting app.

—Knee pain today during practice. Heading to get an MRI now. Can you come by?—

—Not good. Where do I go?—

—Stop in at the front desk. Rosalie will call someone to take you to doc's office—

Once he was finished, he handed the phone to the

imaging tech to be removed from the room. An hour later, he sat on an exam-table, waiting for the results. His gut clenched tight. Had his season ended before it even began?

A knock sounded on the door, and Alice entered, deep lines marking her face. "What did you do?" She flicked her gaze down to his exposed knee.

"Nothing." He shook his head. "I threw the ball and must have taken a wrong step. They're telling me not to panic but I'm imagining the worst."

She sat on the small stool placed by the exam table. "Are the team and staff freaking out?"

"Not really." He shrugged. "The athletic trainer talked to coach and calmed him down, and as I hobbled off the field, one of my offensive lineman called me a big baby." He laughed at the scowl on her face. "Just his way of showing concern."

Alice ran a finger down the long scar on the outside of his knee. "Have faith in the strength of your body. Sometimes, pain is your brain's way of alerting you to a problem before it gets too severe. You likely overworked the muscles, and they sent off distress signals for protection."

Tingles of pleasure from Alice's touch dulled the pain. Her calm voice smoothed his worry. "I hope you're right."

The door burst open again. "Micah." Cassidy rushed toward him. "What happened? Did you hurt your knee again? Why didn't you call me?" She pushed past Alice and the incoming doctor.

"Take a breath." He smiled and turned his gaze to Alice. "Let's hear what the doc has to say."

"Micah, your knee is fine." Doctor Curtis patted

his shoulder. "The sudden pain is your body's way of telling you to take it easy."

With a wink and a grin, Alice rested her back against the wall.

His heart flipped and tripped at the sight of her, so perfectly poised and confident.

The doctor bent over to take a closer look at his knee and pressed two fingers into the side of the joint. "You may feel a sudden, sharp twinge from time to time, but the pain is nothing a little ice and rest won't fix. The muscle tone around your knee is strong. I can tell you've worked hard over the off season."

"I have my trainer to thank for being in top-shape." He pointed at Alice. "She's put me through an untraditional workout plan."

"Well, whatever you've been doing, keep it up. Go home and ice your knee for the rest of the day. You should be fine by tomorrow." The doctor shook his hand before grabbing his paperwork and exiting the exam room.

Biting at her lower lip, Cassidy squeezed his hand. "You need to take it easy and lay off the training."

Micah scooted off the exam table, easing weight onto his injured leg. His knee twinged with a dull pain—nothing like the shocking jolt earlier. "I'll listen to my body, but I'm won't stop training now. Not so close to the beginning of preseason."

"Looks like you're in good hands." Alice stood and walked to the door. "I'll catch up with you later." Her long stride placed her out of the room within a few steps.

"Wait." Micah limped after her but wasn't fast enough.

"Come on. I'll drive you home." Cassidy held his arm.

In an attempt to support him while he walked, she placed herself too close, making each step awkward and uncomfortable. He brushed her off and moved quickly into the hall, but Alice was gone. He clenched his fists. *Darn.* He'd catch her when he got home. Turning back to Cassidy, he held out a hand to stop her full-court press. "How did you know I was hurt?"

"Andre texted me. He knew I was in town." She rested a hand on his arm. "You're glad I came, right?"

What he needed to say, he wanted to say in private. Micah escorted her outside and to her car. "I appreciate you traveling all the way from New York to see me, but I think we both know the time's come we say goodbye."

Her normally smooth brows wrinkled, and she opened her mouth, then pressed her lips together. "You're really giving up on us?"

"You'll always hold a special place in my heart." He took her hand and raised it to his lips. No spark. No attraction. "I broke our relationship. You should move on."

"I'm too late." Cassidy rose onto tiptoes and gently kissed his lips. "She's a lucky woman."

"I'm the lucky one." Warmth filled his chest. Meeting Alice Liddell had been a touch of fate, and he wouldn't let her slip through his fingers.

One corner of her mouth lifted. "To be honest, I'm very jealous."

Remembering with fondness good moments they'd had together, he placed a finger under her chin to tip up her face. She was so beautiful but now a friend, and his heart only swelled with thoughts of Alice.

"Take care, Micah." She secured the straps of her purse over her shoulder. Sliding inside the driver's seat of her rental car, she waved, then drove away.

By now, practice had ended for the day. He'd head home. Hopefully, Alice would be there. He'd use the twenty-minute drive to prepare what he'd say. Maybe he'd use sympathy to break down her defenses. Or push her buttons to get her emotions fired up.

Either way, he needed to convey how deeply he loved her and convince her to stay. A sure win or doomed to defeat? Only time would tell.

Chapter Nineteen

After Alice arrived home from the stadium, she changed and went out for a run through warm, humid air. Ignoring the deep burn in her legs, she kept pushing onward. Her goal was to finish five miles—her longest run since her injury—far less than she'd completed in the past, but she'd snatch any small victory.

Years ago, she'd completed fifteen-mile hikes through the woods around Fort Bragg. By the time the final miles loomed, she'd ignored her bloody feet squishing inside her boots with every step. At a certain point, her body and brain had gone numb. She'd pushed past the pain and fought through to the end. Alice knew she'd never again be at the same level of physical fitness. Even so, she wouldn't use the fact as an excuse to sit around and grow soft. She was a fighter and would recuperate some of the strength she'd lost to the IED.

Minutes later, she slowed to a walk in front of Micah's house, breathing in and out in a deep, steady rhythm. After pushing the code for the gate, she made her way down the long driveway and back to the little guesthouse she called home. Opening the front door, she went straight to the kitchen for a glass of cold water.

Around her sat reminders that the space felt like home—Micah's training calendar, the pictures Kate sent of Maddy and Joshua hung on the refrigerator, her medals of accommodation used as motivation whenever she felt like giving up. Realization nudged that she'd become too comfortable here. Seeing Micah with Cassidy had reinforced the truth—she didn't belong in his world. As a visitor, she would soon be gone.

Tell that to her heart, which never wanted to leave.

The time had come to tell Micah her stay was over. She'd grown too attached to the hot-shot football gunslinger who loved another woman. During her run, she decided she'd gracefully bow out, stating her work with him was completed. If his knee was still giving him problems, he needed professional guidance. What more could she do? She'd return to her apartment in South Carolina and begin the next chapter of her life.

A knock at the door disrupted her ruminations. Through the picture window, she saw Micah, his hands stuffed in the front pockets of his shorts. She quickly grabbed a glass from the cabinet, filled it with tap water, and took a long gulp.

After opening the door, she lowered her gaze to his knee. "You should be sitting with your leg up, icing your knee." The leg didn't show evidence of swelling— a good sign.

"Then let me in." Micah stepped past her into the front room. "You're dripping with sweat. Go for a run?"

Sighing in resignation, she lowered onto a little wooden side-chair across from the sofa. In her icky, post-workout state, she wanted to avoid contacting anything upholstered. "I went out right when I got home. The weather's great today."

He sat and propped his injured leg on the sofa,

before stuffing a pillow underneath his knee. "You left in a hurry."

"You were in good hands." She detected a hint of bitterness tainting her voice. A feeling she needed to get over—now.

"What if I wanted to be in your hands?" He arched a dark eyebrow.

She exhaled an exaggerated sigh. "Stop teasing."

"Why won't you admit that you got something for me?" Both dark eyebrows wiggled.

His grin would have melted a lesser woman. "I'm getting a headache from you, if that's what you mean." She warmed by the second and started sweating again.

Micah lost his grin. "At the stadium, Cassidy and I said our goodbyes. I've made my feelings very obvious, and she recognized my heart belongs to someone else."

"What do you mean…obvious?" Her heartbeat accelerated. Did he really push away any chance of reuniting with Cassidy?

"I'm obviously in love with you." He adjusted his position on the sofa so both feet were on the ground. Leaning forward, he studied her. "Say something."

Alice felt her chest squeezed with disbelief. He couldn't possibly be in love with her. Not after he'd ended their kiss in the hotel room in Ohio. During the time since, he hadn't tried again. "I should leave." Fighting dizziness, she stood and escaped into the kitchen.

"You're not going anywhere until we finish this conversation." Micah followed and now stood inches away.

"You don't need me here anymore." As she set the glass in the dishwasher, she worked to control the trembling in her hands. "You have the team trainers to work with...people who know what they're doing."

"Didn't you hear what I said?" Micah grabbed her arm and spun her to face him. "Yes, I have the Warrior's staff at my disposal, but you're more than a trainer to me."

"I've decided to accept the position at Fort Bragg." Her words flowed out in a rush. "The contract is only for a year, but I'll have time to figure out what I want to do with the rest of my life." Last night, she'd tossed and turned, waking that morning with a clear choice—she'd become part of the historic training program for female combat soldiers. The position would serve as a bridge from military to civilian life and finally allow her closure. An added benefit—she'd stay too busy to cry over a broken heart.

Her decision regarding Joshua and Maddy's future churned in her gut. Soon, Kate would press her for an answer, and Alice was ready to accept them into her life and home.

Micah set a finger under her chin and tipped her face to meet his gaze. "Alice, I'll support you no matter what you decide." He narrowed his gaze. "Just don't leave me now."

Everything inside her begged to throw herself into his arms and announce she'd stay forever. Was she really good enough, though, compared to Cassidy? His ex was a beautiful fashion designer and a custom-made partner for a professional athlete like Micah. "I told you I don't do serious relationships. And after everything I've admitted to you about my family, you should understand I'd never open my heart to a man who still held feelings for another woman." *Stay strong.* She closed her eyes, finding a few seconds of peace without the temptation of Micah's handsome face hovering above her. Her short-lived respite shattered when his lips connected with hers.

He held her waist with strong, large hands. His obvious claim was too strong, and she shuddered against denial. As she savored the feel of his kisses moving along her jawline, Alice gave her heart permission to soften into submission. She slid a hand up his bare arm then moved under the sleeve of his T-shirt. She kneaded the muscles on his shoulder, enjoying his throaty sounds of pleasure.

He hooked both hands together behind her back, trapping her against him. "Tell me now that I want any other woman but you," he murmured against her neck.

Logic mixed with fear flooded her brain. She set both hands on his chest and pushed.

"Don't run away," he whispered.

Desire sounded in his voice. The enjoyment of his embrace was too great, and her resistance faded. "Micah, you don't mean it when you say you want me." *I don't understand how to make a real relationship work. I'll only hurt you in the end.*

"Stop telling me what I mean, what I think, and how I feel." He dropped his arms to release her. "Why don't you take my words at face value?"

"Because I think you're confused. You're worried about the upcoming season and see me as a miracle worker when in reality, I'm just a screwed-up veteran who can't figure out her own life." Her voice cracked. Tears burned her eyes, and she fought to keep them from spilling.

"I'm too shallow to understand the valuable gift

235

I've been given?" He shoved a hand through his messy, brown hair.

"No." She couldn't stop her emotions from bubbling to the surface. Taking a deep breath, she forced a calm she didn't feel. "These past few months, I've tried so hard not to fall for you because I knew a relationship could never go anywhere. I'm the perpetual female friend, and in most cases, I'm good with the title." She shoved her hands into the pockets of her running shorts. "You were the first man I ever considered breaking my rules for."

"Break your rules, Alice." He stepped close and encircled her waist with his hands. "For me."

She sniffled back tears. Visions of her days as a young, scared girl filled her head. She folded her arms across her chest, placed a barrier between them. "I saw my mother live with a man who would never love her. Not the way a wife deserved. I'm so afraid to let myself be that vulnerable."

"Trust me. I'll care for and protect your heart." Micah gently kissed her temple.

Her pulse quickened. "My heart has always been mine alone." She pressed a palm against his scruffy cheek. "I think moving back to South Carolina is the best for both of us. I have some things to take care of before I make the move to Fayetteville. The most important is finding a house big enough for myself, Maddy, and Joshua."

Stepping back, he crossed his arms over his chest. "You promised you'd stay until training camp, which is at the end of July. So you owe me three more weeks. If you need to go out to Fort Bragg for a few days and house hunt, that's fine, but I'm not releasing you from your obligation."

As her blood boiled, she searched for something to toss. Something not too hard, like a pillow—she wouldn't want to hurt him, much. Just a stinger. "Micah—"

"*Ahhhh*!" He waved a hand in front of her face. "I get three more weeks to win your trust and your heart. If by that time, you can't tell me you love me, then I'll let you leave without a fight." His lips curled into a huge grin. "But I'm personally not worried."

"Why?" She snorted. "Because no mortal woman can resist your charms?"

"As true as the statement might be, my irresistibility isn't the reason." He swept a finger across her cheek. "I love you, Alice. I'll spend the next three weeks proving it."

With a weak smile, she'd accept his challenge, not confident even Micah Palmer could break down all her barriers. And if not, she'd leave, reinjuring his healing heart. She wouldn't let him be hurt. She'd rather bear the heartache than inflict more onto him.

****

The next morning, Alice looked inside her coffee mug. *Empty*. While mindlessly watching the morning news in Micah's kitchen, she'd finished two cups. "Is there any coffee left in the pot?"

Micah, dressed in plaid shorts and a pink polo shirt, walked over to the counter and inspected the coffee maker then carried over the pot and poured the remaining drops in her mug. "You okay spending the day by yourself?"

"Yes, for the hundredth time." She lifted the mug, simply enjoying the warmth on her hands. "Go have fun with the guys on the golf course. I have a book I've been meaning to read."

He sat beside her, and his fingers skimmed down her bare arm. "I have some reading material, if you're interested." He grabbed a white folder from the other side of the table and slid it toward her.

"What's this?" Flipping open the folder, she spotted a stack of news articles tucked inside.

"Me. Or at least those news stories were about me. I don't want to hide anything from you."

She gazed down at a grainy, black-and-white picture of Micah with a beautiful woman on his arm. Her vision blurred, and her breath caught. The headline of the article spoke about his rocky relationship and alleged substance abuse. "I haven't been living under a rock. Your bad behavior isn't anything I don't already know." If Micah really wanted to build a relationship, why dig up old news?

"Reagan shoved this folder at me at the end of last season." He slumped in his chair. "The next day, I agreed to check into rehab. He managed what no one else could do…open my eyes."

Giving a silent prayer of thanks for Reagan's dogged persistence, she closed the folder and slid it back across the table. "Irrelevant."

"I need you to understand who I was." He tapped a finger on the folder. "The truth is ugly and nasty, and I wish I could erase that time in my life. But if I'm to do right by you, then I have to be totally honest."

She checked the time on her watch. "Get moving or you'll be late for your tee-time." Alice stood with him in unison. If she had to inevitably fall for someone, she was grateful her heart had the good sense to pick a worthy man. "You don't have anything to prove."

Micah embraced her, and his lips grazed her mouth. "I'm proud to call you my girl."

She laughed. "Go." Shooing him out the door, she pressed a hand to her chest as it filled with tender emotion. Why did he have to be so—so—Micah? And now he wanted her to see his troubled past. As if anything in these news articles had anything to do with the man he was now.

But he'd requested she read the contents of the folder, so she'd skim through it to appease him. She already knew about his addiction and bad-boy behavior.

After pulling out the first sheet, she closed her eyes and took a deep breath. With Micah's willingness to be totally transparent, she should do the same—easier said than done. Buried deep were too many dark spots in her memories. Each one would require time and patience to dig without cutting out her heart.

While reading through the articles, she was surprised at the contents of a few. Of course, the media took circumstantial evidence and convicted him in the court of public opinion without proof. They used hype and drama to sell advertising. Nothing she read tainted her feelings. In fact, she loved him more.

Micah was a good man with an honest heart, and she'd be a fool to let him go. But giving up was what she considered. Or were Micah's efforts slowly winning her over?

****

After days of non-stop coaxing, Micah finally convinced Alice to ride on his motorcycle. The Wisconsin weather was as temperamental as an overtired toddler. Yesterday was sunny and in the eighties. Today, the mercury would struggle to reach sixty. A cool wind whipped down the length of the driveway.

He stood beside the black Harley—his pride and joy. His agent hadn't been happy about his purchase, but Micah didn't care. Once he got Alice on the bike, he was confident she'd change her mind.

Earlier, they'd spent an hour in the gym together doing yoga. Alice continued challenging him with her nontraditional training plan.

Now, they both deserved some fun.

Over the years, he'd forgotten the feeling of having a genuine good time. He'd been so wrapped up in earning a spot as a starting quarterback, and then excelling at the game. He'd lost track of everything else and built his life upon one thing—football. When the game was stripped away, he couldn't cope. Drug abuse and late-night partying filled the empty space.

Clearly, he needed time off the field. With Alice, he'd rediscovered joy in a sport he'd competed in at one time for fun. When he stepped onto the field in August, he'd take on every challenge with the same excitement he'd felt as a boy.

Alice strolled down the driveway. She wore well-worn jeans, a hooded Army sweatshirt, and a hint of a smile. "I can't believe you talked me into this."

His pulse kicked up. "You're an adrenaline junkie, just like me. You'll have fun. I promise." He tossed her the spare helmet then mounted the bike.

She secured the strap then swung a long leg over the seat of the bike. Her arms wrapped around his waist.

He drank in the warmth of her body pressed against him. "You ready?" he asked over the rumble of the engine.

As they took off down the road, Alice reverberated with laughter.

With each backroad mile, the weight he carried on his shoulders grew lighter. Simply enjoying the day wasn't enough. In twenty years, he wanted to experience this same rush with the same woman sitting behind him.

When he arrived at their destination, he pulled off into an overlook. He lowered the kickstand and cut the engine, before twisting around to accept Alice's helmet.

Below them, Lake Michigan churned in shades of blue and gray. Seagulls coasted in the air above the beach, their cries replicating an animated and loud conversation.

Alice shook out her hair. "The water is beautiful. This view goes on forever."

He stood behind her and wrapped his arms around her waist. "Over by the bluff is a path that leads to the beach. You up for a walk?"

She bent over to rub her right leg. "A walk would be nice. I need to work out the cramps."

Once they descended from the bluff, Micah and Alice walked hand in hand along the beach, where the cold water lapped up onto the sand.

"When I arrived home from the retreat, I walked on the beach every day." She slowed their pace. "I forgot how healing fresh air and sunshine can be."

He hoped someday he'd understand everything about her—a soul-deep knowledge. "We should come back here on a day when the sun's shining."

"You really love that motorcycle, don't you?" She grinned.

"Not as much as I love something else." He bit his tongue to keep from saying more. Subtlety was a skill he didn't possess.

She stopped walking and turned to face him. "You excel at sweet talk, but I believe actions speak louder than words."

"I love action." Grinning, he lifted her hand and kissed the top.

"You telling me how you feel doesn't mean nearly as much as taking me here today." Leaning in, she gently kissed his lips. "Gambling on a real relationship is a constant struggle."

The brief contact left him wanting more. "Thank you for taking a chance on me."

As she began walking again, she tugged him along. "Have you given much thought to your life after football?"

"Not really." He shrugged. "I'm living in the moment right now, but I'd probably want to stay involved with sports somehow. I imagined a family would need my attention when the time came to retire."

"You thought you'd settle down with Cassidy." She kicked a small rock, sending it hopping across the sand.

Squeezing her hand, he kicked a rock, too. Unfortunately, his fell short of where hers landed. Good thing he'd stuck with playing quarterback in school instead of goal kicker. "Yes, before my injury. Even when everything was falling apart, I held out hope we'd fix things." He hesitated. "Please don't take what I'm about to say the wrong way."

She peered at him side-eyed. "Go on."

"You've been really hard on me and pushed me

passed my normal limits." He grinned at her scowl. "But over the last few months, I've felt like I've gone from wearing old glasses to twenty-twenty vision. Not only can I see clearer, I understand what's important in life. I want more than winning at football."

"You have done well, my pupil." She bumped him with her hip. "Just don't go soft after I leave."

He let his gaze wander out over the water. In the distance, a container ship floated across the horizon. "I can't envision a future without you in it."

"You make it difficult for a girl to resist." She stopped beside a large stack of boulders and moved closer, running a hand down the rough surface.

"Good." He grabbed her and kissed her solidly on the mouth. Alice's lips softened, and she tasted like the apple she'd eaten before they'd left. As he held on, he couldn't stop the aching fear that when she left for home in eighteen days, she'd slip away.

Was he strong enough to secure Alice's heart, not only now but forever?

Chapter Twenty

A week later, Micah did one last set of bicep curls and returned the fifty-pound dumbbells to the rack. The chatter of his teammates echoed through the room. He'd come early, wanting to use the equipment and hang out with the guys. He became invigorated by the ancient right of male bonding over lifting metal disks.

Across the room, Garrett Kantra worked the crowd like he vied for prom king. As if the starting quarterback could be won via popularity contest. Micah had no problem proving his skill against Garrett on the field. The kid had a thing or two to learn yet, though. If only he'd shut his trap long enough to listen.

"Hey." Kantra approached. "How's that knee holding up?"

"Better than ever." Micah wasn't lying. Despite the small setback a few weeks ago, his knee felt strong. He crossed his arms over his chest.

"Cool. Good enough to compete for the starting job?" Kantra grinned.

"I'm not worried."

"Man, you should be." He took a step toward Micah. "I worked with some of the country's top athletic trainers during the off-season and hired a quarterback coach to help with technique. Just a heads up, you should watch your back."

As the cocky jerk strutted away, Micah held his

tongue. The kid could talk all he wanted—words were meaningless at game time.

Reagan Harrison waved him over to the bench press area. "Don't let Kantra get under your skin. DeMarcus and I have big plans for him on media day."

"Linebacker sandwich?" He fought a grin, knowing firsthand what the two linebackers were physically capable of but also had confidence in their professional integrity. They likely wouldn't hurt him—much.

"Nothing too painful. We'll keep him on his toes." Reagan sat on one of the weight benches. "You ready for training camp next week?"

"More than ready." He was eager to start but not ready to say goodbye to Alice. Time moved faster with each day. Over the past two weeks, he'd made some headway but not enough to convince her to fully commit.

Maybe Reagan would have an idea on how to win a cautious woman's heart. Not so long ago, he'd been in a similar spot. "So, how were you sure Julie was…you know…the one?"

Reagan's eyebrows arched almost to his hairline. "Say what?"

He didn't want to raise his voice, so he stepped closer. "How did you know Julie was the one?"

A wide smile formed on Reagan's sweaty face. "I'm not really sure. I got to a point where I didn't want to live without her. I was willing to compromise on things I never saw myself giving up before. True love changes your perspective."

Micah glanced around the weight room to see several guys moving closer, likely straining to listen in. He ignored them.

"Are you thinking about getting back with Cassidy?" Reagan's smile dipped to a frown.

"That relationship is over." He hadn't heard from Cassidy since she'd left Timber Lake. She'd faded from his thoughts faster than he'd imagined.

"Then you have Alice on the brain."

As several guys nearby whooped in reaction to Alice's name, Micah flushed. "Can we talk somewhere more private?" Why had he asked for relationship advice in the weight room?

"Can't. I need to finish these bench presses and get going. Julie asked me to come home right after my work-out and watch the kids. Spot me, okay?" Reagan lay on the bench and reached up to grasp hold of the bar with both hands. With a grunt, he lifted the three-hundred-fifty pound weighted bar and slowly lowered it to hover over his chest.

Micah stood above him, watching Reagan pound out reps without a grunt. "I want to make things work with Alice." He waited for Reagan to finish before continuing. "If she refuses to commit, where does that leave me?"

Huffing, Reagan sat and rested his hands on his thighs. "I have one piece of advice. Don't let her leave with things open-ended. Whatever her issues are, you can work on them together over time."

Micah thought back to his rookie year—the year Reagan had been brought to his knees after a break-up with the one and only woman he'd ever loved. "Julie wasn't very receptive to your advances at the beginning."

"Not smart to bring that up." Scowling, Reagan stood and slapped Micah on the back. "Go home, enjoy your time together, and don't do anything stupid. Got it?"

"Yeah. Thanks." Unfortunately, he excelled at being impulsive and rash.

After a quick shower, he'd head home to see what Alice was up to. And like Reagan suggested, try not to do anything stupid. *Good luck with that.*

****

"Stop shooting at me," Alice yelled over the noise of the TV. While seated on the edge of the sofa cushion, she kept her gaze fixed on the flat screen. Her pulse quickened like she'd stepped into a real battle.

"Killing you is the object of the game." As he speedily tapped the controller buttons, Micah's body swayed.

Her current game strategy was failing, being she was only one shot away from death. Sending her avatar to the corner of a building, she waited for Micah's to appear. When he finally showed himself, he ran full speed into her trap—bam, bam, bam.

His computer-generated avatar collapsed. "That's cheating," he yelled.

"I used a simple military strategy called the death trap." Smiling, Alice set her controller on the sofa. "Never run into a situation you haven't secured first." He stroked a hand up her leg, lingering over the scars and causing her to shiver.

"Good advice. I'll remember for next time." Micah leaned in for a kiss.

As her body charged with attraction, she heard the buzz of her phone set on the side table.

"Ignore it," he whispered into her ear.

She checked the caller ID and stilled—*Kate*. "I

have to take this." She scooted away from the man who was in the process of short-circuiting her brain.

Blowing out a breath, Micah fell back on the sofa and started a new video game.

"Hey," she answered. "What's up?" Blasts of fake gunfire sounded from the TV.

"Are you alone?" Kate asked.

"Let me step outside." She exited through a back patio door into the quiet night air. Moths buzzed around the porch lights, causing her to move toward the dark edge of the patio. "What's going on?"

"Your dad came for a visit today. I don't know how he found my address, but he threatened to drag Maddy back home." Kate cleared her throat. "Joshua told him to leave. The kid is as stubborn as you. Anyway, I called the cops, but they couldn't do anything since Josiah is their legal guardian."

Alice's stomach heaved, and she feared she'd throw up on Micah's lawn. "They can't go back with him."

"They won't. Don't worry. I talked to a lawyer about having you named as legal guardian."

"Getting them removed from their parents' custody will be a legal nightmare." Alice pictured years of red tape and heated with anger. Her brother and sister didn't have that long.

"Your father asked about you, Alice. He said he'd leave Maddy and Joshua in your care and give them their birth certificates if he can talk to you."

Slowly lowering herself onto a patio chair, she leaned over and clenched her roiling stomach. "I can't."

Kate blew out a breath. "You're not sixteen anymore, and he's an old man. He has no power over you."

Yes, she'd faced more dangerous enemies but never one who scared her more to her core. "Why is he demanding to see me? I've been gone for years. I don't understand why he cares."

"He heard of what you've done in the Army," Kate said. "I think deep down, he's proud."

The thought caused her to feel even sicker. "He feels nothing but contempt." She could say the same of her feelings for him.

"He's interested enough to come all the way to Santa Fe to harass Maddy and Joshua."

Resignation settled over Alice like a toxic cloud. She was left with little choice. Either she faced her father or Maddy and Joshua were at risk. "I'll come on two conditions. He only gets fifteen minutes and promises to leave them alone when we're done."

Kate sighed. "Can you be here tomorrow?"

"I'll call and book my flight right after I end the call." When would she finally be free from the nightmare her parents created? The thought of facing her father again, a man she hated more than the terrorists who'd planted the IED, made her want to scream. She clenched her fist, nails digging into the palm of her hand. "Tell the kids not to worry. I'm coming. Oh…and ask them to pack. I'm taking them when I leave."

"Really? I thought you were still in Wisconsin with Micah."

Sadly, not for much longer. "I am but only until the end of the week. I want the kids as far away from their father as possible."

"You're leaving Micah already? I thought you two

were seeing each other…romantically."

How could she explain the jumble of emotions Micah left in his wake? She did love him, probably too much. The strong feelings he stirred scared her. "Micah is a wonderful guy, but I'm not sure this relationship is a together-forever deal."

"When will you finally stop running? I'm sorry, Alice, but I had the same upbringing you did and didn't let my past emotionally cripple me. Marriage has been wonderful."

She gritted her teeth, not feeling up to arguing with her cousin. "You are a loving, sweet person. I'm not. I'm better off alone."

"Bull," Kate said. "From what I saw of Micah at the retreat, he's crazy about you and strong enough to stand up to you…a winning combination."

"Are you done?" Wearing a reluctant grin, she rolled her eyes. Kate was right about Micah being strong enough to push through her stubbornness. Didn't mean she'd admit the truth to anyone, especially Kate or Micah. "I have a flight to book."

"You're lucky I love you, dear cousin." She made a few kissing noises. "Talk to you soon."

Alice disconnected the call and set her phone on the patio table. How would she explain her sudden departure to Micah? *I have to leave because my deranged father is threatening my brother and sister unless I agree to meet with him.*

Her relationship with Micah had been going smoothly. He was kind and caring, without being too pushy. At times, she found herself wanting to throw caution to the wind and give up everything to be with him, but she was too well trained to act impulsively. As deeply as she cared for him, she couldn't take that final step and fully trust him with her heart.

Slipping her phone in the back pocket of her shorts, she walked inside to find Micah still engaged in a video game. He pressed Pause and glanced at her as she approached. "Everything okay?"

"Not really." She plopped next to him on the sofa. "Kate called. I need to fly out to Santa Fe tomorrow. I should be back the following day."

"Why now? I only have you for a few more days." Micah frowned.

"I just need to go." She flinched at the harsh tone of her voice. Taking a deep breath, she focused her energy on remaining calm. The reason she was upset had nothing to do with the kind man sitting beside her. "It's an emergency. I wouldn't go if I didn't have to."

"What's so important that you have to fly across the country?" He rested an arm around her shoulder and squeezed.

She couldn't help but be distracted by his attractive mouth, which was so very close. *Now was not the time for thoughts of making out*. "I have to clean up a personal family matter."

"After all the time we've spent together, you still don't trust me." Micah clenched his jaw, and the muscles on the side of his face twitched. He eased back on the sofa.

The accusation stung, likely due to the truth behind his words. "My keeping something private has nothing to do with trust."

"I've done everything I know to make you understand how much I love you. I'd rather never again step on a football field than hurt you, but you continue to hold back."

Deep sentiment flooded her heart. "You're perfect. I'm the one with the problem." Alice reached to take his hand, but he pulled away. The last thing she wanted was to hurt him.

"Seriously?" His brown eyes glistened.

Maybe with rage. Maybe with pain. Either way, she was the cause. Fighting the sting of tears, she closed her eyes. "I'm leaving for two days to take care of some family issues. I'm coming back."

"Then in a few more days, you'll move home, and then what?" The video game controller cracked in his tightening grip.

"You always knew I was leaving." She reached across to brush a lock of brown hair off his forehead. "Why are you really upset?"

"I might not be a relationship expert, but I do know what we have together won't survive without trust."

She breathed in and out, slowing her racing heart. "I trust you." The words flowed easily, not nearly as difficult as she feared. Shame still locked her tongue from telling him everything.

"Not enough to share your burdens."

Her pulse kicked up again. "I've handled my business alone for a long time. I don't know any other way."

Kneeling in front of her, he stared straight into her eyes. "Why won't you let me in?"

She knew what he wanted—when she'd finally let go of the last piece of herself, the part she'd held back out of fear. "I have to call and book my flight then go pack. Once I have everything set, I'll let you know my schedule."

Micah stood and exited the room without another word.

She was left struggling for breath. In protecting herself, she'd hurt him. Inside her chest, she ached with the shattered pieces of guilt and grief. They pierced her conscience as her mind and heart battled. Eventually, one would win, and she prayed his love was strong enough to demolish her fear.

****

How could you hold onto something you never had? Micah carried Alice's suitcase out to the car and placed it in the trunk. After a brief kiss and stiff hug goodbye, he stood silently and watched her drive away. She hadn't trusted him enough to share her latest family trouble. For Alice, her personal past was a deep vault very few were granted access. He'd been lucky to get a small glimpse inside when he'd met a part of her family at the retreat, and then again when she'd opened up about her polygamist upbringing.

Why couldn't he be grateful for the offering, even if she still withheld a portion of herself? What she'd shared likely was more than she had with almost anyone else.

His Harley rested inside the garage, and he fought the urge to chase her down and apologize for pushing when he had no right to ask any more than she could give. Instead, he went inside the house and sat in front of his computer. He tried to focus on the latest emails from his agent. The Warriors were hosting a media day tomorrow, and his agent wanted him to be prepared for whatever questions reporters threw his way.

Carl also forwarded a written endorsement offer from a popular sports drink company. Blinking, he read the dollar amount several times. Amazing what companies paid for a popular athlete to endorse their product. Judging by the dollar size of the offer, he must be close to reclaiming his status as one of the leading quarterbacks in the league. In another month, he'd run out on the field and prove his worth.

His phone pinged with a text message from Alice.

—*Sorry how I left things. I'll call you tonight after my meeting, and I can tell you more about what's going on—*

He sat for several minutes with his fingers hovering over the screen of his phone.

—*Have a safe flight. Miss you—*

—*Miss you, too. I care about you, more than you know—*

His heart ached.

—*All I know is you left without much of an explanation—*

—*Stop jumping to conclusions. You're such a drama queen—*

He laughed. Somehow, even when they fought, she found humor in every situation.

—*Not being a drama queen—*

—*You're the most handsome one I know. Plane's boarding, got to go. Talk with you tonight—*

He opened the photo tab on his phone and scrolled through the history. After looking through the pictures of his grandma at a Warriors' game, he deleted a photo of him and Cassidy someone had taken at a New York fashion party.

Finally, he found what he was looking for— pictures from the retreat. He lingered over one of Alice, standing out among a group of male veterans. Another he'd taken of her one morning when he'd come to the gym and found her struggling to complete a pull-up. She'd strangle him if she knew he'd taken her picture, but he'd felt compelled to capture the sheer determination on her face.

The last picture saved on his phone was a selfie with Alice. Their faces were squished together to fill the screen. When he'd snapped the picture, she stuck out her tongue while he wore a huge grin.

Micah survived a rocky childhood, a season-ending injury, pain pill addiction, and Cassidy walking out on him. In the end, only Alice had the potential to fully break him, and the reality of how deeply he needed her terrified him. A deep tremor rumbled in his core, and his hands trembled.

Had Cassidy been right when she'd stated he traded one addiction for another? Was his love for Alice pure, or had he come to depend on her as a good-luck idol?

In less than a week, she'd leave for home, and he'd discover if their relationship was strong enough to survive or proved only a fleeting impression, washing away like a footprint in the sand.

Chapter Twenty-One

No amount of preparation could have readied Alice for the meeting with her father. After wiping sweaty palms on the sides of her jeans, she stepped inside the little café and set her gaze on the devil she'd wished to banish forever.

Josiah Wolf sat in a corner booth, eyeing her as she walked in.

In the years since she'd last seen him, he'd aged drastically. His white hair and beard looked shaggy and overgrown, and his clothes hung loose on his thin frame. How small he looked in comparison to her memories came as a surprise. Her father had once been a towering figure whose scowl scared grown men. She'd been on the receiving end of his belt and could attest to the strength of his arm. Her throat tightened.

"Esther," he croaked.

When his hand was only inches away, she flinched out of reach. "My name is Alice." After sitting in the booth across the table, she studied his face. His milky blue eyes held no hint of warmth.

"Okay, Alice." He stared. "You've grown since the last time I saw you."

"Let's cut the pleasantries. Why did you ask me here?" She didn't want to be with him longer than necessary. Even the smell of his cologne mixed with homemade lye soap made her physically ill. Alice remembered being forced to take a scalding hot bath and cleaned with lye soap after she'd done something wrong. Her mother would hold her down while another wife scrubbed her skin raw.

"I wanted to see my daughter." He pressed together his thin lips. "Do you begrudge an old man from seeing his own flesh and blood?"

"You are a stranger who was ready to sell me into marriage to a man older than you." Internally fuming, she pointed a finger at his face. "I don't know what you think you'll accomplish with this little meeting, but when we're done, you will leave Maddy and Joshua in peace."

"You always had such a sharp tongue." He shook his head. "I wasn't surprised when I came home and your momma told me you'd run off. You never wanted to follow the rules."

"I got punished every time I stepped out of line." Under the table, she clenched her fists. Josiah would not see her struggle.

"I was just saving your soul from the devil." He reached toward the back of the table and straightened the metal napkin holder, ketchup bottle, and salt and pepper shakers.

"You are the devil." She lowered her voice so as not to attract attention. "And I saved myself."

His blue eyes glazed over. "Esther…"

"I'm Alice." She pointed a finger at her chest.

"Whatever name you go by, you're still my child." Resting his forearms on the table, he leaned in. "I've always seen the most of myself in you."

Bile rose, the taste bitter on the back of her tongue. "I am nothing like you."

"Who do you think you got that stubborn streak from?" One corner of his mouth lifted, causing deep creases in the tan skin. "I've followed your career in the Army. I know you were injured in combat. I'm proud of what you've accomplished."

The sect was isolated. Somehow, he'd kept track of her. She chilled at the thought that her protective wall hadn't been as thick as she'd assumed. "How did you find that information?"

"We've added a few computers with internet access for use by the church leadership. I'd log in every once and awhile and look up your new name. The head of the church would be very angry if he knew I was here talking to you." Josiah pulled out a napkin and wiped his brow.

Their server stopped to take their order, but Alice had no appetite. She ordered a cup of coffee just to have something in her hands. "Why are you here?" She attempted one more time for an answer. "Even if I was welcome, I'd never go back." Certainly, he wasn't here because of love. Josiah Wolf didn't love anyone but himself.

One corner of his mouth lifted. "Like I said, I was curious about the person you grew up to be. You know you broke your momma's heart when you ran away. And little Matthew cried for a week straight."

She was in no mood for a guilt trip and gritted her teeth. "I'd run away all over again if needed. I'd rather have died than stay trapped on your compound." She stared at the source of years of anxiety. "Our home was a prison, and only you held the key."

He spread open his hands, palms up. "Because as a man, my responsibility is to maintain my house and family."

"You chose that lifestyle. I didn't. Neither did the rest of your kids." Rage filled her, and her body warmed. Why had she let him get to her, after she swore to keep emotionally distant?

"I wanted you all saved." His voice trembled. "I don't want you, or Joshua, or Maddy to go to Hell."

The sincerity shining in his eyes caused her to hesitate. Did he actually believe his church's teaching, or was he using their hard rule of law as a form of control? She leaned forward, resting her forearms on the table. "Hell for Maddy meant being sold off like a heifer to become part of another man's flock. Hell for Joshua meant turning into a man like his father. What you're doing inside the sect is wrong. I've spent years running from the pain you caused, but no more."

She placed the palm of her hands on the table and glared at the man who called himself her father. To her adult eyes, he was no longer a larger-than-life monster. Now, she held the power. "I'm warning you. Stay away from Maddy and Joshua. Don't contact me. You might have skirted around the law for the past forty years, but I will work to shut down your compound."

"The government can't touch us." He leaned back in the booth seat. "And we have a deal with the local police—don't ask and don't tell. Those of us who live at the compound stay because it's the life we want. Our ways are not for you, an outsider, to judge."

Anger burned away her remaining strands of control, and she pounded the table. "Marrying off teenage girls is morally wrong. Being married to more than one woman is against the law." She could argue from now until judgment day, but he would never concede. His beliefs were too deeply ingrained to ever crack.

"I can see our conversation is done." He scooted off the seat and gazed downward. "I'll leave you alone if you leave us alone. I can see you've hardened your heart to me. Just know that of all my children, you've made me the proudest."

With a slackened jaw, Alice sat as her father walked out of the diner without another word. The door closed behind him, and a new peace filled her heart. Finally, she stopped seeing herself as a victim but a survivor.

One who didn't hide behind a wall of her own making—but lived. Her future was open, spiraling into endless possibilities, with one man standing at the center. If only she could convince her head to follow her heart.

****

When Alice walked through the front door of her cousin's house, she received hugs of concern. Kate, Maddy, and Joshua all hovered in the kitchen while Alice fixed herself a snack. After twenty-four hours of stomach-churning worry, she finally felt hungry.

"So, you haven't been arrested for murder." Kate leaned against the counter. "That's good."

Alice took a bite from an apple, nodded, and chewed. Juice dripped onto her lips, and she grabbed a paper towel to clean off her mouth.

"Is he going back home now?" Maddy sat perched on a kitchen stool, hands folded on her lap. "He'll leave us alone, right?"

"He won't bother you again." Alice gave her sister a hug. "He was curious about me. We had a short conversation, then he left."

"I was so worried about you the entire time you were gone." Kate rubbed her shoulder. "When he showed up at my front door, all I could think of was that I failed all of you."

"Him finding your house is not your fault." Alice swept aside her own guilt. Neither she nor Kate was to blame for the destruction the sect created. "I'm glad you called me to handle him."

Joshua stepped toward the center of the room. "Thank you, Alice, for coming all this way for us. Father used to talk about you, like you were the symbol of destruction. But I think deep down, he took pride in your courage."

"I hate that he takes any pride, or credit, for the person I am today." What she made of her life was in spite of him, not because.

"He's not all bad, you know." Joshua gazed down at his white socks. "Sometimes, he was nice and loving. But he had to run his household in the way the church expected. He had to be tough on us."

"Don't make excuses for his behavior." Checking her temper, Alice put a hand on his broad shoulder and squeezed. "No one forced him to join that sect all those years ago."

"I know. I'm just saying that I think he would get out now if he could. His family's falling apart, and he's getting old." Joshua raised his gaze to look at Maddy, then at Alice. "Maddy and I left because we didn't want to be trapped into their lifestyle, but we don't hate our family."

Joshua's statement forced Alice to examine the situation with a fresh perspective. During her time in the military, she'd been taught to base her judgments on logic, not emotion. Contrarily, her gut reaction to anything regarding her family was pure emotional. "You're a much bigger person than I am. I'm sorry I treated you all like you didn't exist. I should have been more like Kate and helped those who wanted to leave."

"You followed your path." Kate took hold of her hand. "I chose to stay here. When we needed you, you came, which is all that matters."

"How much longer can we sit by and let the sect continue unchallenged?" Regretfully, she no longer had the military back-up to storm the compound herself but without proof, the act would be illegal.

"We talked about going to the police." Kate glanced at Maddy and Josh. "But decided an interrogation so soon after leaving would be too stressful for them both. And Maddy was concerned about law enforcement sending her back."

If she had shown more backbone, Alice would have reported the sect and pushed for intervention a long time ago. "Two of the men I served with are now FBI Special Agents. Once we get settled at Fort Bragg, I'll contact them to see if they can pull a few strings and start an official investigation."

"But what about the moms and the rest of the family?" Maddy's eyes welled with tears. "I don't want them going to jail."

"Don't worry. I'll make sure anyone innocent is protected." Alice glanced around the small kitchen, and her stomach growled. Surely, Kate had something around she could throw together for a meal. "I'm starving. What should we do for dinner?"

"Thank you for everything, sister." Maddy's small

hand covered Alice's. "Are we really flying on an airplane with you tomorrow?"

"I need to clear my plan with Micah, but I'm positive he won't have a problem with me bringing you back. We're only staying with him for three days before moving to my apartment."

"We're all packed." Joshua smiled. "Didn't take long. Kate bought us some modern clothes. I really like blue jeans."

Her heart swelled with protective love. She'd forgotten the excitement of the modern world after being confined to a home that resembled the nineteenth century. "You two better get a good night's sleep tonight, because tomorrow's the start of a whole new adventure."

A new adventure awaited them all. Now, all she had to do was firm her resolve regarding her next step with Micah, and then find out if he'd go along with her plan. If not, her heart was in for a world of hurt.

****

With nothing more exciting to do, Micah sat at the kitchen table to review his fan mail. Earlier, he'd picked up a box of cards and letters sent to Warrior Stadium. He was half-way through the pile when a colorful design on the outside of an envelope caught his eye. He opened the top and pulled out a sheet of white paper decorated with a crayon drawing of Micah standing beside a young boy. Wires were attached to the boy's arm. A hospital bed rested in the background.

Micah flipped over the paper and read the letter written in a child's uneven letters.

Dear Micah Palmer,

My name is Aaron. I am eight years old. I am at

Timber Lake Hospital because I have cancer. The doctors are trying to kill the cancer. I am a big fan and excited to see you play.

Could I please have a real picture of you so I can put it up by my bed? Can you sign it, too?

Your #1 fan,

Aaron Johnson

While reading the child's letter, he felt his heart stir. Sending an autographed picture, which the team's staff could do, wasn't good enough. This little boy was confident enough to reach out and ask for a small gift. The very least Micah could do was visit Aaron in the hospital.

He called the Director of the Timber Lake Hospital—a woman he'd become acquainted with from past fundraising drives—and requested his visit to the Pediatric wing be kept a secret from the media. He didn't want reporters and photographers to disrupt the children. Plus, he wanted his drop-in to be totally private.

A few minutes after he finished making arrangements with the hospital director, his cell rang. At the sight of Alice's name, excitement filled him like a thousand bubble bees. "Hey."

"How's my favorite football player?"

"Trying to stay out of trouble while you're gone."

She laughed. "How's that going?"

"Good. I was on my way out the door when you called. One of the guys just invited me over to play cards."

"Oh, I don't mean to hold you up."

He'd always put other plans aside for her. "No problem. What's up?"

"I've taken care of my family issues. My flight arrives in Timber Lake tomorrow, early afternoon."

Anticipation kicked up his pulse. He wanted her here—right now. "Cool. Do you need a ride?"

"No, but thanks for offering. I'll hire a car service. I have another favor to ask. I'm bringing two guests, and I hope they can stay in the guesthouse until I move out."

Excitement brewed at the possibility her guests were Joshua and Maddy, though he hated dwelling on the day she'd leave. "The guest house is your home. I don't care if you have guests, as long as it's not a single male who isn't your brother."

She laughed. "Joshua and Maddy are officially moving in with me. Something happened to push up the timeframe, so they're coming now."

"Will you share what that something is?" He was proud of Alice for pushing away her own discomfort to cover Maddy and Joshua with a protective wing. Now, if only he could convince her to let him fully into her heart. He'd be part of their family and therefore, the teens would be under his protection as well.

"When I get back. Promise."

A small victory but one he'd gladly accept. Just like a football game, he'd push hard, moving ahead one yard at a time, to get him to his goal. "Can't wait to see you tomorrow." After he ended the call, he stood behind the patio door and gazed across his yard to the small guest house. If he had his way, she wouldn't move back to South Carolina. She'd move all her belongings into his house.

Since Alice had flown to New Mexico, he'd made a few decisions. First, he accepted the fact she might never fully let him into her life. Second, he concluded only a portion of her heart would never be enough—either all or nothing. He'd deal with the nothing if necessary, but in the next three days, he'd play hard to win it all.

****

During the drive from the airport, Alice sat by Maddy in the backseat of their hired car, leaving Joshua up front by the driver.

When the car pulled up to the gate, Maddy gasped.

Alice reached out a comforting hand.

"Will we be trapped in there?" Maddy pointed down the driveway.

"No." Alice soothed. "You use a code to get in and out. The gate is to keep out strangers and give Micah privacy." She exited the car and walked to the keypad, then pushed in the code.

The wrought iron gate slid open, and their driver steered the car toward the house.

"Does he live here all by himself?" Slack-jawed, Joshua stepped out of the car. He spun around.

"Don't get too attached to this place. My apartment isn't as impressive." Alice took their bags out of the trunk and escorted them back to their temporary home. After she showed Maddy and Joshua around the guesthouse, she left them to unpack and walked across the backyard in search of Micah. Surprisingly, he hadn't come out to meet them, and she ached to see him after only a few days apart.

She let herself in through the unlocked patio door. Inside, the shades in the great room were drawn, and dirty dishes filled the sink. Micah was never so messy. She lifted an article of clothing off the arm of the sofa—Micah's Warrior T-shirt. Where was he? "Hello?" she called out. Silence greeted her.

Maybe he was at the training facility or out with one of the guys from the team. After closing the door behind her, she returned to the guesthouse to check on Joshua and Maddy. Back in New Mexico, Kate introduced the teens to daytime talk TV and soap operas. Both teens were currently transfixed on *Days of our Lives*. Not the best introduction to modern society, but they'd learn soon enough real people didn't have nearly as much drama in their daily lives. Thank goodness.

With a strong need to stretch her legs after the flight, Alice changed and went outside for a short run. As she moved across the sidewalk pavement, she felt strength in every muscle. Even her injured leg kept good pace without much pain. When she returned home, she saw Micah's car parked in the driveway.

He stood on the patio and waved.

Tingles of pleasure moved along her spine at the sight of him. "Where were you?" Slowing to a jog then to a walk, she stopped before him. She wanted him so much, she ached. Without hesitation, despite the knowledge she was sweaty, she wrapped her arms around his neck and sank into a deep kiss.

"Miss me?" He grinned against her lips.

Leaning away, she backhanded him on the chest and the muscles underneath flexed, causing her heart to palpitate. "Of course."

Micah nuzzled her neck. "I was at Timber Lake Hospital."

"Why?" *No, he can't be hurt!* She jerked her head to look him in the eye, almost clipping his chin. "I leave for a few days, and you end up in the hospital?"

"Calm down. I went to visit a new friend, Aaron Johnson." He entwined his large hand with hers. "He sent me a letter, asking for an autographed picture. I thought I'd do one better and deliver it myself."

"Really?" She imagined a little boy meeting his sport's idol and her heart melted. "You're so sweet. Did you alert the media?"

"No cameras. No reporters. I spent the morning hanging out with the kids at the hospital." He inhaled then breathed out and smiled. "Alice, I felt inspired. Those kids are so brave. They're fighting such grown-up diseases. I hope my visit took their mind off their sickness for a little while."

"That's the most wonderful thing I've heard in a long time." She rested her head on his muscular shoulder, enjoying the solid feel of his body pressed against her. "How did little Aaron react when you walked into his hospital room?"

Micah laughed. "He nearly jumped out of bed. We took pictures and talked football. After about a half an hour, he started growing sleepy. The Head of Pediatrics escorted me so I could visit the other kids staying in the wing."

"You're a good man, Micah Palmer." *The best I've ever met.*

He kissed the top of her head.

Prickles of satisfaction laced together a soothing pattern inside her brain. "Joshua and Maddy are in the guesthouse watching soap operas."

"I bought brats to grill for dinner. We can eat out on the patio and visit."

"I like your plan." She hesitated. "Micah, we need

to talk about what happened in New Mexico."

He rubbed a strand of her hair between his fingers. "Later. How about you shower first?"

If she thought she couldn't fall any harder for this man, she was delusional. Micah wasn't perfect, but he was darn close.

But she might never give Micah everything he deserved—commitment, full trust, and a no-holds-barred love affair. What would happen if she couldn't take the last step? Would he accept her moving away with only lukewarm promises?

Yesterday, she'd faced a man who'd haunted her nightmares for years. If she conquered her biggest fear, she should have no problem tackling the others. Right?

Held securely in Micah's arms, she thought about Maddy and Joshua, who were now dependent on her. She thought about her new civilian position with the Army and how large a commitment the program required in order to succeed. She considered how most successful relationships took a lot of work under the best conditions.

First things first, though. She stepped away from Micah and sniffed her shirt. He was right—she needed a shower. Then after dinner, she'd come clean about her meeting with Josiah, requiring she bravely peel back one of her last remaining layers of self-protection.

With a kiss and a promise to find him once she had showered and changed, she headed to the guesthouse.

Doubt nagged her mind. Could she really fully open herself to another person? One she'd only known for a few months? Guess she'd discover how deeply she desired Micah and how far she'd go to keep him in her life.

Chapter Twenty-Two

After a dinner with good food and even better conversation, Joshua and Maddy explored the property then headed off to bed, leaving Micah and Alice alone in the backyard. His desire was more physical, but he knew a deep conversation was needed.

While Micah waited for Alice to speak, he enjoyed the fresh, night breeze. The late July night air clung with heat and moisture. In four days, he'd check into training camp. In less than thirty-six hours, he'd say goodbye to Alice. Sadness soured his gut.

He sat beside her on a lounge chair by the pool. Bull frogs croaked somewhere under the cover of night. The movement of the wind rippled the surface water of the pool.

Alice cleared her throat. "I went to see my father." She rested a hand on his arm. "He'd threatened to take Joshua and Maddy back home if I didn't meet with him."

His anger ignited at the man who dared to threaten Alice and her siblings. "How did he know where they were?"

"From what he said, he's been keeping tabs on me and on Kate all these years. His curiosity must have finally won out. He knew I'd do anything to protect Maddy and Joshua." She clenched a fist, which rested on her lap.

"Even agree to meet with that monster?" Thankfully, all three arrived in Timber Lake safe and sound.

Nodding, she nibbled the corner of her lower lip. "He looked different than I remember. The years have not been kind. Ever since I left, I've pictured him as a Goliath when in reality, I carried memories of a little girl. I'm taller than him now and stronger. Sitting across the table, I felt angry, but I wasn't frightened."

"Good." Micah lifted a hand and planted a kiss on each knuckle. Alice Liddell really was a warrior princess—his warrior princess. "Thank you for trusting me enough to tell me."

She sighed. "I'm a very private person, partly due to shame and partly for self-defense. I never told my CST sisters about my upbringing. I'm uncomfortable lifting the veil covering my past."

"I admire you for the woman you are today, which means I appreciate the years and experiences that formed your incredible spirit." In his own words, he heard passion and tenderness. Yet, he still waited to hear how she felt about him. She would leave soon, possibly unwilling to give him a commitment. Their relationship was too young to survive a separation without some form of assurance.

Soon, he'd shift his focus to the upcoming season. He didn't want strings of doubt left fluttering in the wind as a costly distraction. "I'm glad you found closure after seeing your father again."

Alice shifted onto her hip to face him. "I don't think I've resolved all my daddy issues, but I'm getting there."

"So, where does that leave us?" Frowning, he'd

push for straight answers and keep pushing.

"What do you mean?"

"When you go back home and then move to Fort Bragg to start your new job, what will happen to us?"

She leaned over and brushed her lips over his. "We keep in touch. I can travel to Wisconsin for a few games. Maybe you can fly out to see me when you have a week off."

"And see how things go?" He sickened. The very situation he feared. No resolution, only thin strands of connection, which could be snipped at any time.

Alice's eyes widened. "I don't know what you want me to say. I signed a one-year contract with the Army. The job will help me transition from military to civilian life. When my year is done, I can decide what to do next. I have two other people counting on me to support and care for them."

"I'm not asking you to give up your job. I'm asking for a commitment. I love you, Alice."

Her eyes widened. "I...ah...care about you, too."

With his male pride stinging, he gritted his teeth. "I won't let you leave our relationship open-ended—either you're all in or say goodbye and walk away."

"Are you giving me an ultimatum?" She pressed her frowning lips into a firm line.

Her temper didn't scare him. Not anymore. "We have two more days together. During that time, I won't bring up the subject. But on day three, before I take you to the airport, I expect an answer."

"Why pressure me?" She stood fast and swayed on her feet. "Can't we just see how things shake out?"

"No." He rose to stand and stared into her eyes. "I'm not the kind of guy who can put his heart on the line then sit around waiting for it to get run over."

Alice's expression softened. "You do have a gentle heart." She exhaled a deep breath. "Fine, but don't forget I have you for two more days of training. I might get payback."

"Looking forward to it," he whispered into her ear then pulled her close. The feel of her body pressed against his comforted his troubled soul. She was solid and real.

"I should get back to the guesthouse." She kissed his cheek. "The kids were a little jumpy about their first night in a new house."

"They're fine." He claimed her delicious mouth, but her small surrender wasn't enough. He wanted her total submission. Though, Alice's willpower was a million times stronger than his own—carbon fiber as opposed to glass.

She nipped his bottom lip. "I really should go. Be ready to run at six a.m."

"Only if you wear those tight, little shorts." He grinned. "I love to chase after you."

"Stop." Laughing, she swatted his chest. "You don't fight fair."

"When it comes to you, I'll fight…but never fair." An assertion he meant. He'd do anything to prove his love and secure hers. She meant more than anything else, including football, which proved the stakes were too high to fail.

****

Alice woke with a start. Her heart pounded loudly behind her ear drums. She sat in bed and looked at the digital clock on the dresser then scrubbed her eyes. The time was four a.m., and Maddy slept soundly next to her in the king-size bed.

She slipped out of bed and tiptoed to the kitchen for a drink of water. The dream she'd awoken from had been different from any in the past. She'd seen no explosions or men dying at her feet, and she hadn't been dragged home and forced to marry a stranger. In sleep, Alice had been completely happy. The feeling clung like the melody of a familiar song. She wished to stay wrapped in imaginary joy. Was her subconscious demonstrating a point? Yes, she could live a contented life without a man. But without Micah, her life would lack color. How could she wake every day without the secure knowledge he was a part of her soul?

Something still imprisoned her heart. She'd spent her adult life strong in her commitment to never be in a position of dependence. In the Army, she'd trusted her life to other soldiers, but never trusted anyone with romantic love. Her innermost self had always been locked away, and Micah was the key. Did she have the strength to take the gift he offered?

Why did he have to make her choose? In her heart, she knew he was right, but fear remained an eager jailer.

Several hours later, Alice stood over Micah in the backyard, watching him work out. "Hustle, Micah. I don't have all day."

He adjusted his grip on the handle of the sandbag. "You do have all day, as a matter of fact." Huffing, he lowered the bag to the ground then lifted it back to shoulder level. "How about instead of yelling at me, go grab a bag and do some of these yourself?"

Watching his arm muscles ripple, she leaned against the wall and smirked. "I don't have to survive two weeks of training camp. Don't worry your pretty little head, I'll get my workout. I just hate sandbag power cleans." His growl had her laughing. She'd miss their combative camaraderie. No one else could get her blood pumping like Micah—for more reasons than one.

After the morning's series of exercises, Alice went home to shower and check on Maddy and Joshua. As she walked through the front door of the guesthouse, she noticed the kids coming toward her, towels in hand.

"Going for a swim?" Growing up, she'd learned to swim only because she'd snuck off to the little pond three miles from the compound. She remembered hot days when she'd strip down to her long underwear and jump into the cold water. The first time in, she'd almost drowned. After that experience, she quickly figured out how to keep her head above water.

"Kate bought us swimsuits and took us to the outdoor pool by her house." Maddy wore a pink one-piece, which showed through a long, white T-shirt. "Micah won't mind, will he?"

"No, of course not. He wants you to make yourself at home." Alice held open the front door. "Go have fun. I might join you after my shower."

Maddy and Joshua walked side by side to the gated pool area, and then stopped when they approached Micah.

Alice stood at the open door and observed them talk. No surprise, he acted as a welcoming host. Micah invited them to stay without asking anything in return—another sign of a good man.

But with her, he'd asked one thing—the only thing she'd still felt reluctant to totally surrender.

****

The next day, Micah directed all three of his guests into his truck. He wanted to give the kids a tour of the Warrior's Stadium before they left for South Carolina with Alice. He parked in the lot, underneath the shadow of the massive building and remembered bringing Alice here not that long ago. She'd met several of his teammates, and her appearance had tongues wagging in the locker room for days.

Joshua opened the truck door and jumped out. "Wow! I saw a football stadium on TV, but I had no idea how big it is." He raised his gaze upward. "You play football here, Micah?"

"A dream come true." Micah held open the door to the player and staff entrance. "Playing football isn't as important as what your sister did in the Army." He flicked a glance at Alice. "But I still feel very fortunate to earn a living doing something that I love."

"And you're not pinchin' pennies, as Ma used to say." Maddy smoothed the yellow material of her T-shirt.

"I can't complain." He studied Joshua's and Maddy's new, modern clothes—jean shorts and screen-printed shirts—and wished he had more time with them. He'd love the chance to take them for an afterhours shopping spree at one of the city's department stores.

As he walked the group through the locker room, down the tunnel, and onto the field, he noticed Maddy and Joshua stayed quiet. Whenever he brought someone here, he always viewed the stadium through new eyes. Pride filled his chest. This shrine to football held a sense of history and pride. The Warriors had been a part of the Timber Lake community for eighty years, with the stadium serving as the town's most important landmark. Micah wasn't taking this second chance for granted.

The teens wandered onto the grass and across to the other side.

"You ready for all this?" Alice motioned to the surrounding empty stadium seats.

"Yes." When he ran onto the field, leading the team, he'd be better than ever. Not only had his body improved during the offseason but so had his mind and soul. "I've stopped worrying about my performance. I want to enjoy myself again and play for the pure joy of the game."

"I hope to see you play." Alice squeezed his hand.

"Nothing would make me happier." Imagining her sitting in the stands during a game, he kissed her cheek.

Alice turned her gaze to a large man striding toward them and smiled.

"Mr. Turf said I'd find you out here." Reagan's gaze focused on Alice. "Hey, Alice. Nice to see you again."

"Nice to see you, too." Her grin widened.

Micah didn't miss the telltale creep of blush on her face. Why did every woman on the planet think Reagan Harrison was the most handsome man alive? The dude was married with four kids. "What do you want?" Micah asked the hulking linebacker.

Reagan held his smile until he turned to Micah. "We're having a pool party Saturday to celebrate the kick-off of the season, and Julie wanted me to invite you and your guests."

Micah's stomach plunged at the thought of leaving her at the airport and the possibility of a final goodbye.

Laurie Winter

"Tell Julie thanks for the invite, but Alice is flying out tomorrow morning and heading home."

"Oh." Wearing a grin, Reagan glanced from Micah to Alice. "This guy getting too much to handle?"

Alice laughed. "My time of employment is up. Micah's ready to kick some football butt, and I have a new job. I'm kind of like Marry Poppins—time to move on to others in need."

"Micah, you're an idiot for letting this one get away." Reagan slapped him hard on the back.

"Trust me, I'd lock her up if I could," Micah grumbled. Now, along with a tender heart, his back throbbed from Reagan's "friendly" pat.

Joshua and Maddy ran over to join them on the sidelines.

"Hi." Reagan reached out his hand. "I'm Reagan Harrison. I play defense for the team."

"I'm Joshua Wolf, and this is Maddy. We're Alice's brother and sister."

Maddy tipped up her head and stared open-mouthed.

"Nice to meet you. I have to run but hope to see you all again very soon." Reagan waved and headed back to the tunnel.

"You on babysitting duty?" Micah shouted after him, wanting one final jab.

"What did you say?" Reagan turned and pointed at Micah. "You want to make something of the fact I'm an awesome dad and my kids adore me?"

"No, man. Carry on." Micah chuckled as the big guy disappeared into the dark tunnel. He should know better than to pick a fight with a two-hundred-fifty-pound linebacker right before training camp. He was

278

sure Reagan would find a way to pay him back. Good thing they were good friends. Hopefully, Reagan wouldn't hurt him too badly.

Maddy tapped him on the arm. "Do you want kids someday?"

She spoke in a soft voice. "*Ahhh*…maybe, after I settle down with the right woman." He stared at Alice, whose gaze was everywhere except on him.

"I think you'd make a wonderful dad." Maddy's cheeks turned pink. "I mean…you've been very nice by letting us stay. Thank you."

He wrapped an arm around her shoulders. "Hey, that's what friends are for, and I have no doubt you'll make lots more once you get settled with Alice at Fort Bragg."

As they started walking toward the tunnel, Maddy pulled him to a stop. "But that's just for a year," she whispered. "I want to live someplace that feels like home."

His chest squeezed with protective concern for this girl. "I'm sure Alice will build a great home for you. When she's finished with her job contract, you can decide the next step together, as a family."

"I know what I want." Her hazel eyes gleamed. "I want her to stay with you. I can tell you love her very much. She shouldn't leave you."

I wholeheartedly agree. "Maybe you could tell her. Alice doesn't listen to me."

"That's because she's like our father—thick-headed and stubborn as a donkey. That's what my ma said." She giggled.

"You should probably keep that opinion to yourself." He stifled a laugh.

Maddy dropped her gaze to the green turf under her sandaled feet. "Father said he always knew she'd run. He'd say Alice was too big a force to stay trapped in the sect. Like trying to lock a tornado in a box."

If he thought his love for Alice couldn't get any stronger, he was wrong. "Your father had a valid point." But wasn't trapping her exactly what he was doing? He'd put her in a corner and forced her to make a choice—commit her heart or leave with nothing.

Tomorrow, she'd tell him exactly where he stood, and he hoped it wasn't alone.

Chapter Twenty-Three

A knock sounded at the door. Alice finished tying her shoelaces and went to answer.

Micah stood, backlit by the glow of the rising sun. "Come on, girl." Grinning, he held out a hand. "One last run."

Ignoring the hitch in her heart, she placed her hand in his and followed him out to the road. A mile jog led her to the beginning of a trail they frequently used on longer runs. Micah turned and headed down the wooded path. Today, they only had time for a few miles.

All her belongings were packed and ready to go. Boxes lay strewn around the guest house, which she'd have shipped home. Maddy and Joshua had been extra quiet last night. Even though they'd only been a guest at Micah's place for a few days, she knew they were reluctant to leave. Then again, so was she.

As she ran, Alice remained a few paces behind, desiring a chance to admire the athletic man. He was everything she wanted, not only physically perfect but he possessed a noble soul. In all her years of serving in the Army, she'd spent time in the company of a lot of men. None of them had ever created feelings of deep devotion the way Micah had.

Instead of throwing herself into a passionate romance, she was ready to say goodbye. He wanted more than just a see-you-later kiss. Micah wanted all of her heart or nothing. He'd been clear about not settling for a half-way love affair.

The time approached when he'd ask for a decision. Was she ready to remove the final obstacle and give him everything? Or would she leave, knowing she'd destroyed her shot at true love and broken his heart?

"Tell me another story." Micah slowed to jog alongside her. "About your time as a CST."

She took a few deep inhales to regulate her breathing. Running still wasn't as easy as before her injury, but she was getting there. "After our CST training was finished, we all were scheduled to deploy. The Army loaded us on a transport plane and flew us over to Afghanistan, where we'd be taken to our assigned Special Ops teams. Throughout the whole journey, the other soldiers didn't know what to make of us—a large group of female soldiers traveling together."

"I bet you set them straight."

"Sometimes. Other times, we let them think we were an Army softball team, or the base entertainment, or a core of nurses. No one ever guessed what we were really sent over to do."

"Your group formed a tight bond." Micah decelerated, then stopped.

She stood beside their favorite spot—a little pond edged with weeping willow trees. Chirping robins hopped from branch to ground, likely in search of an early morning snack. "We were not only fighting the enemy but the entire institution of the military. With the combat ban lifted, front line jobs are more accessible to women. My new position is exciting, because I want to help level a very rough path."

"You've already given the Army eleven years of your life. You really want to go back for more?" He wiped at the sweat dripping from his face.

The cool air chilled her damp skin. She rubbed her arms, warding off the gooseflesh. "I never had a chance for closure. I was on the battlefield, and then my career ended. Going back, even only for a year as a civilian, will help me close that chapter of my life." She grabbed the hem of his shirt and pulled him close. No standing on tiptoes needed to reach his lips for a kiss.

He pulled away and shook his head. "I can't kiss you. Not yet."

"Really?" *No fair*. She stuck out her bottom lip, disliking the change in his demeanor.

"You are not leaving until you answer my question."

Narrowing her eyes, she stared back. "So, you'll lock me away." His grin looked very mischievous.

"I hadn't thought about that option so yes…I might lock you up."

"Then you'll need to catch me first." Alice took off, sprinting down the path. His footfalls sounded from behind.

Her time had run out. Micah pressed her for a commitment, and her heart felt ready to explode from the pressure.

****

After showering, Micah dressed in shorts and a T-shirt, then stood at the window and watched Alice load suitcases in his truck bed. The churning in his stomach kicked from simmer to rolling boil. He'd failed to convince her to stay and now, he prepared his heart for demolition.

Alice had done a very good job of avoiding answering his question. He would not let her leave without either making a commitment or ending their relationship, understanding the risk he took in drawing a line. In the end, if she left with unresolved feelings, little hope remained for the survival of their newly budded relationship. He'd learned the hard way commitment could crack under pressure. Hadn't he witnessed that erosion firsthand with Cassidy? Although, the fault was totally his own.

He put his heart on the line. He'd already declared his love and would commit his life to her, if given the chance.

Now, she held all the power. What would she do?

Minutes later, he walked outside to find Joshua sitting by the pool, dipping his feet into the water. "You all packed?" Micah sat beside the boy. Joshua's body was tall and lean. He moved with a dexterity that someday might make a good athlete, if given the chance.

"We don't have much." Joshua turned to face Micah. "I don't want to move again. I want somewhere to feel like home."

As much as he didn't want to be away from her, he remained proud of her ambition. "Alice found a nice house to rent near Fort Bragg, and you and Maddy will be enrolled at the local high school."

Joshua kicked his feet, sending a spray of water over the surface of the pool. "She only plans on working at Fort Bragg for a year, then we'll move again. Why can't we just stay in Timber Lake?"

If Micah had powers of mind control, he'd

command Alice to stay and build a life here with him, Joshua, and Maddy. Unfortunately, he loved the most stubborn woman on the planet. "Trust your sister. She believes she's doing the right thing for all of you." His confidence in Alice matched the tone of his voice.

"And what about you? How do you feel about her leaving?"

Micah scratched the growing beard along his jaw line. "Not gonna lie, it sucks. I understand why she took the job, and I think the challenge will be good for her."

"Don't you dare let her leave without saying she loves you." Hunching his shoulders, Joshua frowned. "I know she does. She's just too chicken to say it out loud."

"What army do you intend to call in to keep her here until she spills her guts?" He laughed. At least he had someone playing backup during his endeavor. "Have you seen her when she gets mad?"

Joshua patted him on the back. "I have faith. Just don't let her intimidate you. When my father told us to do something I didn't think was right, I stood up and wouldn't back down. He never said so, but I think he respected me."

"I'm sure he did." Micah rose and shook the water off his feet. "Well, since I need to take you all to the airport soon, I guess it's now or never." His stomach rolled with nerves.

"Alice is out behind the guest house. Good luck." Joshua walked in the opposite direction.

Luck—he needed a miracle.

****

Alice watched Micah stride toward her with clenched fists and a firm jaw, like a superhero ready to face the villain. Her gut felt like someone body checked it into the wall. *Shoot*. As promised, he was not letting her off easy.

"Time's up, sweetheart," he called out. "You in or out?"

Now, he stood before her, a wall of solid muscle—his arms crossed over his chest and an eyebrow cocked on his handsome face. "Micah, you know how skeptical I am about committed relationships." Her voice sounded too high-pitched and lacked its normal bravado. "Why are you forcing me into a corner when I could break your heart?" With his first admission of love, he trusted her with his heart.

"Because I'm not a man who can love someone as much as I love you and let you leave with an *I'll see you when I see you*. I want it all, Alice."

She attempted to push past him, but he was as movable as a concrete barricade. "You can't force me."

Gripping onto her shoulders, he stared into her eyes. "You want to make a bet?"

Was he purposely goading her? She dug her heels into the grass and pushed again on his chest. "Let me go."

"No." His feet stayed planted. "Say it, Alice. Either you love me, or you don't."

Blood rushed to her head, and her temper flared. She kicked and swept his feet out from under him, landing both of them sprawled on the ground. Wiggling away, Alice elbowed him in the ribs.

Micah tightened his grip. "I'm not letting you go until you give me an answer."

"Why are you doing this?" Stifling laughter, she continued wiggling free of his hold.

"Because you're worth the fight," he growled into her ear.

The remaining wall around her heart shattered. The pieces illuminated the air around her. Gasping for breath, she was laid bare without defense. She loved and trusted him with every fiber of her body and soul. Though, she wouldn't tell him that now—not when he physically held the upper hand.

When she noticed the expression on his face soften, along with his hold, she made her move. With one last surge of strength, she twisted his arm and forced him to roll over into a prone position with his cheek mashed into the grass. She lay over his body.

Micah struggled until he sent up a backward kick.

The move caught a tender spot on her thigh. The brief flash of pain made her jump, which removed some of her body weight pinning him down. Now, he had the advantage and spun her off his back.

Legs and arms entwined, they rolled down the small hill until she was stuck underneath. As Micah hovered above her, she felt a stick poking into her back and lay stuck like a bug underneath him. *We must look ridiculous.* Laughter bubbled up. "Okay, I submit," she choked out in between taking deep breaths. "What's your plan? Keep me trapped under you for the rest of my life? Change the code on the gate so I can't get out?" A sexy smile curved at his lips.

"No, I'm not holding you hostage." Micah rose onto his knees and reached down to help her up.

She knelt before him, studying his face. The features she knew so well—every line, every freckle, and every kissable spot. If she admitted the depth of her love, how could she leave? Part of her wished he would hold her hostage and keep her safe in his protective embrace.

But she'd never be happy turning from her latest challenge. Her position at Fort Bragg would only last a year, and then they had the rest of their lives to spend together. "I love you, Micah Palmer." She grabbed onto his shirt sleeves and pulled him close. "Don't ever let me go."

Cheers broke her out of her reverie.

She turned to see Joshua and Maddy off in the distance, obviously having witnessed the entire spectacle. Her heart swelled to the point she half-expected it to burst out of her chest. Love surrounded her, and after so many years of pushing the feeling away, she now felt very blessed. "Kiss her again," Maddy shouted.

Joshua gave a thumbs-up.

Micah cupped her face in his hands. "You are my world," he whispered. "Remember that when we're apart."

The rough texture of his palms brushed against her skin, causing her pulse to race. "I'm committed to the Army for a year. I know Joshua and Maddy have their sights set on living in Timber Lake."

Micah helped her stand, then brushed dirt and grass off his clothes.

"You didn't literally have to fight for me." Alice took hold of both hands and kissed the underside of one wrist.

"Really?" He grinned. "Come on, admit it. You liked fighting."

"Okay, fine…rolling around on the grass was pretty hot. Don't let it get to your head." Narrowing her gaze, she tapped him on the forehead.

Micah slung an arm around her shoulders. "I already have an ego the size of Texas, remember? What's one more victory to add to the list?"

Cocky man. She bumped him hard with her hip. "Am I just another victory?"

"My love," he whispered as his lips swept over her cheek. "Nothing else will ever compare to winning your heart."

Epilogue

"You ready for this?" Alice asked Joshua and Maddy as they entered Warrior Stadium six months after they'd moved away. Micah had flown them to Timber Lake to attend a game. The temperature was subzero, the mist of their breath froze in the cold air. All three were bundled under so many layers, they could barely walk.

An usher showed them to their seats—very close to the field. Alice spotted Micah throwing the ball to warm up his arm. With a shout of his name, she raised her hand and waved.

He glanced up and grinned.

His smile warmed her more than the two pairs of long underwear she wore. Micah wanted them to visit during the kids' Christmas break, and Alice had received time off around the holidays. But to sit outside for several hours and watch a football game was insane. Obviously, Micah didn't seem to mind. He wore nothing more than a long-sleeved shirt under his uniform.

"Can we get a hot dog?" Joshua asked.

"Sure. Just remember where our seats are." Alice handed him some money then watched as they ascended the concrete stairs. In the past months, her brother and sister had learned a lot about the world. They attended high school and slowly found their places in the new social structure, but she still worried. Both Josh and Maddy lacked street smarts and easily became overwhelmed in large buildings like Warrior Stadium.

"Excuse me," a man said as he approached. "Would you mind coming with me?"

She studied his name badge, noting he worked for the Warriors. "I can't. I'm waiting for my brother and sister to return with food."

"Micah must not have told you." The man sighed and glanced at the field. "We're doing a special veteran appreciation ceremony before the game, and we'd like you to come out on the field."

She ground her teeth. Funny, Micah hadn't told her about this push into the public eye ahead of time. Likely, he'd been worried she wouldn't show for the game. "All right, I need to make sure my brother and sister get back to their seats."

When Maddy and Joshua returned, they wore smiles.

"We'll be okay, Alice." Maddy patted her hand. "And don't be mad at Micah. If he asked you, he knew you wouldn't agree."

"Traitors." Fighting nerves, she moved into the aisle, then followed the usher through a jungle of hallways before arriving at the entrance of the field to join the small assembled group.

"The announcer will introduce you before the singing of the National Anthem. Just walk out to the fifty-yard line and wave."

With her heart beating rapidly, she strode onto the field and made her way to where several service members stood as flag bearers. She noticed Micah standing off on the sidelines, and she sent him a glare.

Over the stadium sound system, the announcer read the names of each of the ten veterans. The crowd cheered before standing for the singing of the National Anthem. Looking around, she felt chills having nothing to do with the weather. Her pride in her service to her country hadn't diminished in the time since her separation from the military. In fact, the distance made for an honest appreciation for what she'd accomplished.

With the closing notes, four F-18 fighter jets flew over the stadium in formation.

While Alice shook hands with the other veterans and active duty members standing on the field, she felt a light tap on her shoulder. She turned and faced Micah.

In one hand, he held his helmet. His other held a small, black box. He dropped down to one knee.

She inhaled, and her heart pounded wildly. "What's going on?"

"I'm wondering what you're doing for the next, like…fifty years." With a thumb, he pushed open the box.

The shine from the diamond inside almost blinded her. "You still think you're Rocky, huh?" she asked while fighting tears.

"Marry me, Alice."

The sounds of the entire stadium faded until Micah's was the only voice she heard. "And what if I say no? Will you tackle me, hold me down, and put the ring on anyway?"

He arched his eyebrows and smiled. "Crazier things have happened, but I'd never force you." Rising to his feet, he took her hands. "So…what do ya say? You want to become Mrs. Palmer?"

She swallowed down the large lump of emotion forming in her throat. "I've changed my name before...to run away. This time, I'll be coming home." She kissed him hard on the lips. "Yes, Micah. Put that ring on my finger and get back to your team. They look ready to win."

"Finally." Grinning, he slid on the ring and kissed her hand.

Her insides glowed with emotion. She glanced down at the large ring on her finger and couldn't stop the spread of a wide smile. As she returned to her seat, she felt a flush spreading up her neck and onto her cheeks. Maybe she wouldn't holler at him for embarrassing her with a marriage proposal in front of seventy thousand people. She'd find a better way to pay him back. Heavy tractor tires and a rope hanging from a barn beam came to mind, and she smiled at the possibilities.

A word about the author…

Laurie Winter is a true warrior of the heart. Inspired by her dreams, she creates authentic characters who overcome the odds and find true love.

She keeps her life balanced with regular yoga practice and running. When not pounding the pavement or the keyboard, she's enjoying time with her family, who are scattered between Wisconsin and Michigan. Laurie has three kids and one fantastic husband, all who inspire her to chase her dreams.

Visit her at:

http://lauriewinter.com

Other Titles by the Author
in the "Warriors of the Heart" series
After All
Home Field
True Horizon
Winner Takes All